The Thing with Willie

The Thing with Willie

STORIES OF TWO FAMILIES

Karen Sagstetter

BERGAMOT

Washington, D.C.

© 2012 Karen Sagstetter

BERGAMOT
www.bergamotbooks.com

Editor in Chief Gail D. Spilsbury
Designed by Leslie Dickersin

ISBN: 978-0-9760905-8-8

Cover photo by Erik Karlsson/Flickr/Getty Images

Printed in the United States

For Bruce

Contents

The Thing with Willie 1
Galveston 1932

Wild Water 13
Galveston 1900

The Wall 29
Galveston 1903

Creation 46
Oaxaca, Mexico 1900

Me and Mama 63
Galveston 1932

Konnichiwa, This Is Texas 66
Pennsylvania 1930s

The White Car 78
New Orleans 1930s

Speaking Up 86
Galveston 1940

Sunday Dinner 90
Galveston 1950

Sapphire Street 97
Houston 1980

Looking Good 165
Houston 1980s

Letters Home 178
Saigon 1970

Night Work 227
Washington, D.C. 1990s

The Best Doctor 243
Galveston 2000

Acknowledgments

These stories appeared as follows:

"The White Car," *Connections* magazine, Spring 2010.

"Me and Mama," *BorderSenses*, Fall 2008.

"Sapphire Street," finalist, Cleveland State University Poetry Center, Ruthanne Wiley Memorial Novella Contest, Spring 2008.

"The Best Doctor," featured fiction, *storySouth*, Spring 2006.

"The Thing with Willie," in *Creative Writer's Handbook*, eds. Philip K. Jason and Allan B. Lefcowitz, fourth edition, Pearson/Prentice Hall, 2005.

"The Thing with Willie," *New Stories from the South: 2000, The Year's Best*, Algonquin Books, 2000.

"The Thing with Willie," *Glimmer Train Stories*, Spring 1999.

"Looking Good," *Potomac Review*, Spring/Summer 2002.

"Konnichiwa, this is Texas," *Antietam Review*, vol. 20, 2000.

"Konnichiwa, this is Texas," *Frederick Magazine*, August 1999.

I am grateful for a 2005 fiction award grant from the Maryland State Arts Council.

John Balaban, trans., excerpts from "When I Got Back to Base," "The Painting," and "King Star," from *Ca Dao Vietnam, Vietnamese Folk Poetry*. Translation © 2003 by John Balaban. Reprinted with the permission of The Permissions Company, Inc., on behalf of Copper Canyon Press, www.coppercanyonpress.org.

Special thanks to Gail Spilsbury and Mary Kay Zuravleff for expert attention to these stories, and to Jody Bolz, Terence Winch, and Sarah Burnes. Thanks also to Wendy Schleicher, Caroline Weaver, and Wendall Williams. I am grateful to Debby Copes, Diane MacEachern, and Nancy Safer, along with many other friends. I offer appreciation in memory of my mother, Margaret Young Sagstetter, and grandfather, Fletcher C. Young. And abiding thanks to Bruce Hathaway, my husband, for his singing and for his wonderful ideas.

Families

GALVESTON

Anna Beaumont (*b.* Sept. 1884)   *m.* (1902)   Howard Clinton
    CHILDREN:
    Lucy (*b.* 1905)
    Louis (*b.* 1915)   *m.* (1937)   Violet Lumiere (*b.* 1917)
       CHILD:
       Tom (*b.* 1948)   *m./div.*   Abby Preston (*b.* 1951)

Patty Wilkens (*b.* 1900; *d.* July 2000)   *m.*   Willie Wilkens (*d.* 1932)
    CHILDREN:
    Beverly
    Edward
    Serena
    Ben and Reginald, twins
    Raymond (*b.* 1927, *d.* 1932)
    Charlotte (*b.* 1932)

PENNSYLVANIA

Eva Harris (*b.* 1919)   *m.*   Scott Preston (*b.* 1919)
    CHILDREN:
    Abby
    Louise
    Natalie

OAXACA 1900

    Guillermo   father
    Laurena   daughter
    Luís   fiancé

The Thing with Willie

Galveston 1932

On a fishing trip with her father, Anna faced her first authentic test of faith. It was 1890, near Galveston, and the boat had skimmed over the water, out to sea, and his tanned face rocked toward her and away as he pulled oars forward and back, forward and back in a hard, sure rhythm. She later recalled sounds of waves slapping the boat, and his voice, telling her facts about the ocean; for instance, how a flounder lies flat on the bottom, two eyes on the same side of his head like a person, not like a fish.

They dropped lines; right away there was a yank on hers, and he helped her manage a snappy little trout. He'd packed sandwiches and cold tea, and he fed them to his child, talking about everything under the sun. When it got hot, he steered toward home, saying that the coast stretched like a lazy cat all the way to Mexico.

Twenty yards from shore, her father reached over the side of the boat and plunged his hand into the water; his sleeve was dark and wet, soaked to the shoulder. He pulled it out, sand dribbling down his arm in rivulets, and unwound his fingers to show her: a craggy, pear-shaped shell. He rinsed it well in the sea water, taking his time, pushing mud from the crevices with his thumb, and with the force of his knife pried it open fast, like a man who knew what to do about things.

Inside the shell was a pecan-sized gray blob. Grinning, he caught it up in his fingers. "Sugar, open your mouth!" She opened up and a fat oyster swam down her throat, tasting like salt water. It was her first completely fresh morsel of seafood.

But in the 1930s people were fishing not for fun but for their lives. So many jobs had disappeared in Galveston, everywhere in the country. When the thing with Willie happened, Anna remembered her father's oyster. Probably that was the moment when she had first become so extremely particular about her seafood.

Willie, clean me a half-dozen flounder, three or four croakers, and a couple of dozen crabs, will you?

Yes ma'am.

How's your wife? Okay?

Yes ma'am.

Your children? Gettin' big I'll bet.

My little boy Raymond isn't too good.

Oh sorry to hear that. What's wrong?

He don't walk yet. Doctor don't know what to do.

How old is he?

He's four, ma'am.

That must be a worry. Sometimes they take their time. How about the others?

Oh they're mostly fine. Taller every day. Eat plenty.

Don't I know it.

Your boy okay, ma'am? Your girl?

Yes, fine, okay. Lucy's fine. All grown up. Louie's a mess sometimes.

She almost said, Can't stay still, but didn't so not to hurt his feelings about his own boy.

Willie was the colored man who worked at John's Seafood. He had a bunch of kids, and his wife Patty kept chickens and a vegetable garden to help out. Because he was a true professional, he and Anna got along, but her husband Howard didn't like him.

What's your problem with Willie?

He's slow.

He's not slow. He's fast when he cleans a crab.

Doesn't answer sometimes. I don't like that. Not polite.

He's busy. Tired.

I couldn't do what he does. I hate fish guts.

I don't mind. I'm thinking of what I'll make later.

It's a good thing you have work to like, isn't it?

Howard had lost his job; his car dealership had folded. He wasn't all that prejudiced but he disliked the idea of a black man having work when he didn't. It came back to his wife making the money for the family, too. Willie was part of that. Anna Clinton was a very good cook, and she was a hit with farmers and fishermen, who paid to enjoy her thick sauces with the red pepper and garlic.

Scales and shells didn't bother her at all. She liked to watch Willie clean fish because she was looking forward to the money she'd make cooking those fish for the hospital or church. Willie tended his knives so they were sharp and shiny; a gleam ricocheted off the ceiling while he worked, his fish heads scuttled to the edge of the counter, scales showered upward, and you had a beautiful fillet in thirty seconds. The same with oysters—he shucked to beat the band. Where he paused was right at first, to prod the edges of the shell and find exactly the right spot for the oyster knife to go in. Then he pushed it hard and quick, the shell opened with the sound of a small belch, like a secret getting out, followed by a scrape of the knife that made her mouth water as the oyster tumbled into a jar.

Still, she could see Willie was exhausted. He was six feet tall, with short-cropped inky hair and a sweet expression. Bent over, like his shoulders were not carrying just him, but invisible weight, too. Sometimes he'd be moving a chaos of entrails into a heap, and he'd stop to prop himself with the broomstick and yawn. Sometimes he forgot to answer and would only nod, which a black man normally would never do in relation to a white lady. Unless he was swaying at the brink.

Anna had a big order coming up—the Valentine's benefit at the firehouse was two weeks away. As if she needed trouble, the teacher stopped by to discuss her son Louis. She commented that he had a decent mind. Could read well, so what was the problem with his math?

Howard talked with him man-to-man on the front porch. The end of that week was bingo night at St. Aloysius, the Catholic church, a new client. Meaning they needed to progress from mounds of okra, crabs, shrimp, onions, tomatoes, and rice, by virtue of elbow grease and correct calculations, nevermind inspiration, to gumbo. Anna said, Here's a recipe for twelve, and Howard said, You specify how much okra, how many crabs, how many onions we need to prepare dinner for forty salivating people who have Friday night appetites and want to win the jackpot, and write it down for your mother.

Louis reacted by looking bored and rolling his eyes, a very dangerous thing to do because that bored look always caused Howard's forehead to turn red and he wasn't going to put up with it for an instant. *Now!* he shouted.

Louis scrammed, leaping away like a hound, over the ottoman in the living room and around the side table with the recipe squashed inside his pants pocket. While his mother planted twenty caladiums in the front flower bed and ironed four shirts, Louis toiled in his room. When he emerged clutching a large sheet of lined paper, the sass had subsided. He'd been stuck on okra because no one knew how many pods were in a bushel. But he'd written:

The Thing with Willie

Gumbo for Forty
1. *Okra: 2/3 of a bushel basket*
2. *Crabs: 4.95 dozen*
3. *Oysters: 33*
4. *Onions: 19 and 4/5 @ 4 inches in diameter*
5. *Chopped parsley: 16 and 1/2 tablespoons*

Of course, Anna had never in her life used a precise recipe for stews. For her famous cakes, yes, and she had to be fussy about whether to add one teaspoon of vanilla or one and a half. But gumbo came about after an evening at the kitchen table chopping okra while you were sipping iced tea. The idea of 19 and 4/5 onions was amusing, but in the spirit of the math lesson, Anna followed it faithfully.

At John's Seafood, she and Louis shopped together. Anna told Willie that her son figured she needed thirty-three oysters and 59.4 crabs.

That right, Mr. Louis?

Yes, Willie, the way I calculate it.

Well, you got it. You watch me.

I'd like for Louis to practice his timekeeping, Anna added.

Yes ma'am.

You're so fast with the oyster knife, could he practice with the stopwatch right here?

All right, Miz Clinton.

Louis observed that Willie shucked thirty-three oysters in four minutes and fifty-seven seconds flat. He made a note of this. Instead of 0.4 of a crab, Willie suggested they take half of a giant blue crab's body.

The rest of the week, Willie wouldn't prepare Anna's fish without asking: did your boy figure this for you, ma'am? If she said no, he'd say, well ma'am, won't he be disappointed if you don't check with him?

Before the '29 crash, Anna had been a professional baker. Now her business wasn't weddings and birthdays but Easter lunch at the hospital or fried fish for the city plumbers' late shift. She usually prepared extra because in Galveston, like all over, there were people who if they didn't hook a flounder that day, they did not eat—regulars at her back porch who would sweep or rake in exchange for a bowl of soup.

After a long day cooking, she liked to go walking on the beach. Anna had never seen a mountain or even a hill. She'd never seen snow. But she'd been born to the Gulf of Mexico, and when she was young, all she wanted to be was wet. On the island, summer heat was treacherous, and her mother didn't object even back in the nineties when she waded into the surf in an old dress. She liked the mush of sand between her toes—hot sand on the beach, wet sand at the water's edge, cool water inching over her feet to her ankles—and she'd push at the tide as it was grabbing her stomach, her breasts, and rising up and over her back while she moved against the friendly resistance of the ocean, like roughhousing with her uncles, wild and safe at once, deeper and deeper until the water surmounted her shoulders, swells were nipping her cheeks, and her skirts were billowing to her hips. She walked slowly, savoring, and didn't mind the fish nibbling her ankles; they made her smile to herself. She'd plunge her face under, shaking her head from side to side and snorting out the salty water like a dog in a bath. Dogfish, her mother called her. And she'd swim and trot along, riding the current back, taking a long time for it. She wanted her hair soaked, dripping, wanted water to sink clear through her scalp, and whatever slab of worry was weighing on her chest, well, it dissolved.

No denying it was a nice break to be getting business from the firehouse—fifty chicken and dumplings suppers for the annual Valentine's benefit. Louis studied the situation and constructed the shopping list. This led to Anna's visiting a chicken farm to select thirteen and two-thirds pullets which, since she was purchasing them live, was going to be difficult. (Louis' fractions were the current family joke.) She'd arranged to have them dressed, so she left the birds squawking and scratching at the butcher's, and stopped in at John's. Anna and Johnny chatted about the mild February weather and the price of flounder, and then he mentioned that Willie's wife Patty was pregnant with her seventh baby and that Willie hadn't shown up for work for two days. What's wrong, she thought. He needs the money. And who'll clean my fish for me? That was Wednesday morning.

Thursday was the day before the benefit. In the evening the whole family—Howard, Anna, Louis, and sister Lucy—were hacking chickens into stew-sized pieces and tossing skin, bones, and fat to the center of the kitchen table, when Willie knocked on the back door, a child in his arms.

The child had to be Raymond. He was small. Cocker spaniel sized. Not malnourished—his skin was a strong coffee color and he wasn't skinny—but he was limp. A bag of limbs. Bones bundled together, but not holding him up. His head rolled around on his neck, and he was drooling.

Evening, Miz Clinton, ma'am. Don't mean to intrude. This here's my boy Raymond.

Why hello Willie. We're cutting all these chickens up. There's a big mess in here and an awful smell.

Can't be as bad as fish.

I don't mind the fish smell.

Really she didn't. To see trout and redfish laid out fat and glistening on ice, begging her for butter, garlic, and lemon, was a pleasure.

The young son Raymond wasn't just slow or sick. He had something terribly wrong with him. He made a constant noise, whimpering and howling, and Willie couldn't shift him around frequently enough to quiet him. Raymond was four years old and had never uttered a single word. He was wearing a diaper.

How is your wife, Willie?

She's all right. Expecting her seventh. We just found out.

Oh, well, that's nice.

Yeah. I suppose. Listen Miz Clinton, I was wondering. It's Raymond's fifth birthday on Saturday. Patty ain't feeling so good right now, and I want a cake for my little boy here.

As Anna talked with Willie, she kept turning her ear toward her family. The kids and Howard were still at the chickens in the kitchen; the hammer of the cleaver and their chatter created a comforting stir in the background. She had a queasy feeling, watching the idiot child. Willie's shoulder was soaked, and she produced a towel.

What sort of cake, Willie?

I'd like to buy one of your great cakes I've heard about. Chocolate icing. And I want you to write Raymond's name on it. With icing.

Why sure, Willie. Of course, I'll make it. What color icing?

You decide. You can make it pretty. I've heard.

Howard didn't like the interruption and snapped, How did she think she was going to get everything done? Things were on his nerves.

Getting that cake baked in the midst of the chicken bones and biscuit dough with the fire chief's wife stopping in every hour to check on things—the idea got on Anna's nerves, too. But she determined to do it.

She labored over her broth, intensifying it with more and more bones, extra onions and green peppers, boiling it down, and down again. She and Lucy sautéed the chicken pieces, set them aside in bowls, kneaded biscuit dough for the dumplings, and around eleven, they put the house back together. With the big mop, Louis washed the kitchen, living room, and hall floors, and Lucy swept the back porch, where they'd been throwing chicken skin, onion peel, and celery ends onto spread-out newspapers. That is, when she wasn't leaning on the broom yawning. Anna was going to assemble and simmer the stews Friday morning and afternoon, and the event was at seven p.m., so the only time for the cake was that very Thursday night, late, after the kids and Howard went to bed. Without exactly lying, she gave Howard the impression that she was contriving a treat for the fire chief.

What's the cake for?

I'll give some to people who help us get our dinners together or maybe to the fire chief, since he's trusting us with the job.

Not a bad idea.

Since the crash, Anna had been working with chicken guts and fish parts and hadn't made many beautiful desserts. "Weddings by Anna" had become known because of a particular specialty: her four-layer spice cake with buttery almond frosting and on top, a burst of white sugar calla lilies with yellow stamens and pistils in a surround of blue asters. But now people who had been wealthy in the twenties were driving old Fords and dispatching their children to the justice of the peace to get married. So her longing for the finest lately was expressed with extra spices and sensational gravies.

In the good solitude of the dim kitchen, Anna sifted her best white cake flour twice, so it would be silky and light. She had always known, as if angels were whispering how, about creaming the butter and sugar thoroughly. About using sweet Ware's Dairy butter in the first place. About superior Mexican vanilla and fresh eggs. She still possessed a few bars of premium Swiss chocolate, which she grated and swirled into the batter for a marble effect. She whipped six egg whites and folded them in quickly so the cake would be airy, divine.

At two in the morning, aroma flowering from the oven, she took the risen cake out to cool. The frosting came easy. For that she used regular baker's chocolate, melted in the top of a double boiler and then mixed into the already combined confectioner's sugar and butter. She spread the cake with the chocolate icing and divided the reserved, not-chocolate icing into three mounds, adding green coloring to one, pink to one, yellow to the other. With her French cake decorator she dripped pink sugar roses, the size of a baby's puckered mouth, in a circle on top of the chocolate frosting, and in the center she wrote, in looping script, *Raymond*. She crafted perfect green stems and leaves and added yellow centers to the roses. Then she removed her sapphire ring (her birthstone), licked the frosting from it, carefully rinsed and dried it, and put it back onto her right ring finger. She believed that something pretty could usually make you feel better and she felt inspired by its confident beauty, its perfection. "Clear minded" was what the sapphire stood for, and she always wore it while she worked.

Her fourth apron of the day was splattered with god knows what, and she smelled like ground-up animals and plants. As she ran a dishrag around the drainboards, her arms cramped; she was dead on her feet; her feet were somewhere below, far away from the rest of her body.

Really, she thought, one more rose would make it look better but she stopped at six because it was the boy's fifth birthday: five and one to grow on. Finally, she arranged the cake in a covered cooler so the roses wouldn't subside. At three-thirty a.m. she fell into bed.

Late Friday afternoon, Anna and Lucy were packing serving utensils for the last run to the firehouse hall when Willie rapped at the back door, crumpling a dollar bill in his fist. He was alone.

But Anna had decided that this cake was not for sale. She told Willie that her husband was very strict about how she disposed of her cakes, and he had given her instructions that because Willie had helped so often when they needed a rush order of shrimp or oysters, the cake was to be a birthday gift to Willie and his family. Well, Willie would not have it.

No ma'am. No way. I have the money right here and you have to take it.

But you gave me a chance to show my stuff, Willie. Nobody's asking for pretty cakes these days. You did me a favor.

The Thing with Willie

Your cake is just beautiful. Beautiful. His name and all. I don't know how you do it, but it's just right.

Anna couldn't take cash from such a poor man. But there was no arguing with him (My feet are planted here till you take it), and she didn't have time for a prolonged discussion. He insisted. Okay, she said, I'll take a nickel, and held out her jar of change. He kept dropping coins in until she retracted the jar, so he must've deposited two or three. For a long time after, the clink of his nickels stayed with her, like a deep shiver.

With the cake in the bakery box, Willie disappeared into the alley, and they got busy with the firehouse supper. Some time during the evening, Anna told Howard the cake had gone to Willie. She wanted to clear that up; she didn't like unfinished business. Howard was enjoying the cheer in the firehouse hall, so all he said was, Why'd you give him the whole thing?—to show he could still question her decisions.

By ten o'clock they must have wiped their hands on their aprons a hundred times, splashed gravy onto the floor fifty times, and said you're welcome two hundred times. But they would surely be hired to supply more benefit dinners; the fire chief's wife all but said so, and with four of them working, tidying the mess wouldn't be that bad.

Very early Saturday morning, while Anna and Howard, Lucy and Louis, were sleeping hard, Willie carried the pretty cake and his little boy Raymond to a pier. There, tied to a piling, was an old but spacious rowboat, belonging to someone, he didn't know who. The weather was perfect: cool, clear, blue sky blooming with pink and orange clouds.

Willie tied his son's legs to the seat so he wouldn't be tossed over in a swell and joined him in the center of the boat. He rowed east toward the sunrise, passing shrimp boats, cotton ships, and fuel barges, and on and on they went straddling waves, jumping waves, bouncing, riding all the way with the Gulf. After they were beyond sight of the beaches, he aimed a pistol at Raymond's head, pulled the trigger, and then pointed it at himself.

By late Saturday afternoon, the boat had drifted back to shore. The cake was still in the bakery box, secured with ropes in the hold between the two bodies. It was intact—fragrant and colorful— except that it had been neatly cut. Two large slices were missing. All the pink sugar roses, with the perfect green leaves and yellow centers, were gone too.

Soon it grew hot again, and hotter still, March to July, and so on. Anna started going to the beach in the early mornings, walking ankle deep in the small waves. Howard found a job selling typewriters, and he and Louis were the ones who on Sundays delivered Anna's étouffées to Patty. She had a baby girl at the end of the summer.

Wild Water

Galveston 1900

Everybody knew that Anna Beaumont dog-paddled before she could stand upright, and by the time she was five, she'd mastered a proper crawl and a swift sidestroke—as if she had not been born in a bed, but washed into town straight from the ocean. She was part of it, joined with it, never had any fear of water or wind. Anna's mother soon understood that her girl was perfectly able to steam through the breakers and into the sunset, and therefore she paid attention. Sitting plump in her maroon beach chair, studying Anna's strokes, she'd tug her pinstriped railroad cap down against the flare of the sun and hail her daughter, triumphant in the sea.

The Gulf of Mexico did not give Anna any trouble, but by the time she was fifteen, it was trouble she wanted. She was tired of being a good little student, a great girl. It was 1900 and on the edge of that century, all was calm, all was bright, and Anna's mother and father took her terribly for granted. Her parents were submerged in endless matters of house. Family dinners were torture.

"Papa, can we take the train to the city on Saturday?"

"What?" Mr. Beaumont didn't look up from the paper. He continued to scratch the mosquito bite on his neck. Mrs. Beaumont didn't seem to hear, either.

"Did you pick up the flour yet? What about the feed? The chickens would starve if it was up to you."

They would've cared more if she'd been a rosebush; at least they would've pruned and fertilized and admired her. She wanted something to happen, something with a boy behind the oleander hedges, or just something.

One blazing May morning, the kind of morning when heat grips you by the head and sweat pools behind your ears, Anna and her mother stretched after gardening, brushed mud off their skirts, and decided to take a dip. They walked to the beach, waded and splashed, shared a sandwich. After an hour, Mrs. Beaumont reminded Anna of the rule that she must not swim alone and left her to nap under the beach umbrella. She ambled toward home, squishing her own bare feet in the cool wet sand until she had to turn left, away from shore, onto the street, out of sight.

Well, Anna plunged in to swim against whitecaps and practice her crawl. She knew how to sidestroke inside the trough between waves so they encompass you, and she rode along within that embrace, her body melting away, becoming tide and surf, and then rolling back to shore in her own good time. She kept in the water, happily immersed to her shoulders, for a good while. The gulf was beautiful that day—clear enough in places to see crabs darting and long curling waves to rock you. Eventually, Anna flew in on the rise of an impertinent breaker, landed a mile or two up the beach. And though she knew Galveston Island as well as her own house, now, freed from her mother's worry, she determined to know it even better.

She licked the salt from her lips, pushed tangled hair off her forehead, and shaking herself dry, turned to see where she'd landed. Not a hundred feet beyond the dunes was a heartstopping sight: white tents stretching down the beach, fanning into the hot distance—the immigrant settlement she'd always heard of, a tent city full of foreigners. Anna shivered, hardly believing her luck, and grinned, bowling along.

At first there was no rhyme or reason to it. She spied a short, brown man in a head scarf, and ten feet away, a pale blond fellow in a straw hat. Dozens of children. A shirtless boy. A woman with a long black braid and dark skin, in a tight white blouse and gathered skirt. A girl in orange and white, her outfit wrapped around her like a sheet. Chinese, together in ten or twelve tents. Negro people, too, maybe not from Texas or Louisiana, maybe really from Africa?

Her father rode to the encampment sometimes to find yard workers, but instructed Anna to avoid the dirty people who lived there. "You don't need to know them. They don't need to know you." But instead of gloom and squalor, she found a bustling small town, conducting itself in a confusion of languages. Boys were hefting buckets of water; children with pails full of eggs or fish scurried around; women were hanging clothes up to dry and stacking kindling. She just hadn't expected it to be so convivial and intriguing, and she felt excited, but speechless and staring, like a latecomer to an odd ark.

About twenty feet in, she noticed a sizable tent with the flap tied open. A pretty woman was grinning at something behind her; in fact she was crouching and trying to duckwalk outside, through the flap, but someone pulled her back in, toppling her over, and she laughed. The flap flopped shut, and Anna could see the shadows of a couple rolling about inside, which gave her an anxious but not unpleasant feeling in her stomach.

A woman in a checked dress was leaning over a wooden crate, setting up for a meal. Weren't those dishes rather fine? The bowls were decorated in a border of lavender flowers, and there was a medallion in the center of each plate. She placed a vase of flowers on top of the crate. She was chatting to another woman, who was stirring something over a fire, ten feet away. Were those silver forks and knives? Anna's family didn't own any silver.

From what her relatives were always saying, she'd expected scary, misbegotten vagrants. But here were people who had the nerve to enjoy themselves, quite apart from the good citizens of Galveston. Anna was stunned to have accidentally defied her parents twice over—first by swimming alone and drifting off limits and then, by deliberately visiting the forbidden camp—and amazed to be rewarded so richly. She'd caught her mother and father red-handed wrong!

She brushed sand off her feet and tried to tie her hair back and straighten her outfit so she'd resemble something other than a drowned chicken. She approached the women setting out the food.

"Hello. I hope I'm not interrupting, but I just came off the beach. I live in town."

The two women looked blank, but they smiled.

"Where are you from?" asked Anna.

"Poland."

"Those are beautiful dishes."

"My mother's. I couldn't leave behind. Sorry, my English."

"What's your name?"

"Anna."

"Anna? Really? My name is Anna, too."

"Two Annas. Nice! Nice! You are Polish?"

"No, no. I'm from Texas. Right here."

As she cleaned fish on her back porch, the Beaumonts' next door neighbor, Mrs. Brady, had opined that the port of Galveston needed to curb its Ellis Island act, processing thousands of foreigners on their way west. "Too many. Staying way too long; it's one thing for them to stop here for a few days, but living in tents for months is ridiculous." Foreigners' children were urchins, in rags and starving. Newcomers squatting in tents were undesirable; established citizens had to keep up standards. But Anna was now noticing that these wretched tent people were not particularly smitten by her inherent superiority.

"Over there is English," smiled the Polish Anna. "A doctor. He speaks."

Anna saw another big tent, a baby crying, plus four more children. A woman was slapping her own arm.

"I hate mosquitoes," Anna offered.

"God, yes," the woman answered. She was maybe in her late twenties.

"I do hate 'em and I hate slapping myself like an idiot. We didn't have so many in Galway."

"Excuse me. Where is that?"

"Ireland, dearie."

"Are you with your family?"

"Yes, we're together, all seven of us."

"I'm new here. Are the men at work?"

"Some of 'em are working, if they're lucky."

"Your husband?"

"Yes. Yes."

"I heard your husband is a doctor."

"No. Not him. There's one in a tent around the corner."

"Where does your husband work?"

"On the piers. Gets two meals a day that way."

"What's his job?"

"He unloads cotton. Sugar. Whatever there is. You're full of questions. Where do you live?"

"In town. Near the beach."

"Everything is near the beach. It's an island. What's your daddy do?"

"He works in a shop."

"We're moving out of this place in a week or two. We finally got enough money to rent ourselves a real roof."

Anna sidled through on the makeshift paths, picking her way among the fantastic people. Everybody was occupied hanging laundry, sweeping sand out of tents, reading to children, cleaning fish. Most smiled or waved as she strolled among the rumble of languages. She sniffed at bunches of dried lavender and noticed ropes of chile peppers hanging alongside jars of red, yellow, amber, and black spices, like potions from other continents carried here just to entice her away from the boring world of history classes and yard work.

A young woman with long dark hair, gold necklaces dangling on her forehead, bracelets on her ankles, wearing an aster-blue wrap-around dress, stood beside a whistling kettle. She had a bare midriff, like a circus performer. Anna herself wasn't allowed to wear jewelry. She stared, wishing for such beautiful black hair, forgetting herself.

"Hello, miss," the girl said. "My name is Mita."

"Hello, Mita. My name is Anna." Anna held out her hand. "Where are you from?"

"From Asia. And you?"

"Galveston. Right here."

Anna was out of her depth. The only Asians she knew were Chinese dockworkers. They had a language so totally peculiar that no one could learn it. But this girl didn't look Chinese, and her English was perfect.

In the next instant Anna was pushed off her feet—her face in the sand and the breath whacked out of her. Her leg twisted and throbbing. A small boy was scampering away, laughing. He'd kneed her from behind, like a bull terrier, and taken her down. He also bit her on the elbow! Immediately, a sweet-looking, dark-skinned man in an immaculate white cotton shirt approached her. He had black hair and a lovely mustache.

"That little brat, Roger. I saw him trip you."

"I didn't see anyone. All of a sudden I was knocked over."

"Does it hurt?"

"Yes." She was teary from the pain; her ankle was bruised.

"My name is Vikram. I am a doctor; I live here. May I help?"

Mita seemed to be running after the brat and disappeared into the sprawl of tents.

Vikram knelt beside her, took her ankle in hand, and turned it very slowly to the right and to the left. The other Anna appeared; she bent over and patted Anna on the arm. "Don't worry."

"Do you have shoes, miss?"

"No, I swam here." She felt ridiculous in her silly bathing costume and bare feet.

"Yes, you are wet, all right. From where?"

"Near the midway. My mother and I ate a sandwich and she left and I decided to go for a swim."

"Without your mama watching you."

"She had to go. She had things to do at home."

"Best not to swim alone. Some of those currents are strong."

"The next thing I knew, I was here."

"I think you should support that ankle. It's very tender already. I can wrap it for you."

"I'm not supposed to be here."

"Righto. Dirty immigrants. And one of them has your foot in his hand."

Dr. Vikram took a length of bandage from inside his tent. He touched the sore ankle lightly, compared one foot to the other. He wound the cloth around and around the bruise. She liked the feel of his palm against her foot, and how he made her feel better without fuss. He had calm black eyes with starlight in them. She felt a tingling up through her back, all over the skin on her shoulders. There were no doctors in her family and no fine china, either.

Of course, she had to get back somehow and suddenly, as though a basket of eggs was about to spill, she was scared about going home. Maybe she could swim; it would take hours to walk with a sore ankle.

"Listen. I know someone with a pony cart who won't mind giving you a lift home. You'd better not walk." Vikram smiled. "Don't even think about swimming."

She saved the bandage, washing it out with perfumed soap. At night, in bed, she would imagine his hands around her foot, his eyes full of concern. She'd feel hot and uncomfortable and would get up and try to read or tidy something. He filled her mind and imagination. No matter what she was doing, he beckoned, and she welcomed him. She was preoccupied, forgetting her chores. How many times did her mother have to say: Anna, try to remember the laundry today, will you? She did badly on a math test, prompting Mrs. Connell, the teacher, to call and inquire if Anna was all right, she usually was such a good student. Mrs. Beaumont ventured that maybe the ankle, which Anna had twisted on her way home from the beach, was keeping her awake, making her tired.

She reenacted the bandaging of her foot. After a week, the exact features of his face began to blur ever so slightly, but when she ran her fingers lightly over her still purply-black injury, when she held the bandage up to the light, examining it for torn places, when she laid it on the floor to smooth it perfectly, then slowly wound it over the bruise, adjusting it as if hers was the only ankle in the world—his face came back.

There was a medical school in town, and she hobbled to the registration office, asking if there was a student called "Vikram." The clerk didn't think so. She had a friend whose mother took in boarders. The entire second floor of the house was occupied by medical students. Since Vikram was a doctor, perhaps he'd like to stay there instead of in the tent. She asked Mrs. Agee how much the rent was and if they had any openings. Well, not right now, Miss Anna; maybe later in the term.

Until she got better, she couldn't go back to find him. She accepted her mother's cold packs, but refused to go to the family doctor out of deference to Vikram. But her ankle was taking forever to heal, and she was furious at the wait.

"Who exactly lives in the tent city?" she ventured at dinner.

"What about it?" said her father.

"Where do they come from?"

"Misfits from Europe. Most of them check into immigration at Galveston and then keep going. Oklahoma or Utah or somewhere." Her heart plummeted. She knocked over her milk glass, and her mother turned to get a towel. So Vikram might be leaving Galveston, and soon.

"Will they get work out west?"

"Sure. Lots of track to be laid and metals to be mined."

"But I thought they lived in the camp for a long time. Aren't some of them bankers? Or doctors?"

"No, they're not. Why would a real doctor live in a dirty camp like that?"

"I think you got heatstroke out there. You better forget that brown doctor, sugar," warned Lizzie, Anna's friend at school.

"It's nothing. I need to thank him, that's all." She wanted to know somebody from Europe, too. Somebody handsome, who wasn't just from her dumb old street.

In geography class, they were studying Mexico. She asked the teacher if they could study Europe instead.

"You had England last year. And in sixth grade, you had the Continent of Europe."

"I know," said Anna. "But we're older now, and Galveston is a big port. Ships come here from all over, including Europe."

Lizzie took Anna's arm in hers as they left the classroom. "I'm going to go out there with you myself," she whispered. "I want to see the camp. I want to see your brown doctor."

Anna's ankle improved, and she could finally walk to the beach, but slowly, with Lizzie or her mother; she could babysit Mrs. Brady's kids without them being able to escape from her. One Saturday morning a month after the accident, she was pushing little Joseph's carriage along Broadway, past tobacco shops and drugstores. They kept on down the street to the midway, toying with candy and postcards. She took off his baby shoes and hers too so they could go wading, stopping in first at a popcorn booth.

There he was. Wearing a work shirt and rough trousers, he seemed to be loading boxes. She smoothed her hair back and bit her lip for color, forgetting about the baby in her hurry. "Dr. Vikram! Dr. Vikram! Hello! Remember me? You helped me with my ankle!"

He glanced away from his heavy work, looking puzzled. She was terrified that he wouldn't recognize her.

"I'm sorry to interrupt you; I just wanted to thank you, that was all."

"Oh yes. The wet one. The great swimmer."

"I shouldn't have been prowling around your camp like that."

"No, it was nice to meet you. You must be strong, to swim so far and to recover so beautifully. You are walking well now?" His accent was refined; he didn't sound like the other people from Europe.

"Yes. Fine. Thanks. You did a good job. Could I ask you one thing?"

"Why of course." He continued to organize his boxes as they talked.

"What country in Europe are you from? We're studying Europe in school."

"Me? Oh I'm not from Europe. We are from India. Madras. I spent time in South Africa, then London. Then here." She had no idea where Madras was or what India looked like on a map. Of course she had heard of Africa.

"But you speak English."

"And Hindi, Tamil, Afrikaans, and Spanish. The Spanish is just lately, from the camp. I like to be able to communicate with patients directly."

So he really was a doctor! Why was he working at the midway popcorn stand?

"So you help out here, sometimes?"

"My dear girl, I —"

She didn't like "my dear girl." It sounded like something her father would say. She interrupted him.

"I'm really not a girl. I'm almost finished with school!"

"I'm sorry. What is your good name?"

"My name is Anna Beaumont. Your name is Dr. Vikram."

"You have an excellent memory! Vikram is my first name. Vikram Rajinder. What I meant to say was that I work anywhere I can. I need the money. Foreign doctors don't get hired so easily. But I keep my skills up, out at the camp." The owner of the popcorn stand was frowning at them, and the baby let out a yell. Anna jumped. "I have to go."

"Is he your child?"

She could feel herself turning an awful shade of deep red, as if a renegade sunburn was rushing up the entire length of her chest, her neck, her cheeks and forehead, her ears. She spun away, saying hoarsely, "No. He lives next door. To my parents. I live with my parents, in town." The owner of the popcorn stand cleared his throat.

"Vick. I need those boxes pronto."

On Lizzie's second-floor bedroom balcony, the girls conferred in detail about Anna's beautification potential. They combed her long blond hair all the way out, perfecting how it would fall. At the drugstore, they found hair shine, tooth whitener, and perfume. Anna stayed out of the sun all week and avoided gardening, hoping to keep her skin pale. They picked a soft blue cotton dress, with buttons that cinched the bodice tightly and a skirt that brushed her leg just at the ankle, so that she'd have to pull it up a bit to reveal that ankle, in case anybody inquired. She daydreamed of strolls on the beach and evenings on the piers. Perhaps after talking for hours, he would put his arm around her waist. He was so smart, so handsome, that he would know what to do next.

Finally Lizzie and Anna borrowed two ponies from Lizzie's father and embarked early in the morning, figuring that if Vikram was working at the midway, his hours would be later in the day. Trotting over wet sand and letting tide pools splash the horses' legs, they felt like a million dollars, daring and modern.

Lizzie was shocked to see so many tents.

"They go on forever." It was true. Up on horseback, Anna had a better sense of the expanse of the encampment and tried to get her bearings. They dismounted and tied the horses, slowly walking past the first few tents, not recognizing a single word people were saying. The exotic foreign beach, so close to home, parents, and the American flag, thrilled Anna. Lizzie wasn't so sure. "Nothing bad's going to happen, Lizzie. They're friendly. They just don't speak English yet." But she couldn't find her Irish lady or the other Anna, with her fine china and silver. People were stirring oatmeal over small fires, scolding chickens, crabbing. A clear sky was laced with cottony clouds. Three tents were being struck, the occupants evidently ready to move on.

No one took notice of the two young women; it was a busy place. Anna asked an old man, sitting on top of a woodpile, if there was a doctor around. He chuckled: "No English! No English!" The fourth person she tried, a sweaty, grimy but cheerful woman, used hand gestures to direct them through the maze of animals, children, crates, clotheslines, folding chairs, rowboats, and lean-tos. Soon they were lost and had no idea which direction they'd come from. Just ahead was a spacious tent. They could hear talking. Was this the doctor's home? Did Vikram have sisters and brothers here?

Sure enough, there he was, sitting cross-legged on a mat in front of the tent. He spotted her.

"Oh, Miss Anna. How are you? How nice for you to visit! And your friend. Please, will you have tea?"

The tent flap opened and the beautiful Mita, draped in flowing green and gold silk, stepped out, carrying a baby girl and trailed by two small boys. "This is my family," announced Vikram.

Anna hadn't connected Mita to Vikram; she'd forgotten about the friendly young woman "from Asia." She averted her gaze to the tent flap, the sand at her feet, the campfire, the arrangement of seashells on the table. She felt hot and cold all at once, her foolishness, like lightning cracking a sky, overwhelming everything.

Mita and Vikram served strong tea harvested in Darjeeling, a town in the Himalayas of India, and then showed the girls a trove of spices they'd never heard of—cardamom, turmeric, cumin, and a peculiar kind of butter; there were bolts of cloth from their home city of Madras. Vikram drew a map on the sand, marking where India was and the route their ship took from Madras to South Africa and from Africa to London, Louisiana, and Texas. They had planned to go to Colorado, but liked the climate in Galveston and were thinking of staying. There were Spanish people here with skin like theirs. Maybe they'd emigrate to Mexico. They weren't sure yet, but they were glad travelers, free to choose from the whole world.

How could she, in a hundred years—in a thousand years—have imagined that Vikram would be remotely attracted to a blonde person in a light blue dress, so clumsy she let a ragamuffin knock her down, so provincial she thought it was daring to take the ferry to Houston? Maybe the chill in the surf that day had banished all reason; the bag of her mind had flopped open and her common sense tumbled out like dried peas. Vikram gave them each a bundle of cinnamon sticks, tied in red string, and asked: How is your ankle? Would you like me to have a look? That was the last thing she wanted; what she wanted was to go. Next to Mita, she was pale and boring, a child.

They took off at a gallop, arriving home for lunch. Being her best friend, Lizzie didn't rub it in. After her comeuppance, Anna felt nothing at first—as if none of it had ever happened. Her head cleared and other things skipped in: a party next week, a history exam, a hem for her apron, a church supper, her mother's rosebushes. She liked to go fishing with her father, and he had offered a trip in his rowboat. Where had those matters been for the last few weeks? Now they rushed back like overdue bills. She noticed that her mother had a cough; the porch needed sweeping; and where were her sheets of music? She suddenly missed them intensely. Well, remarked her father, we all looked for your songbooks last week. Don't you remember? She did not. Mrs. Agee sent her a note, to Miss Anna Beaumont, announcing a vacancy for a medical student, which fortunately she intercepted before Mrs. Beaumont got a look. She didn't miss Vikram or his touch; her desire for him had been banished by humiliation, stuck now, warm and red, in the pit of her stomach.

Everything else in town, however, was, according to the vast majority of citizens, absolutely splendid. If you listened to Mr. Beaumont and his friends: the great port of Galveston was hosting crucial peanut and sugar ships. There was money to be made; the latest inventions were racing into stores, such as the electric fan the Beaumonts had just purchased. The newspaper advertised "youth restored by electricity while you wait." Broadway, the main street, had become millionaire's row. In school, Anna was able to positively identify Madras as a city in India and India as part of Asia. The Pagoda Bathhouse was packed with visitors, and the midway lured hundreds of vacationers for crabs and beer, postcards and candy. To make wider beaches, the twelve-foot sand dunes that protected Galveston Island against unruly storm waves had been shoved away.

The first Fourth of the new century drew masses of picnickers. Thousands of people crowded merrily on the beaches, heads cocked in celebration, as fireworks broke the night sky and its moon into shooting stars and colored light. For the first time since she and Lizzie galloped away from the encampment, Anna remembered in a rush the smells that enfolded her there: cinnamon, mint, and jasmine mingling with salt air, and she knew she was proud of that long swim to the forbidden camp. She knew wanderers from Asia and Africa! She knew the scent of cardamom!

The following Saturday night, after a supper of bland oyster stew, after listening to her father tell all about tobacco sales, Anna washed the dishes, fed old bones to her puppy, read her book, and kissed her mother good night. But she couldn't sleep, for her adventures had come back in a new form, tingles of pride replacing waves of embarrassment. Once the lights were out, she sat up in bed, wrapping her arms around her knees.

After a while, she heard a voice—her father's friend Jack Richards on the front porch. She pulled on an old checked dress and tiptoed barefoot down the outside staircase, quiet as a mouse.

Anna's father and Jack were laughing and jostling one another on their way to the front gate. They clanged it open, paused to talk some more, and marched down the street, toward open water.

She had never sneaked out at night before, and she had certainly never dreamed of trailing her father in the shadows. But this night, right now, it seemed inevitable. She let the men ramble a block ahead; then, like a freed pony, trotted through her front yard, breached the gate, and crept along. Anna knew her father gadded about on Saturday nights with other men, but what did they do? She followed, slipping behind hedges and the corners of houses so Papa wouldn't see her, and after a few minutes along Bath Street, they reached the great Pagoda Company pier, arching like an enchantment over the Gulf of Mexico, still full of rowdy quartets and strolling couples, everybody silly under the fat moon.

Mr. Brady, from next door, and Mr. Knight, the locksmith, were waiting, and soon, Abe, the colored man who worked in neighborhood yards and played piano on the midway at night, showed up. They shook hands and yakked about a fishing trip and the heat and politics; popped open a bottle and passed it around for swigs. It was cool there, paradise, and all of them loved the wonderful small roar of night waves brushing shore, and how, in the dark above, stars had blurted forth, tiny surprises in all directions. Eventually the men sauntered to the end of the pier, where an electric light was swinging out over wild water.

To Anna's total astonishment, her father, Hugh Beaumont, unbuttoned his shirt, pulled off his trousers, pulled off his underwear. The other men stripped their clothes, tossed them like weeds in a pile on the pier, and leapt into the surf one by one.

She'd heard about skinny-dipping off the midway, but her papa? Who talked endlessly of mortgages? Racing naked to the end of a pier, arms flung open? The men were ecstatic: swimming hard, catching the long waves like insouciant minor gods, riding high back to shore where they nipped hilariously at the bottle. What time was it? Who cared?

Anna moved down the beach in a wide arc, away from the men. She unbuttoned her collar, raised her gown to her knees, waded in. She backstroked, and her skirt, her hair, floated, buoyant.

The Wall

Galveston 1903

Rustling sheets of paper startled her awake. Must be a mouse hurrying across her desk. Well, it was time to get up anyway.

Howard slept soundly next to her, hardly shifting after they made love the night before. He was unperturbed by the whine of mosquitoes or later, by the buzz of a fly or the ping of water dripping from a leaky vase down to the floor and later still, the wind swirling the curtains out into the room and an uproar of thunder, the clack of rain on the roof, the house provoked by lightning. There was the clock chiming madly—a silver hammer beating the side of a bell to mark the hours, stylish but way too loud. That was how Anna knew that the storm came and went between midnight and three a.m., after which the night practically went dead. Curiously, Howard's breath came faster then, as if he were climbing a ladder in his dreams. All the while, he slumbered right through the ripples of the night, barely stirring, except once to lob an arm across her waist.

Who said mice were quiet? Anna heard papers shuffling, and

shuffling again, as though a small clerk were filing her documents, tiny feet pattering from one side of her desk to the other. No doubt he was punctuating her letter to Aunt Margaret with droppings. She heard him bump the ink bottle, and of course it rolled over the edge and thumped to the floor. There would be ink splattered on the rug unless the screw top held, which it probably hadn't. Still Howard slept like a saint. He'd once whispered that his sleep was heavenly because he had an angel to sleep with. She reached for his hand and kissed all its little hollows.

She'd better get up. The curtains luffed out from the breeze, a welcome signal of coolness in hot old Galveston. Anna folded back the covers, sat tall. Pulled on her cotton gown and robe and blew a kiss to monsieur mouse, who at the sight of her let off a tiny shriek and frantically ran up the curtain, shaking the rod, bringing it all down in a heap on the floor. How the mouse would entertain himself for the rest of the morning, she didn't know.

But now the windowpane was unobstructed and she could exult in the dawn: streaks of orange and yellow made the clouds glorious. She hugged her robe closer around her shoulders and padded in her slippers toward the kitchen, first retrieving the ink bottle, which actually had not spilled. There was no hallway inside the house, just a porch that wrapped entirely around. She stepped out to this gallery, enjoying the salty, moist air, walked around the corner to the back, and unlatched the door to the kitchen. She pumped water into a saucepan, which she set onto her stove for boiling. On the drainboard was a note from Howard: *Put towel back on rack.* (She'd folded it, instead of hanging it.) Another note read: *Wipe up coffee drip.* There was a brown droplet on the floor. Why couldn't he wipe it up? His attention to such things proliferated when he was short of money or had a bad stomach.

From the kitchen she could see all the way through to the front door, for theirs was a shotgun house. Someone was standing on her porch. At six in the morning. She was pretty sure.

She splashed hot water into the coffeepot and waited while the coffee steeped. Then she strained the grounds and poured herself a cup, carrying it with her as she moved through the house. Like most doors in town, the front wasn't locked, and Anna was more curious than afraid. At first she didn't see anyone, so she opened the door and stood with her coffee, enjoying the sky for a few minutes, waving to the milkman passing in his cart, delighting in the lights flickering on, one by one in upstairs bedrooms, along the block.

Evidently the visitor had circled the house while Anna was out front, and now she materialized—Sister Jeanne Marie, from the orphanage that had been destroyed. She lived in a rented room, but she wandered around town; people gave her cups of coffee and glasses of milk and invited her in for lunch. In her black robes and nun's headgear, she appeared to be sailing along the streets, especially at night, for she moved expeditiously as if on her way to an important appointment. The sad thing was, she no longer had a nun's collar; her hem was frayed; loose threads dragged from her sleeve. Serene, efficient Sister Jeanne Marie, teacher of geography, Latin, and arithmetic, was getting a reputation.

But she wasn't half-witted at all. Nor was she insane, a criminal, or a beggar. She didn't have a fever. She just thought it was her fault that so many children had died.

All of the orphans at St. Agnes School, a block from the beach, had perished in the great hurricane of September 1900. So did all the sisters who cared for them, but Jeanne Marie survived. Six thousand residents of Galveston drowned, but Sister Jeanne Marie was saved. Confronting fifteen-foot waves, she had tied eight children together with a rope, thinking it would help them stay afloat. Instead, the rope became tangled in debris, dragging not one, but all, down. People thought grief had made the sister deranged. But Anna didn't think so. She was merely sad beyond description.

Sister Jeanne Marie sat down in the rocker, next to Anna, on the porch. She had dropped in before, but never at six a.m.

"Sister, are you all right? It's dawn." Anna tried to keep her voice unhurried, soft.

"Yes, fine. Sorry if I alarmed you. I was getting tired. I went down to the camp during my midnight walk, and I guess I fell asleep out there. I slipped away so they wouldn't think I was one of the immigration people. I can't sleep at night any more, only around noon, it seems."

"Maybe if you took some wine before bed?"

"Yes, but I felt I was drinking rather too much. I'd finish most of a bottle and wake up three or four hours later. So I stopped. Besides, it's costly."

"Let me give you some warm milk. You can rest inside."

"Thank you, Anna. I will accept your milk. You know I met some people in tents on the beach. Looking for work. They saw that I was wearing a habit and wanted to talk to me about church. I told them my church was gone and my children lost. That usually shuts people up." Sister Jeanne Marie yawned.

"Come in," suggested Anna.

She led Jeanne Marie to the sofa in the darkened front room and offered her an embroidered pillow. Sister sat down, sipping the milk, then slid lower and lower into the cushions, her head faltering to her shoulder. Anna nudged her so she'd lie down, lifted her ankles from the floor, and stretched her legs out on the sofa.

She curled up there, and Anna played a few bars on the piano, a ragtime tune, but very slowly, until Jeanne Marie actually began snoring. Why does everyone else sleep like a rock except me? thought Anna. She tiptoed back to the kitchen to prepare breakfast for three.

She was absorbed in scrambling eggs when she felt Howard's hands at her waist. He had wonderful hands—strong palms that ran like a friendly animal over her body, first hovering very lightly over her skin at night, trying to stir the tiny, fair fuzz on her naked stomach, meanwhile kissing her breasts, first one and then the other.

This couldn't last long, because it roused her so that they would soon be making love like it was somebody's birthday.

He lingered while she packed the lunches, clasping her from behind. He kissed the back of her neck and bit at her ear and she moved her eggs off the burner and turned in his arms and loved him around the neck. She didn't mind at all that the counter was now in disarray, the drainboard smeared with butter.

"Sister's napping on the couch. I found her on our porch this morning."

"How many times is it?"

"Five or six. I'm not sure she remembers the other times. Howard, can she stay here for the weekend while we're gone to Houston?"

"I'll think about it. Well, what harm can she do? Why not."

On the devastated beach, on the island of Galveston, Texas, in the spring of 1902, Anna Beaumont was helping labor crews build a seawall. The new wall would protect the floating city from the next catastrophe.

As they worked, the men disinterred from the sand the remains of lives blown apart by the hurricane in 1900. Houses, churches, shops, and boats had been destroyed. Hundreds of bodies had been lost. There were mountains of trash along the beaches, where seawall construction was going on.

Anna Beaumont wanted her city back, with its cotton exchange and shrimp boats, its what-have-you markets, the jetties and pleasure piers, the frisky midnight bathers. She wanted to be part of the crew, to pass bags of concrete along to her fellows. Mr. Lechien, the foreman, wouldn't let her do any lifting, even though she was nearly eighteen and strong, so she got a job cooking breakfast and lunch on site. Most mornings, she stirred oatmeal, tended the coffee, and watched gangs of men struggle with the sand and ocean. One Tuesday, a Mr. Howard Clinton was clearing a massive dune. Four men were helping him—Vernon, from the country; Wu, of Asian origin; Patrick and Alberto, who lived in tents on the beach. They were able to pitch the sand a shovelful at a time away from the staging area, where the wall would be framed in. But sand is sand and doesn't stay put.

Howard plunged his shovel into the hill. Hit driftwood, tugged it from the sand, tossed it away. With the next probe, he bumped something white and hard: an old sink packed hard with mud, so he had to stop, scoop the sand out, and then haul the sink to the junk pile. What else was trapped in the impossible beach that Anna loved so much? That she'd explored a thousand times, squishing her toes down and down, her feet enfolded by brotherly tides, crabs squiggling out of their holes? Now where families had picnicked, there was an everlasting mess—a construction site and an embryonic wall; the arc of the shore gone bestial and its gray mother, the Gulf of Mexico, a graveyard.

As Anna sorted, chopped, and tasted at her station, Howard and the others found crab shells, a chair back, a soaked Persian rug, a candlestick holder, five shoes, and a femur.

She kept water cups brimming. Trenches flooded with seawater and had to be dug out, redone. In miserable heat. Sweat poured from every forehead, dripped down noses and chins. But there was a provocative breeze and a blue sky.

After lunch: a pitcher, a hammer, piano keys. Then something huge. The crew had to stop and focus on pulling it free. Anna approached the men. She had on a sunhat, old dress, work shoes.

"Let me give you a hand."

"Miss, we'll handle this. It's heavy."

"No, I want to. I'm just standing around."

The boss Lechien was not in sight. Howard glanced at Patrick.

"I don't see anything wrong with her helping, as long as we're careful," he nodded.

Howard studied her small shoulders, trim hips, tanned arms, and caught her gaze.

"Well, okay."

She tied her skirts around her waist, exposing her legs, and put on work gloves. Her arms and shoulders were muscled from carrying her own pots, setting up serving tables, and hoeing her vegetable garden. And from years of swimming in the Gulf. Though she had not been swimming since the hurricane. Two years now.

"Do you know how to tie a good knot?"

"I can try," answered Anna, remembering masses of tangled clotheslines at home.

"Tie the rope to the edge, here. Then we'll heave."

Anna produced a knot, fast. The six of them pulled, and the object budged slightly. The small crowd that always coached the workmen got noisier. They pulled some more and a big wedge of sand, the size of a calf, fell away.

"It's a piano!" someone shouted.

Alberto, a strong Italian, who spoke no English, dug at the sand, which kept falling into the trenches he'd just cleared. With Alberto's third load of heavy mud, there protruded a hand and arm, a person waving from the grave. The lean, tough Patrick, who had been a sexton in his native Ireland, sang out: "God rest his soul," as Alberto by mistake tossed the bones toward Anna's feet.

"Oh sorry, ma'am," chuckled Patrick. "Back home the monks'd rather have rib cages and skulls. Use 'em for decoration in their chapel. Say, that is a beautiful piano."

Anna had seen lots of bones. You'd be weeding your tomatoes, crabbing off a pier, planting a palm—and a rogue collarbone would turn up. They were common. Everybody had lost someone in the screaming torrent, and after the storm, the decay of flesh had been so dangerous that hundreds of bodies were piled onto barges, taken out to sea, and dumped, only to wash ashore, where most were burned. It was a mistake to dwell on this—better to set to work, build a wall.

In fact, Anna had seen so many bones that she could identify them, and she knew these to be the lower half of someone's arm—the radius and ulna—still connected to the wrist, hand, and fingers—carpal, metacarpal, and phalangeal bones. But she stared. Was this the hand of the piano player? She picked it up, and the wrist buckled, the hand fell limp, finger bones dangling. There was a silvery band with a blue stone on the pinky finger. An odd finger for a ring. She held the hand against her waist, the way she might guide a dancing partner, so the others wouldn't see, and retreated to her serving table. She didn't want onlookers fighting over the ring—that would be too depressing. Anna slipped it off the dead finger, dropped it into her pocket, and pinned the pocket shut so the ring wouldn't fall out. She trudged over hillocks of sand and trash, where she let the bones drop to their rest, and returned to the buried piano.

There were boulders lodged against it. The men shoveled sand away and encountered a camera, a ladies' fan, china plates, a dog's collar, pieces of the piano bench. Finally, after two hours, the piano—a baby grand—stood magisterial on the edge of the Gulf of Mexico, missing half its white keys and numerous chips of inlay. Vernon guessed that it was carved from walnut; it clearly had been resplendent with inlaid irises, lilies, roses. With half a piano bench positioned in front, it seemed to be waiting for a musician to stride out of the waves in a dinner jacket and perform Mozart.

The laborers were leaning on their shovels, feeling curiously proud of their work, though they'd made no progress on the wall today, none at all.

"I wonder if you could play that," remarked Patrick. He touched middle C—there was a boing. He tapped out a bit of "Maple Leaf Rag."

"I'd like to fix it up." Howard spoke in an optimistic voice.

"I'd like to fix it up," said Anna, in the same tone of voice, at exactly the same moment.

She liked that Howard came from New Orleans and that

ambition and adventure had propelled him to her island; he was handsome and a good talker. Three months later they were married. After the ceremony in church, they promenaded to the beach with their guests and drank champagne at the section of the seawall where they'd met. They rented a cottage in town and with the help of Alberto, Patrick, Wu, and Vernon, moved the piano—now polished and tuned—into their small front parlor.

Leaving Jeanne Marie on the sofa, Howard and Anna gathered seasonings for Anna to use making lunch at the wall and left the house together. Though Howard had quite a talent for sales, there wasn't much to sell these days, so he continued to construct the wall, and Anna still served meals to the workers. The seawall people dragged burlap bags of potatoes, carrots, beans, onions, oatmeal, and coffee to her station, and she wrote menus—not the sublime creations that came to her mind's eye like mirages as she toiled in the sand and heat—but tasty feeds nonetheless. The men liked her spicy stews, she liked the compliments, and she and Howard both appreciated her wages. Anna had always expected that when she got married, she would have a baby right away, but she did not now feel any hurry about it. So far, in a year of marriage, there had been no conception, and truthfully she was half-trying to prevent one. People thought storm trauma had affected the birthrate—even her mother said so. But Anna was not concerned; she had a job to do, was consumed by the seawall, for she, like other citizens, fully comprehended that Galveston was not even really an island, but a sandbar perilously exposed to virulent forces. The rest of life would follow—could follow—after the wall was solid.

Toward the end of each week, Lechien consolidated scraps from sites all over the beach, and today Anna faced crab legs, celery, chicken bones. But at least there were fat white onions, and she had her own red pepper and garlic to puzzle together into a soup. She needed rice and ran to the seawall office for it, whereupon an Irishman wove her a garland of marigolds and another tucked it on top of her head. Queen of lunch. Those Irish! Under the tent roof that shielded her cooking station from the shock of the sun, a line of forty workers—friends and neighbors joining to make a great wall against the juggernaut, most in torn shirts and ragged trousers—held tin bowls out to her ladle. The thirty-ninth person who offered up a bowl this Thursday noon was Sister Jeanne Marie.

As she ate, she slurped a tiny bit and smacked her lips, each spoonful evidently a joy to her. The men glanced at each other, but were kind. "Sweet lady," asked Patrick. "Can you help me straighten my collar, please?"

"Why certainly, I'd be most happy to," replied Jeanne Marie, who proceeded to tend the wrinkled collar expertly. Anna pushed a gigantic soup pot across the stove.

"Sister, you know I could really use a little help here. Could you wash that out for me?"

Sister's hands were trembling as she reached for the pot; thank you for asking me, thank you. She washed it, leaving scraps of onion and bone in the bottom, and putting the lid on top of the wrong pot. "Can I do another one?" "Yes, thank you," replied Anna, wiping her hands on her apron. Jeanne Marie cleaned the second pot, after which she arranged it on the sand, under the work table.

"Jeanne Marie, will you put that in the box instead, please?"

She smiled and did so. But later when Anna checked her storage boxes, she didn't see the pot. "Oh, I thought it was better to put it out on the sand, after all," Jeanne Marie explained. "It seemed to belong on the sand. Not in the box. I like things to be tidy."

"But it goes in the box. Let me."

"I thought I might find Julio out here. He loved to swim so."

"Julio drowned in the storm, Jeanne Marie," said Anna.

"I'm sorry," she answered. "I think your soup reminded me of our dinners at the orphanage. Of course, I know we lost him. I forget sometimes. I know I seem strange to people."

"You're tired right now. Want to go for a swim later?"

The sister froze with fear. Her eyes filled. Right after the hurricane, the Gulf had been full of bodies, furniture, clothes, and no one would dream of going in. People still suffered from dread of swimming.

"It's so hot and the water's calm. Come on, why don't you? Close to shore. Or we'll just wade."

Howard would say she was stupid to lure a melancholy nun into the Gulf of Mexico. *You're not thinking.* Maybe he was right.

Later in the afternoon, the clouds blossomed into pink and purple tufts, pure sweetness and light. Anna led Jeanne Marie by the shoulders to the breathing edge of the Gulf of Mexico. In and out, in and out, millions of little tides bussing their feet, soothing their pain, except once a century when that ocean exploded into murderous walls of water. Anna's quarrel with the sea was far from settled, but she thought that today for the first time since the storm, she might be able to swim without shuddering.

"Why don't you sit here and watch me?"

"I don't want to sit."

"What about taking off your shoes? Get your feet wet."

"I can't."

"Let me help you. Come on. It's a calm day."

Pelicans sailed over their heads, two diving straight down, then shooting skyward, each with a fish. A hundred egrets lilted to shore, like angels. What could go wrong?

Anna laced their fingers together, gently pulled Jeanne Marie down, so she was sitting on the beach. She unfolded her friend's legs, extending them out in front of her and patted her skirt. Slowly, as if time were on their side, Anna untied one shoe, the other shoe, loosening and tugging at each, and then pulled off her knee stockings, so that Jeanne Marie's toes could curl into the sand.

"Nice ring," remarked the sister. Anna's sapphire ring was gleaming in the sun.

"I found it on the beach, the day I met Howard. Those are nice boots. Soft leather. Where'd you get them?"

"Mrs. Brady gave them to me. May I see your ring?"

Anna tilted the stone so they could both admire the star inside, a feathery hint of god.

"And you just kept it?"

"Well, yes. I didn't want to turn it over to the boss—Lechien— he would've given it to his girlfriend. Besides, it's my birthstone. For September. And it's pretty."

Jeanne Marie smiled, closing her eyes, inhaling deeply, even chuckling, as Anna buried her bare feet and toes in the wet sand, a glob at a time.

"Now keep an eye on me, will you? I'm going in," said Anna. Jeanne Marie fidgeted with her skirt, shook the sand off her feet, tucked her knees under and sat upright, but she didn't protest.

Anna tied her skirt up, waded to her waist. She fell back into the lovely water, letting it spill over her chest and stomach, and threw her head back until her hair was good and soaked. Then she backstroked a bit, sidestroked, always in the shallows.

That Saturday, September 8, 1900, there were odd winds, it's true. Not the kindly breezes we loved so much, but a whiff of something giant. Papa was in Houston visiting my aunt; Mama and I were turning beds and clearing dishes. It was just normal, except we didn't hang out Papa's shirts, as there was a light rain in the morning. The postman marched by importantly, dropped off our mail-order seeds, and told about huge swells crashing bigger and bigger and spilling over the tops of our piers. I wanted to go see but had to finish peeling potatoes. Of course we weren't far from the beach and could hear a commotion whenever we stepped onto the front porch. When streams of water inched onto our street, I got excited and called to mama, I'm going, and she didn't mind. She always loved thunderstorms.

People were milling about, gawking at the booming surf; some were swimming like it was the Fourth. It was exciting, but the water seemed too big, too angry; I got completely soaked from the rough spray. Then the bathhouses—our fancy, famous bathhouses—split apart from their pilings. They just toppled into the sea. Some people were still wading, even then. Then the sky got darker and still darker and you weren't wading any more, you were up to your waist even on the street.

The Gulf of Mexico—my natural home, my playground—became a wall fifteen feet high, roaring toward us and though I had never known brutality in my life, I smelled it then, and pushed home as best I could through deep water, crowded now with uprooted shrubs, footstools, dead chickens.

My mother hugged me hard, and we grabbed cheese and bread and water and climbed to the second floor. Mrs. Brady from next door, her baby, her husband, and our friend Jack and his children and wife, a colored couple who appeared on our stairs—we were all huddled in my room, far side of the wind we thought—my god there were whitecaps six feet high in the back yard—a horrifying and inescapable force had come suddenly upon us like we were just nothing.

I don't remember everything that happened, it was so black all night. There were a few lanterns but no electricity or gas. The awful pummeling rain sliced through our beautiful Broadway Street houses like a cleaver; the wind lifted our roof and put it back, a pot lid jumping over the boil and the babies were crying bloody murder. A streetcar was hurled at the side of the house and the wall broke to pieces and we were sucked toward the breach. There was glass from broken windows all around; we just fell out of our house into the roaring street, everybody scattered yelling and splashing. Mama was quieter than anybody, she kept her head. I was the best swimmer and we held hands and gripped the edge of a door and held on. There was just terror everywhere and the water was thick with chairs and tables, pots, timbers, picture frames, whimpering dogs, dead cows. A kitten landed somehow on our door and mewed and mewed so loud without stopping, it nearly drove us mad but we knew just how it felt. I saw my teacher Mrs. Connell only a few feet away crouched on a floating sofa; she bobbed up and waved at me and as she rose, a flying chair hit her in the back of the head. She was bleeding and trying to stop it with one hand, but we couldn't get to her; we were yanked in the other direction by rushing water. I held tight and Mama maneuvered onto our life raft, which was the floating door, and then I climbed *on too. We spun around and around in the black dark, crashing into sailing cars and trees, screaming through the downpour to strangers and I did see Mrs. Connell one last time that night. Once when we bumped the side of the drugstore my mama hit her leg and lost her grip and fell in and I reached for her and she held on in that cold water for a long time and finally she pulled herself back on the raft and we rode toward open water but there was nothing we could do to stop it and we rolled out into the gulf, roiled away from the city like sailors in bondage. We didn't see any lights or any other people for at least two hours.*

Finally, we were tossed back to shore, only to face a wall of smashed houses splattered every which way on the beach and you could see dead people stuck here and there in the rubble. The awful decay hadn't yet started.

Toads clung to everything. I remember the surface of the fence post out front was slow-motion jerky and snakes hung in the trees. Our house had broken up but most of the bottom floor was left. We made a sort of roof from an abandoned rowboat, old blankets, whatever we could find, and moved back in, feeling god so lucky Mama and I were alive and Papa safe on the mainland.

There were blocks and blocks where nothing was left: no houses, no streets, only scoured sand. The immigrant camp, the tent city on the beach, was completely destroyed, hundreds gone, everybody lost. I had friends there, a doctor from India and his wife and little children; he was kind to me when I'd twisted my ankle and they'd given me cinnamon sticks. All of them were killed. There was a smell from slime left by the bad sea and to this day, any unfamiliar odor makes me overcome with dread. We were victims of mother heaven enraged, of infanticide. People hardly spoke, there was just nothing to say.

That night Anna mentioned again the idea of inviting Jeanne Marie to sleep in the house for a few days, while they were gone. Howard wasn't usually keen on letting someone stay in their place, even for a few days. He was too private, too possessive. Plus he liked the house tidy. His instinct for order had intensified as he hauled debris and junk off the beach. But he'd already said yes, and to her complete surprise, he nodded yes again.

"Poor wandering sister. I'll write out a few instructions."

The Wall

Anna's stomach turned involuntarily as she remembered the first time Howard had given her one of his lists of dos and don'ts. He seemed fixated on the latitude of the cheese in the icebox and whether eggs were put in order by size, things she would not care about in a thousand years. Yet she knew that he had landed in Galveston just after the hurricane, after the collapse of all contentment, prosperity, safety. He had unburied body parts, silver trays, photo albums, electric fans—nothing in the world had escaped the wrath of the storm, and it was his job to help restore order and dignity to the wreck. Bringing discipline to the kitchen sink was part of it.

Calm down, she told herself. The sister is like a cracked pitcher, ready to spill. She needs lists. She wants directions.

Howard's instructions for Sister Jeanne Marie sketched basics: how to light the stove, where to sleep. And: *We are so grateful you agreed to keep watch on our house. Take care of yourself and make yourself completely at home.* Reading that, Anna felt surges of love for him.

Howard and Anna returned from their weekend in Houston on Monday evening. They'd had fun visiting cousins; eating at Martha's Beef House; shopping for supplies. Jeanne Marie seemed happy, even radiant. She was obviously rested, but she declined their invitation to dinner. "I really have to go. But I do like your pretty house. And your piano." And off she sailed into the hot night.

"There might be a little rain tonight." Howard opened the kitchen cabinet to get a cup. "Where'd you put the cups?"

"Look behind the sugar," Anna replied.

"China cups are here, but I don't see the breakfast cups. I don't want china right now." He frowned.

Who cares? she thought. Just get a cup. She was tired and didn't want the nuisance of his touchiness. Howard, too, was tired and only wished for a bit of coffee and to relax with his wife. As she watched him retrieve a china cup, her irritation rounded the corner

43

inexplicably into affection. She filled her grandmother's cup, hand-painted with roses, with her best brew and thick cream. They held hands under the table while they sipped.

After, Howard dragged upstairs to get ready for bed. Anna cleared the dishes, leaving them in the sink and opened the cutlery drawer to return the sugar spoon. In the drawer was a pile of toothbrushes. She thought: you gripe about putting things back and then you don't do it yourself. She dropped them in her pocket and took them upstairs to the washstand by the bed.

Next morning, Howard was fumbling with his shirt. "Where are my old socks?"

"Don't know, sweetheart. You can go find them, can't you?"

"I guess." He scowled. "Your nightshirts are in my sock drawer."

"No, they're not." She was sure of this. She remembered folding the laundry. Why would she put nightshirts in his sock drawer?

They'd purchased a camera in Houston, and Anna was fiddling with it, looking through the lens at Howard's shoulders. Handsome man! she grinned. She aimed the lens at his naked chest and stepped toward him, focusing all the way, and finally snapping a picture just as he embraced her, covering her neck with kisses. She flirted back, let him swing her around and tease her breasts from behind. Plait my hair? she asked.

While Howard toyed with her long blonde hair, she continued to peer through the camera and adjust the lens. She pointed at her desk. The ink jar came into view, but there was no ink in it. With her camera's eye, she roved around to the window. The curtains were not pure white anymore, but splotched in dark blue. She put the camera down and pulled away from Howard, reaching for a robe.

Flushed with dread, they flung open all the bureau drawers. Nothing was as before: the missing breakfast cups were in the top drawer, the salt in Howard's desk. Up and down stairs she and Howard ran, checking closets and looking under furniture. The house had been rearranged seemingly at random, yet with considerable care: the face towels had deliberately been placed in the wood pile—folded in neat squares and tamped into a space of perfect size among the kindling.

Ink from the ink bottle had been meticulously poured into another small jar and waited, ready inside the medicine cabinet. Two pairs of Howard's shoes lay just outside the back door, as if waiting for him to step into them and go off to work. With a gasp, Anna realized that three piano keys no longer had ivory on them; the slivers of ivory were stashed in the potato bin. "Oh, god, nothing seems right to her. She's trying to put things back in order," she sobbed to Howard. She was gazing into the black hole of the sister's hopelessness; she couldn't stop crying.

Just other side of the parlor window, Howard noticed the swaying of the swing. It was six a.m.

On the front porch, her legs tucked under her, a pillow on her knees, Jeanne Marie was relaxing. She was balancing one of Anna's plates in her lap on which bloomed a huge, hot muffin, drizzled in butter; she raised it to her mouth and bit in, smacking her lips with contented pleasure.

Creation

Oaxaca, Mexico 1900

Guillermo's daughter was heartbroken. Had locked herself in.

"Laurena, come out. I need help with the flowers. I can't tell what goes with the yellow ones."

No answer.

"Come on, dearest. Please."

He heard the springs creak, the soft slap of covers thrown aside. Those sounds meant Laurena was in bed at four in the afternoon, no doubt lumping the pillow over her face. It was unbearable.

A minute passed. She opened the door a sliver. Guillermo knocked at the air by her nose, a tiny joke, and with his palm, pushed his way into her room. Her eyes were puffy; her hair in strings. She had flung on an old dress.

Guillermo smoothed her shoulders, took her hand, and pressing her arm under his, led her to the kitchen table, prepared coffee. *Café de olla*: first pouring the strong, dark brew, then, with a flourish, a ribbon of boiling milk, from the kettle held high. He always made a small performance of coffee.

"Just roasted. From the market."

Really, the aroma was irresistible. She studied the cup, sipped. Her father rummaged in drawers, pulled out a hairbrush.

"Sit back. You are a mess!" Her eyes scanned the floor, and she shifted slightly.

He loved touching Laurena's long black hair, and he did so, just quickly. He began to brush, something he had been shy of since she was twelve or thirteen. Guillermo untangled a handful at a time, brushed each skein, starting at the top of Laurena's head, slowly tugging through the whole length to the hint of curl at the ends; then, sorting the strands, he started weaving a braid that twisted and hurried like a charged river all the way down her back.

His wife had died when their one child, the beautiful Laurena, was only three years old, Laurena, the beating heart of his life. So intelligent and kind! And a hard worker who hummed through her chores. Eighteen years old and her life a new flame, ahead of her. But this had been a very bad week.

Because Laurena had finally had enough of Luís. Luís *el guapo*, the handsome, the impetuous, Luís with the maybe future. She'd met him when they were five years old, in the Oaxaca Christmas procession; he marched behind her, tickling his brother and snickering while she, solemn and deliberate, carried the baby Jesus to the creche. When, in a totally mortifying moment, she tripped on the hem of her lace dress, Luís had skipped forward to catch the Jesus.

She loved him, and their families long planned for the two to marry. He made her laugh, with his birdcalls and imitations of thunderclaps and barking dogs. But he drank too much, and she didn't like his sometimes cruel mouth. Or how he would seize her hand and pull as if she were a farm animal. One evening, after he spoke sharply, like a bad policeman, to his own mother, and an hour later, cuffed his young brother across the face, she came to a decision. In a hail of shuddering sobs, she begged her father to let her break off the engagement. He did so without hesitation; he could not stand to see her suffering.

Laurena insisted on telling Luís herself, but it was terrible, as though she were, herself, the match deep inside the volcano. She had come home crying and had been a wreck ever since. Luís pounding on the front door after supper last night didn't help. She'd let him in, but would not go walking. He pleaded with her to give him another chance, but she twined her fingers through his and told him no, she would not marry him; it was over.

"Laurena, dearest, you don't seem to have a fever or anything."

"Yes, father."

Tears leaked out, as Guillermo brushed and braided.

"Please eat something. I hate seeing you so upset."

"I don't know what to do. What am I going to do? I've known him so long."

"You know I like him; he is fun, but he's a child, a brat. You'll be fine, better off without him. There are other men in the world, good, considerate, handsome men who will love you and treat you with respect."

Laurena thought of the empty plaza, the country church, the dead, dark streets at night. Nowhere in this picture of her village did she spot even petty men looking for wives.

"And always, always," continued Guillermo, "of course, you can call this your home."

At that, she burst open, wailing anew.

At 9:15 the next morning Luís advanced on Laurena's front door, which normally opened immediately to the sidewalk and the main street. He howled like a wolf; he crowed like a prowling bird. He tapped, knocked, then hammered, in a crescendo of love, possession, and rage. He did so again on Monday, Tuesday, Wednesday, and Thursday, and each morning, Laurena ran out the door and closed it behind her, hoping not to disturb her father.

"You know you love me!"

Creation

"Of course I love you! Since I was five years old. But I will not marry you!"

In a low shriek, Luís implored, "I'll go to the priest and he'll help me with my temper. Please forgive me."

But she had heard this before. She had even, in a fit of doubt, asked the priest if Luís had ever sought help for his bad moods. Father Dagobert had shaken his head.

"I'm sorry, dear Luís. It can't be." She kissed him fast, on the cheek, and locked the door against him.

"You have no soul! No one will ever love you!" he shouted, and up and down the block, the families she had grown up with, the good women who tended her through her baby years while her father worked with gemstones, listened from behind the curtains of their side windows, wishing that Luís would shut up and go away. Señora Margarita and Señora Luisa, to name only two, had already expressed that opinion to Laurena, the preceding evening.

But right now Laurena did not want to discuss Luís with the neighbors. Or with the priest or, god forbid, Luís' mother. She didn't want to hear that she still had a great future. She did not feel pretty or smart or industrious. She did not want to go to school lessons or church, where instead of embracing geography or god, her mind spun and spiraled to her faltering life. Now when she fingered her embroidered sleeves and collars, they seemed hopelessly lacking style or grace; she was known in the village for her delicious cakes, but lately she believed them overly sweet and lacking spice; her chile rellenos were heavy and poorly sauced. She thought it better she would not be married, as she wouldn't have been a good mother anyway; even her beloved cats seemed jumpy and preoccupied, not purring at her much at all.

Luís showed up again on Monday morning.

"I'm sorry, love, I'm sorry for shouting. I just miss you so much!" he hissed through the cracks in the door. He had a handful of orchids. Orchids grew wild in the high canyons—he must have spent hours gathering them.

But when she said she couldn't come out this time, that she had work to do, he banged his head against the door. He yelled: "*Mala chica*! Bad girl! How dare you leave me? No one else will want you! I'm going to tell your father where you let me put my hands." Señora Margarita and Señora Luisa, along with the rest of the neighborhood, spilled their mango juice and cocked their heads to listen harder. Laurena gasped, double-bolted the door, and ran to her father.

Guillermo stepped out of his workshop, situated on a high back porch, where he was feeling stimulated as always by the intense sunlight and dry air, and his view of the valleys and fields. He did not intend to admit Luís to his sitting room. Instead of going into the house, he strode around the side to the street.

"Luís, amigo. Stop it, please."

Luís continued beating his head against the house for a full minute. Guillermo folded his arms in disgust; Luís finally stopped.

"You've been like a son to me, and I hope we can make amends and be neighbors. But there will be no marriage. You must move on."

Guillermo was an old man with vivid memories of his own disappointments. Still, Luís seemed too wild, and Guillermo was alarmed at his behavior.

"It would be better if you didn't come around here any more, for a while."

Luís let the white and pink orchids drop to the ground, and stumbled, a lone dog, a bad dog, down the hill, dodging bricks and stones that threatened to bruise his feet. Up and down the block, neighbors heard, murmured *thank god,* and shifted from the drama in front of Guillermo and Laurena's house, back to their sweeping. Some of the orchids were saved to a vase by Señora Luisa; some retrieved by little girls and pinned to their hair; others were chewed by foxes in the night.

A week later Guillermo had business to conduct, and he rode

along the dirt road into Oaxaca where he would buy a new stone-cutting blade and deliver bracelets and earrings to the fine shops in town that sold his jewelry.

Laurena often worked alongside her father at his workbench. She had grown to love the silent hours, as he sat absorbed in his bits of metal and mineral chips. He called himself a minor craftsman, not an artist, but his pieces were prized in Oaxaca, and a shop in Mexico City was carrying his hibiscus brooch and orange-blossom bracelets. A broker from a Veracruz shipping company had come calling. She was proud of him.

When Guillermo went to town, she had the house to herself, and she usually tidied and weeded and cooked. After these weeks of torment, she had finally slept almost through the previous night, only waking up twice. "You're looking slightly better," her father had laughed, as he took off. This day, she was scrubbing floors, but when she reached the middle of the kitchen, she put down the mop without intending to, and stepped back to her room. She opened her pine jewelry box and picked out the best of her own gemstones: a rough piece of corundum, hardest of minerals except for the diamond. She rolled it around in her palm, put it in her skirt pocket.

Guillermo kept a basket of uncut stones—yellow-hued, pink, violet, crystal, blue—that after cutting and polishing became rings, bracelets, brooches. Since she was a baby, Laurena had played with the seconds and fragments he tossed to her, shooting them across the tile floor of the kitchen like marbles; teasing the kittens who chased the slivers into corners; or arranging broken aquamarines, peridots, and topazes in the swept dirt yard to outline kitchen, bedroom, and dining room of a doll's house. Once she piled her pretty rocks, one by one, in the bathtub outside, to form the craggy spine of a waterfall. On her twelfth birthday he presented her with what appeared to be an ordinary pebble, scarred and nicked all over. He didn't pitch it her way, but wrapped the stone in lace and told her to keep it safe. A deep blue center shone through the opaque surface and bits of mud still hung on, the mud of the mine in Ceylon.

Near Ratnapura, you have the most beautiful view of green highlands. Tea plantations and Adam's Peak, the mountain where Adam first set foot on earth after being cast out of heaven, or some say, where landed the foot of the Buddha. Seams of illama, the gravel-bearing strata, found in lowlands, valley bottoms, riverbeds. A family. One brother working a pump to keep water out of the illama; a brother to collect the muddy gravel; a brother to wash it; a father to check the debris for precious stones; a grandfather to pay for the pumps, shovels, and trays; an uncle to organize the stones, another uncle to market them to merchants and shippers.

One of the children discovered the gray, muddy, jagged rock certain to contain blue corundum, or sapphire, in the gravel bed, loose among boulders, right next to his father's bare left foot. His father smiled very big and took it from the boy, rinsed it, dropped it into his pocket, instantly realizing the rock's value. He packed a cloth bag with the day's finds and sent the bag to town by oxcart with his brother, who was refreshed along the way by the mountain views. He sold it, over a cup of black Ceylon tea, to an exporter soon to embark on a trip to America, with stops in Veracruz and Mérida. The ship would be dispersing raw gemstones and tea.

Even though Guillermo swore the story was true, Laurena always had questions: how could he know how many brothers and uncles were in Ceylon? His description of the mountains sounded suspiciously like those in Mexico, except there was tea growing all over the hillsides, instead of coffee. He claimed that the importer in Veracruz, who brought the stone to Oaxaca, was a personal friend of the Ceylon family, the family who had been mining gemstones for decades. As proof, Guillermo provided facts: Ceylon was a teardrop in the sea, off southernmost India; it was Buddhist and British all at once; parts of the island were just one big tea plantation, green and fragrant like the coffee farms in Mexico.

"See!" she'd call out. "You're making it up!" Laurena would

put her hands on her hips and race next door to collect eggs or borrow sugar.

But today, Laurena did not skip over the beds of white geraniums or red impatiens as she used to, but rather paced herself, circling the grapefruit tree heavy with yellow globes, and wandering to the porch-workshop. Guillermo's workshop was open on three sides, its slatted roof thick with purple bougainvillea, so that the brilliant sun of the Oaxaca plateau danced through the vines. He could turn his gaze west toward Monte Alban, the ancient city from which the Zapotecs had once ruled, or north, in the direction of Orizaba, the high volcano. Guillermo was himself half Zapotec.

Laurena had many times watched her father working with gemstones and occasionally had cleaned or cut them herself under his supervision. When in his absorption and joy in his pursuits, he required quiet, she jokingly called him *"el artista."* But today she understood. She wanted to lose herself, not in the chores of chopping chiles or checking the accounts, but in something uncharted, bigger.

Inside Guillermo's porch with its wonderful view and precision tools, she reached into her pocket for her stone and positioned it on the table, rotated it up, down, over, under. Held it to the sunlight. She placed the stone on the cutting stand, wiped away the mud, saving a few crumbs in the piece of lace, then found her father's small chisel and hammer. She began to tap, gingerly at first, then with a vigorous hit, she split the stone in half. The cleavage was perfect: she had been lucky. Now she would work the larger piece into a convex shape called a cabochon, an oval, ideal for showcasing certain properties. If this sapphire bore feathery inclusions, it would be up to her, the jeweler, to release and reveal the star inside.

She secured the cabochon on the end of a dop stick; using a gentle sharpening stone, she proceeded to grind carefully, to correct the perimeter. Many times she had listened to her father talk about how one should simply round it off to resemble a large pearl, which would allow the inclusions inside to be easily seen. If this were a diamond, faceting would be executed to bring out its extraordinary ability to reflect and disperse light; it took years to learn how. But this was a sapphire, and she was a beginner. She would be thrilled if she could successfully enhance the natural light within. She prepared a piece of felt, sprinkled with abrasive powder, and proceeded at first to dab at her stone slowly, and then realized more force was needed.

The more Laurena's sapphire gleamed, the more skittish she felt. The stone, a trinket from childhood until today, was becoming magnificent, yet she was inexplicably wary, as if the jewel was threatening to lift off the table in a shower of divine light, scaring everybody. As though she had, through skill untested but undeniably her own, discovered the glow of the ages—but that there must be some mistake. She stopped a dozen times to run to the kitchen for coffee, finger the foliage on the geraniums, fold laundry. She was afraid to polish without her father's advice, but she had the whole afternoon ahead of her, and she simply couldn't leave god's creation, now stirred to life by her own hands, untended. After her third coffee, amazingly, she felt calmer, and more in love with her task by the minute.

Guillermo returned in the evening, expecting a warm stew and some of his daughter's good custard. These he was given, along with a star sapphire, resplendent in a silk-lined silver box.

The next morning, the two labored together to perfect Laurena's sapphire and to design a silver setting, for Laurena had decided she wanted to craft a ring. "You can wear it!" grinned Guillermo. "It will be stunning on your finger."

"I'd like to wear it. For a while," she replied. "Maybe I could sell something later on, after I get more experience." Guillermo thought his daughter's ring was beautiful but not quite professional enough. He was astounded that she was already thinking about selling anything. But then he thought: why not?

Laurena's leaving shrouded Luís like a hangover because he was sick over it, sick to the core, and also because he had been drinking a lot of mezcal lately. Living in his town meant constantly breathing fumes of humiliation. Neighbors, cousins, mama, and grandmama averted their eyes out of pity; his father blamed him for the failure; his younger brothers taunted and defied him. When Luís wasn't despondent or drunk he was beset by a testy desire to abandon his village with its pathetic church and crumbling school, to forget about the town of Oaxaca, where he and Laurena had intended to spend their lives, and go where no one would know he'd been spurned. He would comb his hair just so; put on a starched shirt, a leather vest, shiny shoes, and proudly approach a new boulevard in a new city.

He passed through the spring—all of April and May—in a stupor of exhaustion and anger and one noon Father Dagobert observed him napping on the steps of the church. The priest shook him awake, invited him to his own rooms, and offered him a cup of chocolate. The conversation unfolded in monosyllables until the priest, in an inspired moment, leapt to his bookshelf for a primer for learning English. Luís had finished several grades of school and could read and write, one accomplishment he was sure of. The father said, "I can help you. Come in the mornings and we will practice." Luís was aware, in a rush of hope, that the idea could be a path toward something distinctive, or just toward something, since he already knew Spanish and Zapotec and, as Father Dagobert reminded him, he had an ear for mimicry.

"But you cannot tell anyone about this," whimpered Luís, terrified of another defeat.

"I won't tell a soul. This is between you, me, and God," promised the priest.

Luís' mama crossed herself each time she saw her son enter the church, and his trips soon increased to three or four times a week. Jibes from brothers continued to jump at him, but less often. Guillermo, Laurena, and other citizens took note, skeptical of the miscreant getting religion, as there was no evident improvement in Luís' attitude; he was still touchy and often rude.

One morning after a poor lesson, when the priest's corrections were driving Luís mad—*I can never get this! I won't! Leave me alone!*—Father Dagobert decided to push him even more. He grabbed the boy's shoulders.

"You *will* learn, but you need to go somewhere where they speak English. A family in Veracruz. Or, there are ships from Veracruz that dock in Cuba and America. The Gulf Coast. New Orleans. Think about it, you little idiot!"

Even though he had had this very fantasy himself, Luís became more enraged, as though he were being rejected, asked to leave his own home. But the idea filled him, like warm soup, and began to soothe him and give him energy. Over the next days and weeks, he battled less, listened better.

Late in July, Luís sent Guillermo a message, asking permission to stop in to say goodbye, for he was departing for Veracruz to look for a job.

Laurena was greatly relieved. Her own grief was by then slowly tilting away, like the movement of the earth's poles. She welcomed Luís with coffee and chocolate tart. He told her he had been thinking of a job on a ship, possibly going to America for a while.

"Here, Luís. Please take this with you." Laurena handed him the sapphire ring, the one she had made in the spring.

"This is beautiful. Where did you get it?"

"I cut and polished the stone myself and my father helped me with the setting."

He spun it toward the sun. "Is it valuable?"

"I don't know. But I was wondering if you'd take it with you to Veracruz. Or to America, if you go there. Maybe try to sell it. I also made a bracelet and a pendant and another ring. They're in my jewel box for now. I'll give you a commission."

"Never!" he interrupted. "I wouldn't take your money!"

"That's kind of you," she answered. "But let's see what happens. I'd like to surprise my father with my earnings, so if you get a good offer, go ahead and accept and you can give me the money when you come back. Will you let me know?"

Laurena had considered the fate of the ring carefully. It was a good sign that Luís had a plan, a destination, but he still looked haggard, sullen. She thought if she gave him a job to do, on her behalf, that it might ease him. Plus, she wondered how much her ring might be worth.

Luís had thanked the priest, kissed his family, and borrowed a mare, Dulce, from his father for the trip to Veracruz. Luís was to sell her if he decided to go on to America.

The high Oaxaca plateau offered only primitive roads and trails, and he would have to be keen as a hawk. He would proceed north toward Cuernavaca, cutting east to Puebla, on to Ojo de Agua where mineral springs would cleanse him, then northeast around the great snow-capped volcano of Orizaba, before the descent to the coast and the port of Veracruz. Such a journey could take fifteen days or more.

He set forth on the first of August. Elated and apprehensive, he rode like an amateur, trotting erratically through incredible forests of saguaro cactuses and wandering among scrubby pines, but then he learned to pace Dulce better and to conserve water in the wilderness. He arrived in Puebla, where for the first time in his life he stayed in an inn, a barnlike room with a dirt floor to sleep on, smoky oil lamps, and a hot evening meal of beans, fowl, and rice, and bananas and coffee in the morning.

He'd been warned to be alert for robbers with big hats and guns in their belts, but he was fortunate and encountered none. He'd tucked the sapphire ring into his boot for safekeeping; except for Dulce, it was the only valuable thing he owned.

He traveled on to Ojo de Agua where he bathed and drank

like a rich man, then crossed the *mal pais*, the evil land, barren and dreary except for the occasional hamlet, and dotted with lava flows and rocks. He had to circle north of the majestic Orizaba, and there were precipitous stretches to negotiate. He was used to dry country, but near the massive 19,000-foot mountain and around the village of Las Vegas, virtually all trees had disappeared. He camped, savoring sunset and sunrise, finding that watching the luminous cone, snow streaming toward the valley, calmed him. He couldn't move his eyes off the beautiful Orizaba, even exclaiming about it to Dulce, who, he swore, seemed to be listening. When trees obscured the view, Luís rubbernecked so he could see and see.

He was astonished by the transformation, as if by enchantment, in the land as he approached Jalapa, green and wet, its steep streets lined with blooming flowers he had never seen, such as floripundio, fragrant and lily-shaped. He was pleased by the lush city and by the countryside: canyons, waterfalls, coffee plantations tumbling into the distances, the coffee interplanted with bananas for shade; by the mango and orange trees; then he trekked through increasingly sandy terrain and to Veracruz and his first experience of the sea.

He spent two nights in Veracruz, and he didn't like it. There was the danger of yellow fever, and the houses were black from mold or smoke or god knows what. After the tidy streets of his village where everyone for miles had known him since birth, he felt lonesome, and intimidated by the raucous shipyards and crowded markets. But Laurena faded from his mind for as much as an hour at a time as he ambled around the hot humid plazas, avoiding grubby men from the docks and watching huge steamers and sailing ships. He saw no wide boulevard where he could stroll and flirt, no obvious place to work or try his infant English. But after a life in the altiplano, he was taken with the Gulf of Mexico. He enjoyed the wet air and constant breezes; he liked being close to expanses of water; he liked the taste of fish and the bustle of nets and boats. When a friendly ship hand offered him a job on a steamer bound for Galveston, carrying cof-

Creation

fee, he sold his sweet horse Dulce, and jumped aboard.

As the ship steered northward, the crew could still see the cone of Orizaba. Twenty-four hours later, the wind reversed and blew them every which way. For three days Luís was too sick to sort rope or wash dishes; he clung to his hammock, thrown back and forth by the swells, so it was impossible to sleep, and he was bruised from being smashed into the walls. The wind pushed the ship away from shore, toward shore, and the captain was too thrifty to give full throttle to the steam engines; instead he brought down the sail and let the vessel rock and shake and plow several days off course. The heat was almost unbearable, and rats and scorpions scurried in the night. As he was too ill for liquor, Luís' mind finally cleared, and he reexamined the idea of going to America, especially when downpours shunted the ship around even more. But he had no choice; it was the season for storms, he was told. He entertained his fellows by mimicking seabirds, learned to laugh when, during chess games, the rooks and pawns slid off the board.

Luís, born in a remote village in south central Mexico, landed at the port of Galveston, Texas, on a Friday afternoon. For unloading coffee and bananas from the ship, he was promised three days' wages, and the crew was given Saturday as a day off. Despite the raw heat and heavy humidity, he immediately felt at home in this populous island city. People on the street seemed prosperous and busy, and his first words of English worked, as when he bought peanuts on the boardwalk that hugged the beachfront. His "thank you" was returned with "gracias," by the vendor, who chuckled, saying it was the only Spanish he knew. But the sound of the word heartened Luís.

Saturday morning, September 8, 1900, was much cooler than Friday, and relief from the heat raised everyone's spirits. Luís felt renewed, alive. He thought the paths overlaid with crushed oyster shells were curious and liked trodding over them. The smell of coffee from the bulk roaster in town reminded him of Oaxaca; the swooping seagulls seemed sweet, the scent of jasmine comforting. The mosquitoes were annoying, but rising wind whisked them away. Weathercocks were spinning a little crazily.

He heard that there was an encampment down on the beach, where immigrants lived in tents; maybe he could stay there until he figured out what to do next. Saturday morning, the tide was bubbling into shore slowly, which reassured him as he was a creature of the altiplano and did not trust the sea, especially after his stormy voyage. But he was fascinated by the beach; it was like treading on a new planet, and though he could not swim and had no intention of ever plunging into the ocean, he did take off his shoes and let waves wash over his feet. What pleasant cleansing coolness! How soft the sand was between his toes! After a breakfast of eggs and redfish, which he'd tried and liked in Veracruz, he ventured out for a long walk, to go looking for the camp. As he strolled, he missed his Mexico: his family, the marvelous things he'd seen on his trip to Veracruz, especially Mount Orizaba and the lava flows, and the canyons and waterfalls near Jalapa.

His longing for Laurena had churned and gone bitter, and the thought of her chilled his heart blue, reminded him he was happy to be in America, not a grub, cocooned in an isolated village. The sapphire ring cheered him. Luís didn't imagine himself a thief, but he'd never had any intention of returning it. On the ship, an officer had whistled at its luster and the veil-like star. He'd schemed to sell it in Galveston and use the money to set up somewhere in America. He deserved that much for being jilted. If he ever went back to Oaxaca, he would tell Laurena the ring was lost on the ship.

For now, he put it onto his little finger, where it would fit, and turned the stone into his palm so it would not attract attention. The wind was gusty, and the Gulf seemed more turbulent; he presumed this was a typical day on Galveston Island: fishermen were managing their rowboats in the rough water, a few bathers were striding into the surf. He splashed along the shoreline in his bare feet, propelling his gaze ahead, watching people of geography and languages entirely different from his own and feeling mesmerized by the most ordinary activities. In his village, he would not for an instant have noticed a person transporting baskets of vegetables, but here, the sight of a man on horseback, galloping along the beach with tomatoes and beans overflowing the saddle bags, caused him to stare.

And, yes, there it was, the immigrant encampment, dozens of white tents rambling into the distances, like something out of *Arabian Nights*. Luís stopped to take in the picture, under cloudy, darkening skies.

People from Poland, England, Ireland, Italy, China, Germany, India, Mexico were huddling inside their tents because of the wind, and a light rain was falling. A young man beckoned, invited him to take shelter. Luís knew instinctively that he was from south of the border, and the two spoke Spanish together with excitement.

"Where are you going? There's a storm coming."

"I am Luís. I just arrived from Mexico, and I thought I might camp here."

"You are most welcome, but we are worried that the waves will be very high soon."

"What do you do then?"

"We'll get out of here."

Some people were folding up their tents; collecting chickens and ducks, piling them into carts. Blankets and dishes flew away in the wind; children ran to hug their mothers' knees. Dogs barked.

Luís, who knew nothing of wind or waves, squatted inside the tent deafened by the rain of god's creation, until he and his comrades wrapped up in blankets and tried to march through the roar to higher ground. Luís clinched his finger, with the sapphire ring—his whole fortune—into his fist.

Rain came that was not like other rain, but an unfathomable cleavage of the heavens, a divine flood, a monstrous gale bashing the hopeful tent city into a sorry mass of canvas and bodies. All night in black water, some hung on shreds of wood torn from dead boats. Babies were lost. Toads were everywhere.

But Luís was spared the terror of battling the hurricane of 1900 that destroyed Galveston, for he was ripped away by one of the first sixteen-foot waves; all went dark in an instant. Later, his hand was pried open by fishes; his fingers wilted but still held Laurena's ring.

Me and Mama

Galveston 1932

Mama had gone without crying for two weeks in a row, but here she was at it again, all morning. It was a mean August and the heat blowing us right down, no breeze, nothing to cool us off. I was ten years old and everybody called me "sweet chile." Sweet chile, do this; sweet chile, do that, never: *Edward could you please hang out the laundry?* No, it was sweet chile cause we were the color of chocolate, delicious and sweet through and through. Also supposedly I reminded folks of my daddy, who was a sweet man, not a sweet chile, and a hard worker and what were we going to do without him, now that baby number seven was almost due to arrive but we wouldn't have a live father anymore because Willie died in a rowboat with my sick little brother, Raymond. Raymond couldn't even sit up and sometimes he would jerk this way and that and I always thought he might've fell onto daddy by mistake and made that boat turn over. I guess when I'm grown I'll find out what really happened that day.

But that Saturday morning, Mama was swelled up huge and I was in charge of the other four children, and I had to cook breakfast and lunch, too, because she asked me to and I couldn't say no to her, not right then. From her bed, she reached for my neck and rubbed it nice with her pretty fingers. We're about to have another chocolate baby, another little sweetie, and I want you to make your daddy proud of you.

But he's dead, I pointed out. Well he's in heaven and he's watching, and he knows you'll do a good job today, helping your mama. My stomach lurched up because I'd got no intention whatsoever of having anything to do with any baby getting born. I'd seen collie puppies squirm out and I'd seen chicks knock their way out of eggs and I saw a calf come out, and what I remembered was the blood, which I wanted no part of. It was okay to stir the oatmeal and get kids dressed and okay to clear dishes and it was okay to bring my mama glasses of water but that was it. Still, she was my only mama, and I loved her when she chased me 'til I squealed and when she played ball with us and we'd run and run until we were so tired we just dropped. Not tired like old people, who are always saying: I'm tired. I mean the good, ragged tired you get from running your heart out for the plain fun of it.

She told me to send little Ben down the street to get Aunt Dorothy so I did and Aunt Dorothy marched in, carrying clean white towels, folded neat, and she kept one and handed me the rest. Sweet chile, we don't have a nickel for a doctor and you're going to help me with this baby so everything's got to go like I say. Mama's had so many babies, she'll be all right, won't she, I asked because I didn't know what we'd do if she died. I was shaking with fright.

So I took our big pots and filled them full of water from our new taps that my father had put in so proud and carried them to the stove and flipped on the burner. You're not supposed to watch water try to boil because it makes it take longer, but still I did. I didn't know what else to do with my eyes. Then I dipped the towels in one at a time, to get them good and hot.

My mama and Aunt Dorothy were talking in the bedroom and

sometimes one of them would laugh and that eased me some. I walked in there with a hot towel and got a good look at her face during one of her pains; boy did she yell. I rushed out and dipped another towel and fiddled with the kids and stalled during the long groans and awful breathing. But Aunt D called me back in, she said it was almost time, and they needed more towels and mama needed me, too. Honey, give me your hand, let me squeeze, it helps with the pain. She squeezed so hard I yelled and that's when my sister's head popped through. My baby sister Charlotte and mess all over the bed. You could see she was pretty, though.

I wasn't good at anything yet, not hoeing or lifting or arithmetic but I knew how to give my hand to my mother, just right over to her and Patty, my only mama, smiled big and whispered: *Good job, sweetheart. Edward.*

Konnichiwa, This Is Texas

Pennsylvania 1930s

In 1936, when I was in college, I fell in love with a ham radio boy. That didn't last long, but the radio did. I learned to work the knobs and decipher *dahdidahdit dahdahdidah,* crackle and static. For some reason I was patient about it.

Oh I loved the regular radio, too. I grew up in Lancaster, Pennsylvania, deep in farm country and many Amish. My family wasn't Amish, just Presbyterian, and I was glad; I didn't want to be quaint and spiritual. I wanted to be modern and that meant the radio.

Not that I minded the horses and buggies, the white caps and long skirts, very picturesque, but when you're in high school you're ready for a little more. Later when I was grown up and living in busy cities, I would dream about my quiet roads catching the hills like ribbons and leaning into the maples and birches—my god in the fall, the golds! I could almost feel myself pulled along again by a reliable bay who'd studied me and knew what I liked—slow and apple-pie nice into the woods.

But when I was fifteen I would've gone completely nuts out

there, except for the radio. Our radio box was colored midnight blue and had fancy knobs, its smart round dial a face alert to the world. My mother let me listen for hours in the living room. Monday mornings at school we'd talk about the shows from Sunday like kids now, silly over TV programs. For us it was Burns and Allen, Amos 'n Andy, the Desoto Sisters.

At Dickinson College in Carlisle, I discovered drama class, French, electricity club—me, Eva, from the countryside! But after my first hour with a shortwave, I knew I wanted my own set. The boyfriend introduced me to his receiver, and we fussed with the thing together. You tapped dots and dashes with your key to send messages, and someone heard your question or your news and answered back. You had to listen hard to get it, to translate the tweet-tweets into letters and then words. You could reach a ship in the Indian Ocean, a ranch in Mexico. Compared to the bleeping music of Morse, the newspaper was boring, and *History of the Romans,* part I, death warmed over. I'd be shivering in my drafty, damp dorm room, hunched over lit books, eyelids slumping closed, and the desire would overtake me. Somehow I'd find myself transported across campus to the rattling embrace of the radio, smitten by the transmitter. Lots of people were doing the same thing all around the world. Which is what I liked: a watchman discourses from a lighthouse on the coast of Malaysia. After staring at the open sea for eighteen hours straight, in a spasm of loneliness and pride, he briefs you about riptides and ill winds. A Welsh shepherd tramps back to his hut to chin at you about the king and Mrs. Simpson, a happy man.

Once I contacted an Amish girl, a twelve-year-old, who'd been sneaking to a radio outside Lancaster, an astonishing feat for a child in that time and place. She was fascinated by Mr. Pickering assembling his radio from a kit. I knew him too—he owned the Mr. P's Hardware and Miscellany. Eventually he let her practice with his rig; she made him swear not to tell her parents—so she wouldn't get "shunned." It would've been hard to be chums in town, but we could chat forever over the waves. She beeped me news of home. *Hello Eva. Apple crop rich this season, ten barrels of cider.* Or: *Windmill doesn't work, wind doesn't come today.* I responded with mean messages like: "Hey Mary! Plug in that windmill. Electrify!" She tap-tapped: *But wind will come. And candlelight is so pretty; you should see my loft. Shadows. Flickers.* You might say that Mary at twelve was more mature than I—a cheeky coed, for sure—but I didn't have any sisters and I grew fond of her. We signed off with "88," code shorthand for "Love and Kisses."

At Dickinson, I scouted for a major, without a clue about what job to train for or whether to finish at all. I worked in the physics department typing for pocket money and that was how I met the boyfriend from the radio club amid the other radio-struck students. Such as Frank, a carrot-topped Irishman, who was receiving from somewhere inside the colored rings of Saturn, a nutball kid scientist. He used to win code-speed contests, and I heard he was an ace in the war—crowding of frequencies and interference were our main problems—sometimes sending a message was like conversing over the static of a cranky crowd and at only twenty or thirty words a minute. We knew that quartz crystals, if cut correctly, could control the transmitter's frequency and keep a message from drifting into space. But preparing the quartz was iffy. Three or four students and a physics professor were madly fooling with rock-cutting equipment, trying to make crystal units for their ham rigs. Later, they became Motorola Corporation.

There was never any time left after classes, my typing job, boyfriends, and weekends home. All the same, I managed to get to the radio set. Late at night was the most fun. When nobody else was around, I navigated the waves the world over. Hamming after hours was how I found Tanaka because at midnight in Pennsylvania, it was noon in Tokyo. I'd blurped out a CQ Japan signal: *Is there anybody in Japan who will talk to me?*

Konnichiwa, This Is Texas

Tanaka-san became my radio buddy in 1939, the year before I graduated as a French major. I had become engaged to Scott Preston, class president and blue ribbon history champ, who had a wonderful voice that could inspire a crowd or croon love messages into my ear. Tanaka-san was a boy of sixteen in 1939 and already good at English.

My father is interpreter at American embassy. We speak English. We like English. OK?

I'd peck at my dorm dinner of salad and stew, like I was a house wren preparing for a lifetime of arranging twigs. After, I'd sit diligently at my desk for some page turning and note taking until time for the radio and contacting Tanaka-san, according to our agreed schedule, three times a week. By then I was an eagle soaring across the planet.

We used abbreviated English or the Japanese words and their Morse code equivalents that Tanaka-san taught me.

What's for lunch today?

Eel, pickle, rice.

Drink?

Tea. O-cha. *Or just* cha. *You?*

Beef stew and cherry pie.

Drink?

Milk. What is the name of your church?

Shinto. What is your church?

Protestant.

What is Protestant?

Christian.

Are you a cowboy?

Tanaka-san knew that I was named Eva, that I was a woman. Because of his father, who was employed by Americans, he certainly realized that all Americans were not cowboys. He was making a joke. But I played a joke too: I gave myself the moniker "Texas." *What does Texas mean?* "Cowboy," I replied. He answered that I should call him *Konnichiwa*—good day, hello—in Japanese. Sometimes I just beeped him as K-wa.

Come in K-wa. This is Texas. How are you today?
Very well. And you?
Fine. Peachy. Means just great. Where were you born?
Tokyo.
What year?
1923. Where were you born?
Lancaster.
What year?
1919.
What is Lancaster? Where?
In Pennsylvania. Northeastern United States. Not big like Tokyo. Full of farms.

I looked up the history of Tokyo. Next time I asked: "1923. Earthquake?" The question pleased him because it showed I knew something about Japan. He told me that the Tanaka family wasn't in Tokyo when the earthquake struck. They were vacationing close by in a place called Kamakura, scene of catastrophic tremors and a tidal wave. But I couldn't quite get it. I copied, through the static, *K A R M A*, a word I'd vaguely heard of but didn't really know. *Karmakura*. Karma had something to do with your soul. I tried to find it on a map. Finally I figured it out. Not Karmakura. *Kamakura*.

I loved that I could listen to trills of code playing to me like a tiny orchestra and translate along in my head, the way I did in French class.

On the ocean. A harbor. Cliffs embracing a cove. Pine forests marching down bluffs to the sea. Mount Fuji on the horizon. I was lucky. I could go anywhere, even to Japan. I could see the sacred mountain in the mist!

Earthquake time. Our house in Kamakura collapsed. My father trapped under beams. But he got out. Broken legs. House in Tokyo broken to pieces. I was a baby. We didn't live in Tokyo anymore. Stayed in Kamakura. My home. I go to the beach. Right outside my front door. Clams everywhere.

Sand stretched alongside the ocean at Atlantic City but I'd never been there or to any beach. I was pretty sure the Jersey shore couldn't be much like the one in Japan. But what did I know? I'd only seen streams and ponds, not infinite expanses of water. From his description I thought beaches writhed with thousands of burrowing clams.

Were you born in a special time?

No. I wasn't.

Surely, to anyone and everyone the 1920s in rural Pennsylvania were 200 meters below dull. What was my story? My memories of childhood clanked with hoes and trowels, brimmed with dairy cows, the price of eggs, the fun we had peeling paint—how we'd laugh if we could produce great curling pieces off the barn. No. Not advanced like Tokyo.

The campus library told me that the Kanto earthquake hit two minutes before noon on September 1, 1923, unleashing firestorms that devastated Tokyo and Yokohama. Thousands of people died.

How do you say fire?

Flowers of Edo. Fires all over the city. Akari, *little lights.* Kasei, *a very big fire.*

I'd sit cross-legged on the floor of the radio room at midnight with a bag of popcorn, my Western civ book open to some war, longing to be interrupted by the piccolo of Tanaka-san.

Come in Texas. Texas, this is K-wa.

Hi K-wa. Konnichiwa.

Hi? Hi. What?

Just hi. Hello. K-wa.

Tanaka-san chuckled by keying *didididit didit—hi.*

Hai *means "Yes" in Japanese. Spell for you: H A I. Sounds like English hi.*

Yes, yes.

Hai. Hai.

So I taught him "hi," "hello," and "howdy," all-American hello.

Tanaka-san clearly adored the wireless and me, and I liked him and his obsession with it, and the knobs, dials, my beautiful brass key, and how my words tapped out from my fingertip to the key and curled like smoke signals into the sky.

My brother died.
I'm sorry, Tanaka-san. Why?
Do not know. In Nagasaki. He was a teacher.
How old was he?
Twenty-five.
I'm sorry. Drink a cup of tea to help a little bit.
Cha.

Tanaka-san was my overseas kid brother. Sometimes he contacted me from Tokyo where he studied at a university, sometimes from Kamakura where his parents lived.

I am getting married.
Very good! Very good! Your husband's name?
Scotty.
How old is he?
Twenty-three.
So! Older than you?
Yes, a little older. Konnichiwa, will you get married?
Hai. Hai. *I want to get married. Children. I want to visit the United States.*
I want to visit Japan now.
Ima. *Now.*
Ima. My dog lives with my parents now.
What's your dog's name?
Nicky.
What kind of dog?
Big white, black, and brown dog. Collie. He has long fur.
What is a collie?
Herds sheep in Europe, K-wa. What is your weather now? *Ima.*
March is windy. Today is windy. Cold.
What is your word for wind?

Kaze. *Wind:* kaze. *How is your weather?*
Snowing. Blizzard.
Blizzard. A big snow?
Yes. A very big snow.

He asked me for a picture. I mailed him one of me and my parents, in Lancaster, snapped on the Fourth of July 1938. My mother and father are downtown, standing beside a horse and buggy, an old Amish lady in apron, black dress, and cap at the reins. Parked next to it is the mayor's shiny Buick, draped in bunting and stars, and I'm sitting on the hood, my legs crossed, sort of oh-là-là. My hair is a bob of curls. I attached a question: *Guess which one is me?* I wanted Tanaka-san to see that America could be simple and at the same time fast and modern. It seemed to me that Japan was like that too. Over the wireless, he answered:

Hello Texas. This is Konnichiwa. Hello Texas. Arigato. *I have the picture.* Arigato. *My sister has a permanent wave also.*

Tanaka-san sent a picture of himself, his parents, and his sister Masako, striding along a beach on a windy day. He wrote on the back: *kaze.* His black hair is blown all over the place; his sister's is curly all right, the sea wondrous and vast beside them. The faces are rather blurred, as if the camera quivered slightly during the exposure, and my friend is carrying something oval and dark. His smile spills over the whole frame, glowing like sunrise. He put a note with the picture—*We are very lucky to live by the bay. I am the one holding the live clam*—and included a hand-painted postcard of the same spot. In the postcard you can see Fujiyama in the distance, blissful snow capping the radiant cone.

When the Japanese bombed Pearl Harbor, I was outraged like everyone else and determined to beat them back. I was also hurt, as if Tanaka-san had personally caused the war. I desperately wanted to know his opinion. I decided to call him at midnight Tokyo time, hoping he might be at his dials then, when it was perhaps safer. But I didn't have to wait. I walked into the Radio Club and heard his *dahdidahdits,* and I didn't need to write it down—I understood perfectly from just listening.

Texas, this is Konnichiwa. Come in. Come in. This is Konnichiwa. Come in, come in. I will find you after the war. Pearl not my idea. Come in, Texas. Over.

K-wa! This is Texas. Stay okay? Okay?

He was almost nineteen and would be drafted. His father must've already been suspect for being an employee of the American embassy, and surely to contact an American by radio would be treason. But we were just hams. It didn't occur to me at first that anybody on the American side would care that I was communicating with a Japanese. But it wasn't long before the government declared the airwaves off limits to amateurs.

I lived in my aunt's brownstone in Philadelphia during the war, translated documents from French into English for the Red Cross, and became manager of the office. Scotty served in Europe for three years. I didn't see him the whole time. Of course, women at home were constantly worried sick. I would feel nauseous and cold whenever news came about German raids and bombs. I only had a few letters from Scotty. He didn't tell me until much later about his miserable missions and all the dead friends.

Meanwhile in Carlisle, every available quartz crystal was needed by the military services for their radios. My friends from the physics department and others got busy with components and then got rich. To be a pal, I invested a little bit.

I held onto my own radio and longed for the days when the airwaves would be free again, when I could cruise for friends with foreign accents and talk about ordinary things, talk about nothing. Like picking apples or chasing ducks or wading in rice paddies. That was one of the worst things about the war: You had to forget about people and think Nazis and Japs. I couldn't imagine young Tanaka as a soldier terrorizing women in Nanking, as a kamikaze pilot over Okinawa. What I remembered was his earnest tapping and study of

English. I brooded over what might have happened to him.

We were thrilled by Jimmy Doolittle's swashbuckling raid over Tokyo in the spring of 1942. By spring of 1945, we learned about the March missions: American firebombs blurting open in mid-air, in the streets. Cracking and hissing all over the city. Seventy or eighty thousand deaths. If you want fires, it is the proper season: early spring winds ride down from the north and west, wild winds that make flames roar and eat everything up. *Kasei*, a monster.

In 1944 I read a story in the *Philadelphia Inquirer* about life in Japan, based on secret reports from some kind of underground. I guessed they might have been messages from hams. Mothers were in mourning over the tens of thousands of boys killed in campaigns throughout Asia, but they weren't allowed to show their sadness; it would be unpatriotic to cry in public. The army was very harsh, and soldiers were beaten and kicked during training. Ordinary people were brainwashed to think the Japanese were destined to rule China, Korea, Burma, Indonesia, even Australia, and were willing to commit suicide in airplanes for the emperor. Those who knew English were forbidden to speak it, and the police confiscated radios and mail to prevent communication with the outside world. I wondered whether average citizens knew what their armies were really doing.

One Saturday afternoon in May 1945, I was fiddling with my set, trying to hear a faraway station, maybe Hudson Bay, when the static rose like the sound of a house aflame. Then the insistence of those crazy beeps.

Hello Texas this is K-wa. Come in. Come in. Texas, come in. This is Konnichiwa.

My fingers were stiff and shaky, like twigs in a shivery gust. I fumbled at my key and dials, frightened by the tide of static. My god I couldn't lose him! How had he gotten through? My eyes filled and I could barely see. I was breaking the law by trying to reach him, but I didn't hesitate an instant.

Konnichiwa, this is Texas. Konnichiwa come in. This is Texas. Are you safe?

Hai. *Yes. Safe. It's midnight. Blew out candle. This talking is against the law. I made a radio. Boxes and wires.*

Yes. Hello. Howdy. Konnichiwa, I've missed you. Are you fighting?

No. I am a sailor but I sit. I watch for enemy landing.

Tears were running over my face; I was sniffling, hoarse. I tried to click click in the right way.

K-wa. Where are you? Where are you?

In cave. In Kamakura. In cliffs. I guard my beach. Far below.

Twenty-two years old, living in caves, his signal straight and clear. I was on the floor, leaning against the table that held my precious radio set. My heart was such a drumbeat I thought I might die, pounded from within.

You are home. Near your family?

I am commander for Kamakura. I do my job. Watch for American ships.

Your father?

Works in zoo. Practice English with giraffes. But no food. Giraffe dies. Elephants sick.

QSL: I acknowledge. Konnichiwa, I'll bet your English is still good. Do you have food?

Hai. *Yes, Texas. Rice.* Cha. *Fish.*

Konnichiwa, this is Texas. Stew for lunch here. No change!

Texas is place, hai? *Not a cowboy?* He tapped out *hi, hi,* the signals for laughter.

Yes, Konnichiwa. I was playing. A joke.

Are we losing the war? Don't play.

Mayday. H A I. Yes. H A I. Yes. Germany has surrendered. You are losing. You are losing. Mayday.

This is truth? Texas, come in. Truth? Do you acknowledge?

Yes. QSL: I acknowledge. Konnichiwa. I am telling you the truth.

Sayonara, Texas. Thank you. Thank you. This is K-wa. Sayonara. Sayonara.

I lost him in a surge of racket, and myself too. I sobbed as I hadn't dared since the day Scotty left for France. As though I were now allowed, after being forbidden. My wails gathered like temblors, shaking the walls all over my city.

The White Car

New Orleans 1930s

My mother was a laundress who kept her rich brown hair tied back in a long braid—everything about her was starched and clean. She worked day and night, tugging clothes through the ringer machine, ironing long after sunset because it was cooler then. From bed, I'd hear the clank of the iron on the stove, metal on metal. And she did tailoring. She could tuck your waists back together after a baby came or repair a zipper by suppertime.

In the 1920s we were a neighborhood of dockworkers, fish sellers, longshoremen—water people in the city of New Orleans. My mama named me "Violet" because she liked flowers. My family's house on Bernadette Street stood six blocks from the Mississippi River and only a few miles from the Gulf of Mexico. Our breezes mixed the tang of salt and sand from the ocean with the smell of good mud from the river.

A balcony, called a gallery, wrapped around the whole second story of our house. To get to my mother's room or to the bath, we'd slip out of our bedrooms through the French doors, walk along the gallery and down the stairs. There were no hallways inside. A friendly magnolia and its partner, an ancient oak dripping in Spanish moss, hovered over the roof and gallery. Being on the gallery was like being in a treehouse. When my three sisters and I were young, we'd scoot down the tree trunks instead of plodding down the steps.

The windows in my room had white shutters, and my mother would adjust the louvers so they turned whiffs of air toward my face at night. There wasn't usually a breeze, just warm touches of air, like her breath, keeping us from a breakneck sweat, keeping us almost cool enough. I loved the squeak of the louvers and watching her open them.

When I was scared or tired, Mama would kiss me sweet and sing out: "Stop crying!" We managed; we didn't feel down and out, just busy. Our neighbors were in the same situation we were, everybody at the end of a rope, trying to make it meet up with the other end.

I had a father. He did odd jobs, would deliver quarters and dimes to Mama, and then disappear for days. "Vanishing cream," my Aunt Claire would say. One of god's experiments, "like the albatross."

"Violet, honey! Sugar plum!" he'd shout from the back yard, where he was raking leaves into the mulch pile. "Give Papa a big hug!" I'd dash from the kitchen, batting the screen door open, and jump into his arms. I liked his rough face, his hefty squeezes, and the way he swung me high over his head. He'd plop me back down and pat my cheeks with both hands, running his fingers all through my hair, like he was looking for something. But by springtime the year I was six, I sensed his hesitation before he lifted me, his grin going limp with my weight.

Aunt Claire had given me a bracelet strung from seashells that was my pride. After Mass one Easter morning, I was playing with Papa and showing off my bracelet. He put his fishing cap on my head, and the brim slid down over my eyes since my head was so much smaller than his. But when I clasped my bracelet onto his wrist I had a feeling something was wrong, because it almost fit. My father was thin like a little girl, but should have been so much bigger than me all over, not just on his head. One morning his sour breath came over my whole face in a rush as he exhaled, and I drew back coughing.

When I was ten and "a young lady," he gave me a quarter and told me to go to Nat's up the street and buy him a bucket of beer. I fetched it but my mother met me sloshing at the front gate. She was red-faced and straight-backed as I'd never seen her. Papa was taking her money from the pantry—*again*. That was the first time I heard her openly mad at him. Her voice was cracking. She told me I was never to get his beer again—*the lazy outfit*. He avoided me for a few days. I began to understand that "odd jobs" wasn't a real profession. Papa's appointments at speakeasies were followed by visits to St. Theresa, the little flower, approximately once a month, when he would, according to his account, confess to excessive sobriety. Father O'Leary and later Fathers Wilson and Georgette knew him well, and after reminding him of his obligations to the Lord and his wife and four children, would assign him a stiff penance of two full rosaries—the saying of which kept him out of trouble for at least an hour every fourth Sunday. After Mass, we'd laugh over it at a late breakfast where we ate biscuits, fried eggs, andouille sausage, oranges, and thick coffee—we were ravenous after fasting from midnight, which was required so we could take communion. Papa usually joined us at the Sunday table but during the rest of the week he was never there for morning oatmeal. That was Papa: a steady diet wasn't for him.

During the Depression, derelicts frequented the back alleys of New Orleans, and in 1931 when my mother finally told my father to go, he joined his fellows in their searches for food. In those days, destitute people would offer families a hand in the yard or garage in exchange for a meal, and Mama and I, and my younger sisters

The White Car

Julia, Cynthia, and Georgia were in the habit of checking the back stoop at suppertime.

"Hello, Mrs. Jones, my name is Steve Thibodeaux, and I'd be glad to sweep your sidewalk this evening." Our name wasn't Jones, it was Lumiere, but that's what the men always said: *Hello Mrs. Jones.* That's how you knew they wanted work and a meal. "Mrs. Jones, it's Douglas from last week. Would you like those bushes by the front door trimmed? I can make 'em match the ones in the back!"

"You know mister, you're right, that althea is a little scraggly. The shears are in the shed—why don't you go fix it up? Just knock on the back door when you're through. Stew okay?" "Yes ma'am. Thank you, ma'am." And Mama or Julia or I would watch until the chore was done and then bring Steve or Douglas a bowl of whatever the family was eating that night—a creole or potato salad or beans and always thick, black, steamy coffee.

Every three or four weeks, while I was measuring cups of rice for a casserole or sorting peaches for a cobbler, I'd hear a hoarse "Sugar plum!" echoing from the back stoop. "Need help with that pie?" If I didn't answer, he'd zing back with, "Miz Jones! Come on! Let me help out." I hated it worse than anything, and my face would screw into a nasty grimace, which I didn't do on purpose, either. Really, I wanted to throw the potato peels and chicken bones at him, and slam the door. Why was I stuck with such a stupid father, a bum? Was I supposed to love someone so slow-witted? Why did Mama say he was lovable? My father was more like the influenza that had stolen my Aunt Claire. I wanted to do charity for sick old ladies, the other men, *anyone* but him.

But there must have been an invisible vine tethering us to each other, and he pulled me toward him whether I wanted to go or not. Well, a Louisiana kitchen could always use a bowl of chopped tomatoes and onions. "Sure, Papa. Why don't you see what's ready in the garden and pick something?" I'd push through the screen doorway, balancing my chopping board and a sharp knife, and settle him at a card table in the back yard. He'd turn to his work with great deliberation, arranging the produce like a landscaper and planning the cuts, first eight slices north and south, then six east and west. Eventually Mama suggested that I give my father cantaloupe and eggplant, because his grip was too unsteady for dicing small vegetables. When he finished, I'd serve him a bowl of red beans and rice, garlic bread, sliced tomatoes, iced tea. He ate outside, like all the others, and he never came farther in than the kitchen.

I know why he didn't ask himself in. I overheard something one midnight when I was fourteen. That day and evening had been scorching, and the air was still a slow burn. It was midnight, the moon bright as a lantern, wide as the river. I was in bed. A voice surged above the ruckus of frogs. That year I thought it was daring and sophisticated to sleep naked and also, I had the excuse that it *was* really hot. So I had to fumble for my nightgown before I could slip out to the gallery to listen from my place among the oak branches. Papa had passed out, I guess, on the grass and had come to, there. My mother was sitting beside him on the ground, her robe belted tight against her. She was talking, and he wasn't answering. She held both his hands in hers and kissed him on the cheeks. She wasn't crying, like you might expect. She was just explaining that he couldn't be her husband anymore; she was firm about it.

By the time I was fifteen, it was hard for me to stay in school because we needed income. I helped Mama with the sewing and swept floors at Nat's for coins but she wanted me to quit and take a typing course. To work in an office would be a big step up for her daughters, and you could always type to make money. This was one of the few things we argued about. Usually I didn't get that mad at her, even when she was too strict or old-fashioned. I think I was afraid to because I knew she kept us going, and I didn't dare push too hard. But I desperately wanted to finish school and maybe be a nurse. I thought it was Papa's fault he was out of a job, his fault I might have to quit school. Most people in those days viewed boozers as sinners or pathetic, not medical cases. What they needed was a spanking and more time in the confessional. But that stuff didn't work on my Papa, and in my heart, there was a terrible longing, deep as the ocean. I wanted to fix the slack red face, the watery eyes, the wheezing, to stitch together the doleful body, make him into a prince or a president.

In addition to my bed, my room was furnished with a rolltop desk, a wardrobe, a dresser with a mirror, and of course my sister Julia. I was raising a banana tree in a pot, which Julia said would never grow indoors, as if she knew! But I used to tug it outside for sun baths three times a week. The long swaying leaves would graze and follow, whisper to me, when I brushed past, and I loved that rustling.

One night I was startled awake by an eerie, whipping noise, and I sat up straight in bed. Late that same afternoon, there had been a storm, with lightning ripping the sky and thunderheads racing over, and this sounded like my banana tree in a wind. I slid into my gown, which was crimped in a heap under the covers, and walked barefoot to the French doors and out to the gallery. Julia was just waking up.

I remember the magnolia was full of white blossoms that night. From my spot among the branches, I looked out over the neighborhood. Our block had one- and two-story wooden houses set fairly close to the narrow street. Down the road, in the direction of the whipping sound, was a glow. People were yakking and milling around, like Sunday morning, but I couldn't hear exactly what they were saying.

I ran inside, grabbed a housecoat, and moved back out along the gallery, down the stairs, and along the street toward where the glow was. What I saw was not lightning. Not a visitation by a saint.

A car on fire. A white car, a limousine. A car big enough to carry a captain in medals and pressed trousers to the christening of his ship. A car to convey the governor down Bourbon Street. A big-Daddy yessir car. Its shining white doors were being licked up by twelve-foot-high flames; the metal was sizzling. Red hot. The crowd couldn't get closer than a half-block, but oh you wanted to see it fry! Crackling sounds, the sound of tearing, the chink of metal peeling off and hitting pavement. That pretty white no-good car cooking hard to a charred twist. Suddenly the gas tank exploded, sparks stormed heavenward, a big smell of gasoline, and everybody scattered for their lives. Porch chairs nicked by embers blurted into flame. Fire trucks snorted their way through the people, who were wandering around in robes and rumpled clothes. My mother was staring from curbside, trickles of sweat on her forehead, concentrating like she was ironing. What in heaven's holy name was that Rolls Royce doing in our street? Nobody was talking much. All the world was hypnotized by the snow car, the black night, the brilliant orange fire.

Papa was standing upright at the corner, his arms folded against his chest, staring at the sky with its divine flames. My arms were folded too, close to me, and I walked toward him. His eyes were teary, and he called out, "Darlin'!" but the smell of wine smothered the air between us and I turned away, back toward Mama. I don't think he could really see anything except the impossible white car.

The white car burned on Monday night. Thursday morning, Father Wilson came over during our oatmeal and told us. Thursday evening, the paper reported it: a thug with a grudge against a rich shrimper had given a Mr. Lumiere $100 to torch the limo. The police, who knew people's situations, had noticed my father spending a wad of new money on champagne and oysters, but especially on champagne.

Wednesday evening, he'd whisked an envelope addressed to a Mrs. Jones under our front door. But after she found out, my mother gave the $25 to the priests. She couldn't see returning cash to that thug. The holy fathers took the cash, said thank you, and never another word about it. The police knew my father wasn't a criminal, just a desperate bum. He'd never been in trouble with the law before, but still they arrested him, to teach him a lesson and to dry him out.

I was the oldest and I had to go. When Mama and I visited the jail, I made sure my white blouse was starched and tucked in straight, my shoes polished and buckled. I pressed my skirt just right so everyone would know the difference between me and him. Mr. Lumiere was confused about what was going on and shivered and mumbled in his cell. Later Mama sent a sweater for him, even though it was 98 degrees outside.

After jail, Catholic Charities took him in and he lived there until he died. I've got my own home now, and that's what matters. I didn't think about him all that much, but sometimes I missed him, his old way of rummaging through my hair, and how he'd let me cry as much as I wanted, when I was a very little girl.

Speaking Up

Galveston 1940

Aunt D gave me the radio when I was eight, and it was by our bed, me and my sister Serena's. My brother Ben said flip it to baseball. Which I did. But to the Mexican station, to *beis,* just to aggravate him. He tackled me, and Reginald, not his twin for nothing, pinned me to the floor, tickled my armpits until I screamed, got the radio, and scooted out of the room.

But *bola rapida, primera base, esta seguro:* the words skipped in my head.

So when Angelique called *buenos dias* on the beach, *buenos dias* burst like a surprise party out of my mouth, right back. Her black hair fell down her shoulders; she had pretty dark eyes, and we just fit each other right away. We were always wanting to swim or play kickball at the same minute, and we seemed like sisters, only in two shades, me dark brown and her light brown, and my hair was not like hers; mine was short and springy. I thought she was so smart to speak Spanish.

I watched Angel's face and hands for clues to what she meant.

Like her eyebrows arched high when she had a question: *"Por que?"* I got it fast. Almost like I knew the words already.

We splashed like cockers in the waves together and rode innertubes to the sandbar and fished, and on the beach we made sand castles, and one time we built a whole sand neighborhood, with a fish market, grocery, church, school, gas station, shotgun houses: *pescaria, mercado, iglesia, escuela, gasolinera, casita.* And a deep, wide moat with bridges and gates, to keep the insurance men out. We had so much construction to do, we didn't notice the time passing and it got to be seven o'clock. Our mamas showed up, in orange and yellow house dresses, you could see from way down the beach. Because we both missed dinner. But they weren't mad when they saw our creation. In fact, that night, everybody on the colored beach came around to inspect. What about a bank? How about some chickens? Serena pasted trees together from driftwood and seaweed. Aunt Dorothy, laughing like always, took pictures.

My mother learned to make real tamales from Angel's mama, and refritos, and when they had extra, they gave us tortillas. Pretty soon I could even torment my brother Ben, not just by hiding his shoes or snapping a wet towel at his behind, but in Spanish: *Apestozo!*—stinky. It bugged him that I turned on the Mexican radio station, because he couldn't understand. There would be the cracking of a bat and the crowd hollering, but Ben didn't know if it was an out or a home run or a joke.

One afternoon I was messing around, walking home from school. I'd spent all my Popsicle money, so to cool off, I zigzagged off the road, to the beach. It was hot, really hot, and I put my shoes in my book bag and let the sand in the tide pools smush between my toes.

Then I heard a strange noise, like a dog crying, and looked around, in a circle, like my mama taught me. *Look straight ahead, look left, look right, look behind* and sure enough I spotted a baby. On the jetty. Or it seemed like the size of a baby from where I was. I dropped my bag running over and splattered my skirt and legs, but I was glad I hurried because it was Angel's little brother Carlos. He was howling, red-faced and puckered up, and lying down funny on the boulders, on his back. But I mean the top of him, his chest and shoulders, were twisted the opposite way from the rest of him. And he was crying nonstop, panting for breath between bawling.

"*Ime calle!*" he wailed. I fell down! "*Ime calle!*"

"*Dondé está Angel? Dondé está tu mama?*" I managed to ask: Where's Angel? Where's your mama?

"*Ime calle!*" Tears came like waterfalls down his cheeks, down his nose.

I could see the sheriff's station behind a split part of the seawall. I was good at jumping the crack, so I ran over, and I was out of breath but I saw a man in the booth and yelled that my friend's little brother broke something and was hurt bad and did he know a doctor. Why sure, the man answered, and he took off his hat and wiped his face with a bandana, and then got around to calling somebody.

Pretty soon, a man was walking fast toward us, carrying a black bag, but I didn't realize at first that Mr. Tsantes was the doctor. He had a peculiar accent of English, and afterward I found out that he was from Greece, somewhere across the ocean. I didn't expect people with strong accents like that to be doctors. He squatted and bent over Carlos.

"You're going to be all right, little boy. Don't worry. Where is it hurting?" Carlos just wailed louder.

"*Dondé te duele?*" I asked him. Where does it hurt?

Carlos was gasping, and he couldn't get his words out.

I pointed to his knee. He shook his head, *no*. I pointed to his other knee.

"*Mi rodilla, no!*"

Dr. Tsantes felt Carlos' left hip. He winced.

"*Todo mi cuerpo,*" he sobbed. All over me!

"Carlos! Carlos, baby." I patted his cheek, touched his shin.

"Te duele aqui?" Is that where it hurts?

"Si. Si."

"I think it is a broken leg," said Dr. Tsantes, "in which case we cannot be moving him very easily, except on a stretcher. Can you go for help?"

I kissed Carlos' cheeks, and then I flew off the jetty, off the beach, and down the street, home to my mama. Somehow in the next hour my mama and some kind of beach buggy with a sidecar on it and Angel and Angel's mother and daddy and a bunch of brothers and sisters from both families were all on the beach, so there was a crowd. Carlos was being lifted onto the sidecar, his little body covered with a big towel. The doctor had forced something down his throat for pain, and he was whimpering, not crying so hard. Mama told me: "Charlotte, go rinse your feet off and find your shoes." To tell the truth I was ready to go home and have my dinner. But Dr. Tsantes stopped me.

"Miss?"

"Charlotte Wilkens, 1348 Oleander Street," I answered automatically.

"Can you come along to translate?"

My mind did a double back flip, and the doctor's words jumped out, all new: *Puedes venir con migo para traducir?*

I didn't know much except I could tell what people wanted, no matter whether their words were in English or not. Translate was a big grownup idea. I felt my face flush red as a pepper. My heart, my whole being, spilled over with pride and fear. Because I knew Carlos' words; I knew how to speak for him.

I looked at my mother. She turned away at first, slightly. Seemed like she was looking at the clouds, then she took a minute to brush the sand off her skirt, and then she whispered loud: *Yes, go! go,* her eyes full of light and tears.

Sunday Dinner

Galveston 1950

Since I couldn't keep quiet about Tomas, Mama said she wanted to meet him and Sunday dinner would be fine. But there would be a baby and animals and Aunt D, and I thought well nothing to do about that except warn him. How about dirty rice and fried chicken? asked Mama. Tomas has a bad stomach, so for once could you do something like salad and beef stew? She sniffed but said okay, I'll tone it down. We'll be coming from church, dressed up, but could you not wear the yellow cotton with the orange lilies all over the skirt? Tomas appreciates subtlety, if you can understand that. At the party last week he was nice about my red chiffon but after, he gave me some magazines to study for wardrobe ideas. He thinks colored girls look good in black and beige, and off-white, especially for work.

I don't wear black or gray, Mama replied.

Beige?

I don't serve dinner in professional attire because I live here. What does this boy like about you?

He likes my mind! My Spanish.

How 'bout the Chinese menus? And the French?

I don't know.

Sunday Dinner

Ten of us came for dinner: Mama, Aunt Dorothy and little cousin Cheryl whom we call Peaches, my brother Edward and Carla and the baby, me and Tomas, and my sisters Serena and Beverly. I wore the silver bracelet Tomas had given me, along with a beige skirt, stockings, my new heels, and my best white blouse. I had earrings on, too, and my necklace with the cross.

My brother answered the door and there he was.

Good afternoon. I am Tomas Ramirez. He really looked nice.

Edward shook Tomas' hand and I introduced him to people. Edward inquired about his health, his home.

I live in a small house in town, with a daylily garden.

How nice, smiled Edward.

I got a skirt with lilies all over it, Mama chimed in, from the kitchen.

How nice, said Tomas.

We never spent much time with our flower beds, continued Edward.

But I don't see why. They are large and well placed on the south side of your house.

The south side is actually a bit too hot. We grew tomatoes and corn, cucumbers and beans there but finally switched to cactus. We moved the vegetables out back.

We kept on with our hellos and iced tea and then sat down at the table.

Peaches, will you please say grace?

Yes ma'am. Dear Lord thank you for this meal. Amen.

Anything else? prompted Aunt D.

She giggled. Thank you for the dessert. My favorite.

What else?

And thank you, Lord, for our guest. Amen.

Amen, everyone said.

Nice job, honey. Peaches squirmed and with two hands captured her glass and downed a lot of milk.

Excuse me, but I wonder if we could turn the fan off? Tomas asked, right after the amens.

It's awfully hot, Carla pointed out.

Yes, but it will blow dust around and also make the food get cold.

Oh, said Carla, reaching for the switch on the fan. She'd been married to my brother long enough to know when to keep quiet, but her eyelids almost entirely closed over her eyeballs for a tiny second.

I am not feeling completely well, explained Tomas, taking miniature portions of everything. There were wide open spaces on his plate.

Why I am so sorry to hear that, chirped my mother. Can I get you some soup or milk? More water?

No, Patty, thank you, I'll be fine, he answered.

I thought he should call her Mrs. Wilkens until invited to do otherwise. Nobody ever calls her Patty at first. It's Mrs. Wilkens.

What is your business, Edward? asked Tomas.

I have a job delivering dry cleaning, and I take a course at night.

Oh. What course?

I am taking a pre-law course, my brother answered.

I suppose that would be at one of the colored universities?

Why did he phrase it like that? I didn't like his tone of voice. And why hadn't he told me I looked nice?

At a branch of the University of Texas.

What's a goiter? asked Peaches. My mama gave her an expression that made her grab her milk glass again.

How old are you, son? Aunt D was sitting next to Tomas. I winced, but Tomas sipped his water and smiled.

I am twenty-five.

And you do what?

I am in business. Retailing. I sell clothes. Men's shirts and trousers. And you are Charlotte's aunt. Where do you live?

Down the street.

Sunday Dinner

I admire your earrings. They are very becoming.

We went on a field trip at school, said Peaches.

Honey, don't interrupt. Why thank you. Aunt D glanced at me. You know our Charlotte studies a lot for a seventeen-year-old, and I'm glad for her to get out more, have a boyfriend. How did you meet Charlotte?

I could feel a sweat break out behind my knees. Did he know he was my boyfriend? Plus, I'd told all of them how we met. What was the point of this interrogation?

She applied for a job at our store. Obviously a very bright and appealing young girl. Unfortunately, there weren't any openings.

Tomas sounded like an uncle, not a beau. They were all talking about me like I wasn't there, like I'd been sent off to bed so they could discuss me. I was more than tired of being the youngest kid in my mama's house. I moved the orange slices in my salad to the edge of the plate.

What's a fetus? asked Peaches.

It is an unborn child, answered Mama.

Can you have a doggy fetus?

I nudged her hard under the table with my knee. I really wanted to put a stop to all of them, to the whole thing. I've decided that after college I'm going to apply to graduate school, I announced.

For what? Tomas cried.

It won't be shoveling Purina at the feed store. Edward spoke up. Girl has always had Spanish and god knows what babbling inside her head.

What in heaven's name for? And what would you do? Tomas asked, his face looking as white as a dark brown face can look. Teach?

I'm not sure yet. Research. Work as an interpreter.

But you could teach children to speak Spanish, couldn't you? Could you not get a job like that?

She's never wanted to teach, said Serena. She wants to study

93

and write and speak other languages.

Peaches raised her hand. I know how to spell *goiter*. I tried to wither her with a look but Mama beat me to it.

Aunt D patted my shoulder. You are amazing! Good for you, girl. Do you have any applications yet?

I have to get through college first.

It was heady to reveal my crazy plan, which I had not spoken of even to myself until this moment, and astounding that my family understood.

Yes, you might not even graduate. Even then, you don't have to go to graduate school, interrupted Tomas.

No, of course I don't have to. But I want to.

Well you may not always get what you want, he said. In a slightly mean voice.

What was he saying? Only yesterday Tomas had been kissing me in little spirals on my upper, middle, and lower arm and singing to me in Spanish. I had to admit the Spanish and having a family in Monterrey was part of why I liked him.

Peaches was cleaning her plate. Before each of the final six bites, she produced a letter out loud: G – O – I – T – E – R.

Hush girl! Edward plopped the baby into Carla's lap and leaned forward on his elbows.

Some wine, Tomas?

No, thanks. I drink only occasionally. Yeah. Like last night, when he put away three gins.

Do you swim? Do you like the beach?

Not so much. The sand is so ubiquitous.

Aunt D's eyes caught mine before she remarked: Well if you don't like waves and sand, you should skedaddle right out of Galveston. With that, my mama stood to clear. Everyone helped; even Tomas carried two glasses to the sink.

Mama had cleaned and pressed her brown skirt and a plaid jacket, with gold and maroon lapels, which she looked very good

Sunday Dinner

in. What Mama had made was pot pie, with her best flaky crust, chunks of roasted chicken, and smoked onions. Bev prepared her spinach and bacon, orange and onion salad, which nobody can make like she can, and Serena made risen rolls, and Edward bought better wine than we usually had, and everybody except Tomas and the baby was soused by the time Aunt D warmed up her peach cake.

Lady, our calico cat, was retrieving eggshells from the garbage, had lifted them out of the peelings and wads, one by one, in her mouth, and was batting them triumphantly across the wood floor, under the table, in and out among chair legs and our pumps and loafers, spinning, here and there, into the far corner behind the stack of newspapers, and out again, the loose shells scuttling behind the potted rubber tree. On one of her trips from behind that tree, she pushed out a real egg, that she'd apparently stored there for safekeeping at an earlier time, a live egg, thumping it so hard that it cracked, and then rolled, dribbling raw yolk along the way. The baby squealed every time Lady skipped by.

Any sudden noise—a teakettle spouting off, a car backfiring, a thunderclap—set off Ava, mama's parrot, her pride and joy. Ava, short for avocado, sort of, had been napping, her head tucked adorably under her wing. But a certain nine-year-old had removed the birdcage cover and she was now, in response to the baby's whoops, screeching Lady! Lady! Lady!

Tomas excused himself to go to the "men's room."

When Beverly arched over the table, coffee server in hand, toward my cup, she dripped little splats, like toe prints, over the tablecloth, marking the route between her and me. I think she did it on purpose. Carla giggled; so did Bev. Bev then proceeded to fill mama's wine glass with fresh, hot coffee. More chuckles. More bird racket. She straightened her shoulders.

Why do you let that boy boss you like that? demanded Beverly, in her big sister voice.

He's not a boy!

Well he ain't a mature male.

Tomas emerged, wearing a different shirt, a brown and white stripe; evidently the heat, since the fan was off, had made him sweat. I guess he kept extra shirts in his car. I appreciated that he was neat and well-dressed, but now he seemed priss-assed and I didn't like him. I didn't like anybody and wished they would all go away.

I shocked myself by saying, Tomas, you know we had a call just before dinner that our cousin was sick and we're going to have to get on and visit soon. Can I stop by the store tomorrow? To see how you're feeling? He gave me a peculiar look, and so did Bev and Aunt D, so did Edward and my mother, so did Serena and everyone in the room, even the baby, even Lady. Ava shouted: Good-bye! Good-bye!

Si, I will depart, then. Thank you so much for a lovely dinner, Patty.

I no longer remembered why I'd invited Tomas or why any of the people at dinner mattered one bit. I pictured myself rolling up a newspaper and whacking them, one by one, on the backs of their hands.

As soon as the door shut behind him, Peaches spoke up: My class went to the museum on Thursday.

Well, well, said my mama. Was that interesting?

We saw a two-headed baby. And a big swole-up leg, cut off of somebody.

Hush! said Aunt D. Not now.

Must not've been an art museum, said Carla.

A medical museum, explained Peaches. S – I – A – M – E – S – E twins. In a jar.

Any ears? or eyes? I asked.

Peaches lit up. E – Y – E Eyeballs! From a mean person, I bet. How about a B – R – A – ...? I said.

A – I – N... nodded Peaches.

Sapphire Street

Houston 1980

Birthday

As a specialist in the care of feet, the lowest rung of the body, Louis Clinton spent much of his time at ground level. When people removed scuffed and spattered loafers and put their stocking feet into his two good hands, he became obliged to earn their trust. With a sale of the right shoes, he could make customers feel snazzy and comfortable all at once, and he didn't charge extortionist prices. Though he managed to sustain a zest for his work, after more than thirty years on the floor, he was now longing for something more elevated. Higher fashion. Jewels.

He indulged his passion by giving presents to his wife, Violet. Left alone, Violet would've stuck with a wristwatch and support hose as the extent of her commitment to glamour. Still, when he decorated her, made her glitter, he could recall her beauty, her youth, and he was sure there existed a necklace or bracelet, a glorious gem, that she could love.

"What's wrong with her?" he asked his son, Tom, over lunch at Maria's Fiesta Grande.

Tom claimed he didn't understand women except for his ex-wife Abby Moonspinner, and on the subject of her character, he could be eloquent and crystal clear. Lately bumming around the country on a Harley, Tom often cut through Houston. Where the kid got his funds, Louis had no idea, but Tom rarely let his father pick up a tab. Tom and Louis both preferred green salsa, not Tabasco, on their eggs; they both hated argyle socks. They liked each other.

"She's being stubborn," he said to Louis as a margarita slid down.

"Yeah—since forever. She liked it better when we didn't have any money. I don't think she even likes her wedding rings. I clean the diamond with ammonia and shine it up, and she thinks I'm a crank. And shallow."

"Well, Dad, you are a little fixated. What's that?"

Propped against Louis' water glass was a promising white box. Louis loved the slide of the cardboard against the linen tablecloth, the tiny puffing sound of the lid leaving the bottom half. Swaddled in the cotton was a shimmering brooch, which Louis raised from its bed and held aloft.

Four days before meeting Tom at Maria's, Louis had left his shop, Clinton's Shoes, for a coffee break. Mid-May could be balmy, but it was stingy-hot; even the steam lay flat on the dusty sidewalks.

As he approached Martine's Jewelry, he experienced the feeling of contentment, like having a stomach full of lemon pie, that shiny objects engendered in him. Here might be the island of divinity he kept longing for while he tried to tempt grimy teenagers with Thigh-Wise running shoes. He noted the security buzzer. He was dressed respectably—in dark brown trousers and a tan sport jacket, and he was sure the salesperson would trust him.

A Mexican-looking gentleman, superb in a navy pinstriped suit, buzzed him in. Oak and glass display cases rested on midnight-blue carpet. The air conditioning was set so that people in elegant clothes would be cool and comfortable.

"Good morning! This a new shop?" asked Louis.

"Yes, sir. My lease began two months ago, and I have now assembled my gems for you to enjoy."

The guy's English was extra-perfect, and Louis didn't want to say too much. Refined foreigners intimidated him.

"Okay. Great. Good. I own Clinton's Shoes, three blocks along Mariella. We give discounts, and I'd be glad to give you a tour of my stock."

"You are most kind, sir." He extended his hand. "My name is Rudolpho Martine. I will certainly visit your establishment."

Establishment wasn't a word usually applied to Clinton's Shoes.

"I'm Louis Clinton. Where you from, Rudolpho?"

"I grew up in Mexico City. I have been a purveyor of gems for ten years there and wish now to try my luck in the United States. May I show you anything?"

"Why not! Yes. For my wife."

Louis didn't often wear jewelry; he wasn't comfortable decorating himself for the public. Instead he inflicted baubles on his wife. Women were supposed to like showing themselves off, and he would've been satisfied to doll *her* up, but Violet wasn't the type. Louis wore a ring, tie clips, cufflinks. But really, earrings, bracelets, and tiaras fascinated him.

"Yeah, well, I'm just looking. Want to know who's doing business in the neighborhood." He moved toward the center display case. Two dozen stones—diamonds, white emeralds, pearls—had been loosed across black velvet, stars and moons floating across a miniature night sky. If only he could hold each one, turn it east and west, take the beauties home, live with them!

Next to the case was a mahogany desk, with a vase of fresh white roses accenting the dark wood, and a photograph of Rudolpho Martine positioned at the corner. In the picture, he was hunched over a magnifier and holding a pair of tweezers in one hand, a sliver of gold in the other.

"That is a picture of me creating this flower," he said. He reached into the adjoining case and retrieved a brooch, which he lay upon a swatch of black velvet. He nudged it toward Louis.

A single purple stone, a half-inch wide, shone from the center of a gleaming blossom. A glitter of gold suggested pollen. Silver petals encircled the stone and enameled green leaves cupped the petals. A dozen petals and leaves had been etched so there was a hint of veins, as in a real flower.

Louis stared for a full minute. His mind danced away. What he imagined was not in Mexico, but India. Two centuries ago, a princess, a wedding. Her young face framed by a gold silk veil and midnight black hair. A caplike headpiece and the purple stone suspended from strands of gold on her forehead.

"You *made* this?" he whispered.

"Yes. The stone is amethyst, and I have crafted a violet, that most delicate of flowers. This is my idea of a white-petaled variety giving birth to powerful lavender hues. For a fine lady."

Louis shook himself back to the present, Mariella Street in the 1980s, astonished at the blazing power the little pin had over him. Later he wished he'd thought of a man-to-man, technical question to ask Rudolpho, such as what tool do you use to incise a web of veins on the tiny green leaves? How could your fingers be so steady?

"I'll take the violet," he said forcefully, as if it were meant to be. The price didn't shock him, but of course Vi must never know. Lately, she had been filing and organizing bank statements, and he caught her watching a "how to make money" show on television. She had a basic terror of spending that meant she couldn't even accept somewhat practical presents. For their twenty-fifth wedding anniversary Louis had proposed a new refrigerator with a musical icemaker and a dial for selecting songs of love, sports, or Christmas. No thank you, she'd responded, her eyes rolling toward the ceiling.

Maybe such an appliance was silly and extravagant. But he felt, with thrilling certainty, that any human being would be enchanted by this wonderful silver and gold flower with its hypnotic violet center. Tom wasn't so sure.

"Look, Dad, it's beautiful, really. She deserves it. But don't be crushed if she doesn't keep it pinned to her sleeve. You don't go out that much and you know how she is."

Louis reluctantly put the violet back into the box.

"Where next?"

"Don't know. Want to see the southwest, the Grand Canyon. Maybe I could scout turquoise for you in New Mexico. My meditation is going really well. I get up at dawn and worship the ground I'm walking on. Better than being married to an acid freak."

"You and Moonspinner had some good times. Where is she now?"

Tom laughed. "God knows. I don't want to know. Listen, Dad, take care of yourself, okay?"

"I hate to sound like your mother, but any plans?"

"Not really. Just odd jobs. I want to do something with my math degree besides crack Viet Cong codes. I know; it's been seven years. But I've still gotta work on getting my head back. Astronomy, maybe. I need a little more time."

A week later Louis had the brooch gift-wrapped in mauve tissue paper. He ordered a corsage of tiny violets, his traditional birthday treat for his wife, and he always took her out for dinner. For this, her sixty-third, he made a reservation at Pier Nineteen on the shores of Lake Houston, a dress-up place.

Really, she looked fine. What they called a sundress, it had a scooping neck and green spaghetti straps. One strap rose from behind, crept up and over her back, and met the other strap, which attached to her front bodice at the top of her breast. As they got ready, Vi asked Louis to tie the straps together for her. He pulled them into a loose bow, so the straps would slide off her shoulders once in a while and ran his thumb over her breast as he worked. She grinned but detoured to the bathroom and re-tied, so the straps were knotted, secure. At least her neck and shoulders were bare, Louis thought, and still pretty to look at. She had an extra fold of chin and her upper arms needed tone. But she was slim and attractive, with short curly auburn hair and deep green eyes. The suggestion of allure—a loose strap, a high-heeled black patent shoe dangling from her arched foot—would have set Louis to whistling.

But this dress. The tight-fitting bodice covered her plump bosom completely and a very full skirt poufed out, like a prom outfit. "Gathered," she called it. That was okay, if a little dated. Except the dress was decorated in peaches. Pale orange peaches, each with a stem and a couple of green leaves, and the peaches were littered all over the skirt.

"I will *not* wear miniskirts or dashikis or sarongs or any of that other nonsense!" Vi declared. "I have a closet full of perfectly good clothes and I'm going to wear them out!" Why did it bother him? What was the matter? She was entirely correct, and on her own birthday she should suit herself.

For years they had agreed to save and plan for the future with Louis insisting on occasional splurges to lighten things up. Then there had been an era in the marriage, just after Tom graduated from college in 1970, when they argued over every dollar. Prosperity was flaring, and Louis meant to stoke it. The savings account was once again growing. Business was good and the house paid for. But she stood firm against him. No backsliding when they were finally on their feet! Those feet weren't shod in sturdy enough shoes yet! She purchased basic colors in clothes, almost exclusively—navies and dark browns—that she kept for years. At a bankruptcy sale in 1960, she committed a black cocktail dress, silk trousers, and a linen jacket to her closet, and just because it was twenty years later didn't mean they couldn't still be appealing. The dress with the peaches was from 1957.

Sapphire Street

After whiskey sours, Caesar salad, crab imperial, and Chardonnay, Louis winked at Randall, the waiter, who, hips swiveling to avoid oncoming tables, chairs, waiters, and diners, propelled himself toward them, elevating a silver tray above his right shoulder. On the tray was a white telephone with a gold dial. The telephone was ringing. In an ever so slight Texas twang, Randall said: "For you, ma'am."

Violet looked adorably baffled as Randall placed the receiver into the palm of her hand and pressed "speaker phone." A smile tweaked the lines around her mouth. From west Texas Tom was singing in his baritone on the other end of the line, "Happy birthday to you, happy birthday to you, happy birthday dear Violet, happy birthday to you."

"Tom! What a surprise! So sweet! How's El Paso?"

"I like it. But gonna get going tomorrow toward Arizona. You know me. I like to keep moving."

The guest phone was removed and a flaming birthday confection—white cake, almond icing, her favorite—expressed to the table. Randall brushed the lady's hand with his lips and presented Louis' gift. Violet leaned around the table to kiss her husband.

"You know I don't want presents! But thanks anyway, dear, for this pretty pin! God, who would've thought I'd be sixty-three years old." She stuck it to her green strap. Louis perfected the angle. "It's a violet, honey." He couldn't take his eyes off it, which created the impression he was staring at her breasts. She wore the luxurious violet through ice cream and cognac and another glass of white wine. In the car on the way home, she nibbled Louis' ear and loosened his tie. He tugged on her straps.

When they arrived home, she put the violet brooch back in the white box and set it on top of the two dozen other diminutive gift boxes from Louis, stacked on her bureau. They slid into bed under a green and white striped sheet, his left leg flopped over her right knee, their upper bodies apart, for a pleasant sprawl. Sometime around four in the morning, the narrow tower of boxes, each holding a tiny jeweled cargo, toppled to the floor. Earrings, bracelets, necklaces, and rings slipped out, like night creatures crawling away.

The Shoe Fits

Monday morning Louis fetched the heavenly violet pin and tucked it into his coat pocket, since he knew his wife wouldn't miss it. He'd return it to her dresser in a day or two, but for now he simply wanted to be near the jewel. In the hall mirror, he conducted his morning inspection. His thinning hair was still mostly brown, salted with silver, and he was trim in the middle. If not a stylish dresser, at least he had taste, and a salesman needed to be sharp looking. Today's powder-blue shirt and midnight-blue tie drew out the sky blue in his eyes.

He drove the two miles from home to work in his old Chevrolet, determined not to let the coughing engine distract him. He planned to review the accounts, place orders, and talk with Otis, one of his three sales clerks, about security.

Louis' job was to hold people's feet in his hands all day. What had gotten into him in 1946? Now it was 1980! He shivered. But he was proud of the way he'd managed the business and, yes, proud of his aesthetic sense, even though in his life he'd mainly applied it to feet. He wasn't a designer, of course, but he had an eye for shape and color, fit and feel. He liked a slim ankle rising smartly into the curve of a sturdy calf, anchored by a deep black town shoe. The same ankle would be all wrong in white flats. Some judgments came easy. Why torture the eye and mess up back muscles with clunky basketball shoes, when lightweight, classy canvas slip-ons were available?

Before he did paperwork, it was Louis' practice to serve the first customer personally each morning and to continue selling for a couple of hours, so he could keep in touch with people and with their feet. Besides, feet were usually more pleasant before lunch than after, because they hadn't been trapped inside shoes all day, churning sweat into odors.

At 10:10, ten minutes after opening, in shuffled a tall, thin young man, wearing one baby hoop earring in his left earlobe, black jeans, a blue and yellow tie-dyed T-shirt, a ponytail dangling down his back. Wisps of his blond hair had been colored emerald green. Whereas in 1955, a person dressed like that was either a homosexual or an artist, in 1980 he might be a veteran like Tom, or a drug freak like Abby Moonspinner; he could be a bank teller, movie maker, or graduate student—it was impossible to know. The main thing, Louis reminded himself, was he wanted to try on some shoes.

"May I help you sir?" soothed Louis, smiling.

"Sure, man. I'd like some sandals. Thick soles, cool, last awhile."

"No problem. I'm with you. See what you can find over here." The island display held thirty-five styles of sandal, poised to clutch onto pairs of feet and stroll out for picnics. Mr. T-shirt picked through the rows of pinks, blacks, whites, and tans and returned empty-handed.

"What kind of business you in, sir?"

"I fly a small plane."

"Tourists?"

"I carry cargo back and forth across the Mexican border."

"What kind of cargo?"

"Rope. Spices."

"Who are your customers?"

"Mostly students. Trouble is they take your plane apart at the border, rivet by rivet, looking for smugglers. I'm losing patience with it."

"That's interesting. I always admired a pilot. I was in naval supply in World War II but some of my buddies were in the air corps."

"Wow!" he said. "I'm Gary."

"Well, Gary, I'm Louis Clinton and I've been in business here for thirty-four years. Now you won't be wearing the sandals while you're flying, will you?"

"No, man. I got tennis shoes for that. No, these are for long walks on the beach with my woman."

So he wasn't gay. "You from around here?" asked Louis.

"No. Oklahoma."

"Not much sand where you come from. You're better off in bare feet on the beach."

"Thanks for the tip. But I still want sandals. Didn't see anything on the table."

Louis repaired to the back rooms and produced the "Locomotion" sandal. It had thick, heavy black soles with wide straps that held the sole close against the bottom of the foot. From L.A., guaranteed to "keep you cool and moving."

"Hey, nice!" nodded Gary. "Got any better colors?"

"Sure." Gary wasn't wearing socks. Louis unlaced his tennis shoe, revealing a naked, aromatic foot, and fitted him with an alternative. Brown soles, flamingo-colored straps.

Gary pulled on the other sandal. He walked around, extending his leg toward the floor mirrors. After about forty seconds, he said he'd take the Locos and that he wanted to wear them home. He must be doing okay with that cargo plane because Locos were not cheap. He gave Louis $90 in cash. Louis packed the old pair in the shoe box and handed it over, along with five dollars change.

"Thanks. See you around."

"Don't step in any ant beds!"

Around 10:30, a small, olive-skinned woman in a green and gold sari, a bright peacock, strolled through his shop. Dozens of wrist and ankle bracelets made tinkling sounds, like a glass harmonica, when she moved. Louis longed to turn up the volume.

"Hello, ma'am," he grinned as she browsed among the tennis shoes.

"Why, hello, good sir," she replied. "You have a notable selection of shoes to don at sport."

"Yeah, yes, I do," he said.

"Please, may I try these?"

It was a pair of navy-blue "Annettes" with extra-thick soles and plaid laces. She sat down and removed her sandals—pale yellow thongs. No support.

Louis loved the sight of her, loved the lilt of her voice. Is a sari more like an evening gown, he thought, or floppy lounging pajamas? Probably the right garment for the hot weather of India—and Texas—but difficult to manage if you were digging in the garden.

"Ma'am," he ventured. "Sorry if this is rude, but I've always wondered how a sari would be around the house. Does that pretty fabric fly into your curry or get stuck in the front door?"

"Yes, yes why not!" she laughed. "Indian women are not always graceful. Saris are beautiful for looking but not practical in all cases. In my home, I have jeans."

Jeans? He held her small foot in his hand and hated the thought of interrupting its sweet curve with a garish tennis shoe. But he eased her toes and her heel inside, laced it tight, and then patted that ankle. Her toenails were painted deep red; she had only to shift slightly and her five ankle bracelets chinked deliciously.

Adjusting her silks, she stood and stepped around the store, testing the fit.

"No, I think it best not," she declared finally, to Louis' disappointment. He was glad she didn't take the tennis shoes, because they didn't go with her at all. But he wanted to prolong his gaze. The violet brooch was in his pocket, and he imagined her pleasure, were he to show her.

"What about another style?" he asked. "I'd be very pleased to find you the right style!"

"No, sir, not today!" She unlaced the tennis shoes, slipping her fresh, fragrant feet back into those thongs.

Yes, there were compensations for being a worker-bee shoe vendor. Everybody needed shoes, from janitors to movie stars. Whether sturdy or fragile, fat or thin, freckled, dark brown, or off-white, the feet he examined each day hinted at distant treks, storied realms.

Beautiful women allowed him to literally sit at their feet as if he were a prince offering a glass slipper.

Clinton's Shoes stood stalwart on a good corner in the Montrose area of central Houston. People could come into the west door and wind among displays and salespeople on their way out the south door. En route, purchasing happened.

The neighborhood was one that had kept its old houses—grand dames built in the twenties and thirties, with wide front porches, upper stories, widows' walks, leaded glass windows, hardwood floors—"run down" according to real estate agents—banana trees swaying lazily in the yards along with oleanders and dignified palms and oaks. It was semi-tropical, semi-shabby. It had "charm."

Louis and Violet had lived on Lincoln Street since the war and many times talked about selling. Their home was paid for but wouldn't draw the offers because people now wanted to procreate in the suburbs. Fanning from the city center in all directions were frame, ranch-style cracker boxes fabricated in the fifties, dropped gracelessly on half-acre patches of dirt that sold at exorbitant prices. Why leave a roomy stucco sweetheart with two floors, rare in Houston where houses tended to flatten amoeba-like on one level? People envied that two-story house! Its aging thick walls kept it cooler in summer, and the friendly front porch sheltered Vi's potted kalanchoe and periwinkle as well as basil, chives, and dill. Four palm trees lined the driveway, and a high hedge of oleander bushes provided privacy.

The area was salted with old and new friends. Doris and Charlie had retired and enjoyed winters in Arizona, but they returned often. Fletcher and Rose had endured a treeless development near the Houston airport for years, but got tired of the incessant noise and moved in next door five years ago. The families grilled chicken together and played Scrabble. Harold and Fran, an elderly brother and sister couple, lived on Cordelia Street, around the corner, and Violet took care to check on them often. Vi and Louis belonged here. Besides, the shoe shop was only a few blocks from home. No long, sweaty commute to work.

Wedged between the small Catholic University of St. Thomas and the venerable Rice University, the area evolved during the sixties into a mélange of old-timers and you-name-its. Many of the great old mansions were rented to groups of college students or had transformed into places where you could stock up on bead curtains, futons, incense burners, tofu, bean sprouts. There were gay bars, vegetarian bookstores, and sports shops specializing in racquetball, lacrosse, and archery, for god's sake. Indian, Vietnamese, Somalian, and Persian restaurants materialized alongside the Mexican, Chinese, and barbecue joints as if the spores of many nations had been suddenly released to fructify in Texas. Then there were people on the verge of being old, like himself, who ran businesses to service the basics of life: shoes, hardware, appliances.

The high-heel and Sunday-school markets dwindled. Louis' block was breached on several fronts by a rush of weirdos and freaks, and he was still there to fit their feet. At first he resisted. Why should he go out of his way to offer a thin, doe-eyed immigrant "Spartacus" sandals that lace up to your thigh and look cool with a miniskirt? "Girls who dress like that smoke marijuana—reefer, honey," explained Vi. "You don't want anything to do with them." Reefer? Reefer had been around ever since there was Mexico, and its current popularity was a source of amusement for Louis, who'd puffed in 1928 during a Boy Scout field trip to the Alamo. "Makes you spit cotton," he'd told Tom. "That's all."

But it was a matter of economics. Louis' store was located in a squat, brick commercial building, which he'd been lucky to find in the 1940s. But in the seventies, the roomy vintage residences on nearby streets began converting front rooms into specialty shops, Tibetan rugs strewn on wide front porches, almond morning tea on tap inside. He was wary at first of attracting a fringe clientele, but the danger was in having no customers at all. He had to compete.

He stocked his store for all persuasions of foot and, coached by Tom, experimented with Friday night promotional events. Foot massages. Acupuncture demos. Shoe jugglers. Tattooists.

The business rallied. Eventually Louis began to see opportunity in the variety in the neighborhood. Customers regarded him not as just another hack merchant, but as someone with imagination. He'd never forget the day in 1976, when a slight Asian man came in, asking for the manager.

"That's me," said Louis.

"Sir, I have a special request for you. May I ask you to consider something a bit unusual?"

"Sure. What's up, buddy?"

"Charlotte Wilkens had suggested I contact you."

"Charlotte! Old friend of my family in Galveston! Lives in California now."

"I met her a few years ago."

"Smart gal."

"Yes. I am looking for a right shoe only. I don't need the left. I have only one foot."

"Darn it. Damn! Sorry about that. I only sell 'em in pairs."

"Of course, I understand. But I wish to purchase a good quality, black leather shoe for dress occasions. My daughter's wedding. Is it possible you could sell the left shoe to someone else? To pay $50 for two shoes when I only wear one—well, you see the trouble." His eyebrows and hands all raised at once, as if the question had overtaken him entirely.

"Are you new in the neighborhood?"

"Yes. I've worked at St. Thomas in the biology lab for one year. I am an assistant." He was dressed in a light brown embroidered shirt and loose-fitting white trousers, immaculate as a cruise-ship passenger. At first glance, Louis hadn't noticed the round wooden peg protruding from the bottom of the left, pressed trouser leg.

"Excuse me for asking, but where are you from? Originally?"

"Saigon."

"Were you in the war over there?"

"Yes."

"But your family got here okay?"

"Many did. We escaped by boat to Hong Kong. Then here."

"Did you have an accident on the way?"

"I lost my leg to a land mine. In Vietnam."

Movie images of jungle explosions blew across Louis' consciousness. As a nurse, Violet was used to torn flesh, but Louis hated the idea.

"Oh no. Awful."

"My wife is a nurse and she knows good doctors."

"Actually, I don't need one particularly right now. But I appreciate your kindness."

"Here, pal. Find yourself a shoe. I'll sell its mate to somebody else. Knowing this neighborhood, somebody missing a left will come in here before long and I'll be ready. Really. No problem."

Word spread that Clinton's Shoes had a supply of lonesome shoes—half-pairs—and would sell your extra, single shoes on consignment to people who only had one foot. Many had been wounded in Vietnam—both Asians and Americans. Some had lost legs to cancer or car accidents. And there was no denying it was good business—Mr. Dao, the lab technician, put free ads for Clinton's Shoes in a Vietnamese-language newspaper. In came the customers.

Some weeks at the store seemed to be all paperwork and no cash flow. But dull it wasn't. Almost every day, someone intriguing, someone bringing a whiff of beauty, a pang to the heart, visited Louis' life for a few minutes. By eleven in the morning, the Monday shoppers had already nipped his natural curiosity and sense of fun. Why then, after three decades, did the runway ahead seem to be darkening?

Saturday Morning

People asked Violet Clinton's advice on marriage, children, and mortgages.

"Hi, Doris!...No, really? Well, old men do that. Up and down all night...I'll bet you *are* tired. You'd better take naps. You don't want to hurt his feelings...I know. I know."

"Hello Penny!...No, really?...You'd better take him...I know, I know....I just think that cough might mean something...Yes? The car payment?...He's got to pay for it...Me? I'm fine. Talk to you at lunch...Sure. Bye."

During a typical evening, the phone rang every twenty minutes. Yet, for all her warmth with friends and patients, Louis didn't think she understood her own husband. Was it only semi-strangers she cared for? Sprains and fevers aroused her, while he was left alone with his foot fetish. He wanted his pretty gal, his longtime companion, to playfully grow old with, not this live-in Florence Nightingale. When he gave her shiny gifts, she said thank you and never complained that he was a lightweight. But he caught the accusation in her eyes.

Violet had savored her two-year course in practical nursing during the war. She wanted to assist in the national effort, and she worked until 1948 when Tom was born. When he was safely in junior high school, she went back, taking on twenty hours a week at C.C. Young Community Hospital, a few blocks from home. Like a game warden among poachers, she kept her eye at the scope, her finger on the trigger, until she was victorious over injury and disease. She had a special knack for inspiring teenagers to buck up and stick with their rehab exercises or liquid diets, while their friends were eating popcorn at the movies or riding waves at the beach. As a consequence, parents adored her, and many patients stayed in touch for years. Last Christmas, Barry Jay, now a rancher in the hill country, couriered ten filets mignons to Violet, one for each season since, at eighteen, he beat cancer "because of Vi force feeding me," and it was very likely there would be holidays with 30, 32, 45 steaks, for the cancer didn't dare come back. Sometimes the sight of her in the nurse's uniform—an outfit resembling a white box—agitated Louis. The promise of *amour* smoldering beneath that starched compassion and good sense made him tremble. But when he tugged at her pressed white skirt and called her "cutie pie" as he had in 1936, she'd twist away. Once he asked her to wear the uniform to bed, so he could unbutton the blouse slowly, and unzip the skirt. Violet was an affectionate person and she kissed his earlobe, but then stated: "Honey, I only wear nightgowns to bed."

He didn't work at Clinton's Shoes on Saturdays. But Vi had rounds at the hospital, and Louis was glad. Saturday morning was when he sorted through her jewelry and confirmed it was clean and polished. He'd smooth his black velvet jeweler's cloth on his desk and scatter loose stones over it—a time for "checking" these nuggets of beauty, alone, without guilt.

Vi usually packed her tuna fish sandwich and V-8 and exited through the garage door around seven o'clock. On this particular morning, her parting words rained at him:

"Why can't you fix the garage door today?"

"Because I don't know how, and I don't want to. I'll call a repair man!" he answered.

"If you think you're retiring any time soon, you'd better remember we have to save money first!"

"I am not fondling people's feet much longer!" Louis stormed back.

"Well, you may have to! We need to upgrade our flood insurance. The new clutch is going to cost $400. Do you have $400? I don't!"

"As a matter of fact, I do! Stop being so cheap. It's time to do what we want for a change. I've been looking at the heel radius on local teenagers for thirty years. I don't have all the time in the world!"

"Stop whining! You're healthy. You may just have to keep working for a few more years. With your la-di-da habits, you'd better. Or else I'll have to figure out a way to make extra money."

Louis' mood of dreamy anticipation had turned fiery. She was not going to stop him. Already, he looked at his watch constantly and hated birthdays. He disliked trips to the grocery store because they meant the purchase of gum medicine and antacids. He had known people who died within months of becoming sixty-five. "Bye, Louie!" Vi sang out abruptly. She always bounced back from spats, while he tended to brood over them. Feeling blue, he went to the guest room, which doubled as a home office, and without exactly intending to, pulled at his University of Texas yearbook on the top bookshelf. The old dear tumbled to the floor in a whoosh of dust. He let it stay there.

Louis took pride in his cherry wood jewelry box, imported from Hong Kong, with its six wide drawers and brass fittings shaped like lions' heads. Like a suitor, he stole ardently to the two top drawers, upholstered in yellow silk and filled with his rings, truly a private pleasure garden. Each piece was vibrant as any orchid, any magnolia. For when he thought of "decorating," he thought of his hands.

Louis opened the top drawer and his head cleared. He chose a sterling silver band, inset with flat slivers of lapis, for his right ring finger. For his pinkie he selected a diamond solitaire, a simple beauty he'd received from Tom's ex-wife, after they divorced. She'd given it back to Tom, with the caveat that Louis, who was fond of jewelry, might like it.

Louis liked red, the red of lipstick. For his middle finger, he picked a wide, incised band, sprinkled with tiny rubies, that he'd discovered at a flea market. The piece was not expensive, and the rubies reminded him of fierce rosebuds. Now, with three rings on his right hand, and only his wedding band (which he never removed) on his left, he had the crazy idea to be gluttonous and to outfit his right index finger and thumb. His college ring, carved with the visage of

Sapphire Street

a longhorn, felt fine on the index; onto his thumb, he slipped an opal, surrounded by tiny pearls and diamonds, his most ostentatious ring. His thumb, as the least handsome of his digits, deserved to be adorned in this gift from the angels.

On his left wrist, Louis arranged his favorite turquoise and silver bracelet, emblazoned with foxes and cactuses, a gift that Tom sent from Arizona. His plain gold wedding band on his left hand could bear but one simple accompaniment, a gold and mother-of-pearl ring he'd haggled from a street vendor, which he slipped onto his left pinkie. For the sheer pleasure of feeling it against the skin of his fingertips, he retrieved his mother's star-sapphire ring (her birthstone), then placed it carefully back, where it shone stunningly against the yellow silk.

Louis occasionally had the thought that he wished he were a woman. He had heard of cross-dressers. But such ideas created worry lines. Louis pushed the thoughts away and put Noxema for Men on the worry lines. For his hands were now shining with the lights of the ages, the promise of divinity.

God, it was easy to see why a thief wanted diamonds instead of shoes. Everybody did. The value of a diamond was beyond compare. In front of the full-length closet mirror, he cocked his hands on his hips, practiced putting them in and out of his pockets.

He kicked off his slippers (leather, with ankle support and fleece lining), bent over, and pulled up his nylon socks, so they felt smooth and tidy inside his trousers. Then he gathered *Cactus 1937* from the floor and settled into his recliner.

Louis paged through freshman week, journalism club, tennis team, and the Aggie game, but his eyes kept focusing on acquaintances who had been killed at Guadalcanal, Burma, Normandy— he'd spotted six faces already, and he was only a few pages into the book. He skipped ahead to class rosters.

Louis had not graduated but still felt kinship with his class, and he had attended a few reunions. In the section on seniors, he ran his right index finger, the one with the college ring on it, among the pictures of class members. He hadn't done this since the twenty-fifth reunion, when he was forty-seven years old, now almost twenty years ago. Except for the studying, he'd enjoyed being in college. There was his professor of history, likely long dead. The marching band—what talent! How they could rouse the crowd at games, make people jumping to win! Here was Ginger something. He'd had a few dates with Ginger but they'd never been serious. He couldn't remember now why not.

On impulse, the rings still triumphant on his hands, he picked up the telephone and asked for Oklahoma City information. He got a number for Ginger Knickerson, her married name.

"Hello, Knickersons!"

"Ginger? This is Louis Clinton from forty years ago. Calling from Houston. Sorry to surprise you—don't know what came over me. Do you remember?"

"Of course I do! Long time it's been, Louie! How in the world are you?"

"I'm fine. Older, a little bald. But no spare tire! Just wanted to say hello to an old friend. Don't know what gets into me sometimes. Are you free to talk for a minute?" He suddenly thought of her husband.

"Sure. I live alone now. Bill died two years ago but I still love to chat. Do you remember I used to get in trouble with Miss Fitz for that?"

"Miss Fitzsimmons! Sure I do. Well I know from the twenty-fifth reunion that you have children."

"Yes, they live right here in town, nearby. Four of them, you know, three daughters and a son, and I lost count of the grandchildren. I love them to pieces. What about you?"

"One son is all. He's a great traveler. He's out in New Mexico about now."

"How is Violet? I remember her picture from the reunion."

"Busy. People really rely on her."

From somewhere in Ginger's house, he discerned barking.

"Hush," she said to the animal. "That's Douglas, my Labrador. Wants me to feed him. What a thing, you calling me like this. I don't know what to say! What's your line? Don't you own some kind of business? Boots?"

"I'm a gemologist. I keep my hand in, but I'm about finished with shoes. Precious stones is my trade. Got more business than I can handle."

"That sounds fascinating. You mean diamonds and emeralds?"

"Well, yes." Pricks of sweat formed on the bridge of his nose. He hadn't lied since childhood, except when trying to skimp out of a speeding ticket. He occasionally fictionalized charitable contributions on his tax return.

"For a shoe salesman from the beach, that's quite something. Didn't you grow up in Corpus Christi?"

"Galveston. What about you Ginger? What's your thing? Weren't you working in an office?"

"Oh yes. Twenty years ago to make extra money. But after that I took up painting. I always was a dabbler, if you remember. I've sold a few artworks and printed a line of birthday cards."

"Why don't you send me one of your cards?"

"Really? You sure?"

"You can send to my business, but let's see, the address is changing. We might be moving. But I'll get it to you. What's yours?"

"3030 North Apple Ridge Road, Oklahoma City."

"Goodbye for now!"

Louis hung up the phone and like a juggler tossed a ballpoint pen end over end, so it hit the ceiling. One by one, he removed the rings from his fingers and returned each to its place in his jewelry box, which he locked. He marched to his Chevy, clicked the key in the ignition, and drove to the post office, where he registered for a post office box. In the lobby, he doodled a few lines on scrap paper, then he went to Instatype and had a business card printed:

Louis Paul Clinton
Specialist in Precious Stones
Houston, Texas

Appraisal

"What exactly is a gemologist?" asked Ginger a week later. Louis had been called to the phone while giving advice to a motorcycle cop whose boots only lasted an average of sixty days. "Pavement is hell," he'd intoned, but quickly shut up to take a "call from Oklahoma City."

He straightened his tie on the way to the office, and he tested his telephonic voice before answering.

"Yeah?" as in detective movies. Or "Yes?"—too curt? "Louis Clinton"—more businesslike? "Hi Ginger!"—friendlier? "Good morning" was what he actually said.

"Good morning back," she replied. "I hope you don't mind, but your card arrived, and I thought I'd call."

"Ginger! This is a nice surprise. What can I do you for?" Louis winced at himself. That was one of those strained, cheery expressions Vi was always using with her friends. What had gotten into him?

"Louis, it was so good to talk to you and so much fun to get your biz card. Could I just ask your advice? Would that be all right?"

"Sure, fire away!" He winced again. What a blurter he was! Then came her question—she wanted to ask about his job. Fortunately he could explain what his profession was.

"A gemologist is an appraiser of gems. A specialist, a rock scientist." She breathed as if she was impressed. "Well, my insurance company has requested an appraisal on my diamond ring and appraisals cost a fortune. What do you charge for a looksee at a beautiful ring?"

"You know, Ginger, it's been hectic lately. I'm still a little busy with the store, but I'll check on that for you. I'd like to help."

"That'd be fine. Call anytime. No hurry. Oklahoma City is pretty quiet. Guess that's why I doodle and read the way I do. Of course you can't be too careful with the terrorism out there."

"What?"

"Oh, you know. Beirut. The Arabs. Fanatics. I canceled a bus trip to Denver last spring just in case."

"Just in case what?"

"In case they wanted to get our bus. You know. The Arabs."

"You were worried about a terrorist attack on your bus?" Was she kidding?

"Not worried. Wise."

"Where'd you get that idea?"

"The papers tell the whole story."

"I don't read much. But I like movies." Actually he rarely went to the movies, but thought he'd like to be a with-it person, up on flicks. The truth was Louis felt embarrassed that he watched so much TV. Nearly every night after work, he flipped on the tube. Sitcoms made him laugh out loud; he liked horse races, baseball, tennis. But unlike most of his friends, he loathed football. Since the Vietnam war he had a distaste for people crashing into each other for no good reason.

"Oh, me too! I love movies. I go on Sundays with my daughter, Sharon. I'd better get off now. It's my nickel!"

He hung up and returned to the floor, scanning for customers.

"Louis, can I have the afternoon off?" asked Otis. "I gotta go to the dog races." Nobody *has* to go to the dog races. Why didn't Otis spend his free time at the library? Or raking his yard? But Louis felt generous. Lord of the manor. "Sure, go ahead."

He waited a week to call her back, from his office in late morning. She answered with a warm "Hi there! How's business today?"

"Great. Just great. Busy. Listen Ginger, I've been thinking about your question. I'd charge about $35 for an appraisal. It's a lot I know, but you really have to understand how a diamond is made, how to spot flaws. That sort of thing."

"Good gracious! They say to appraise it every year. I can't spend $35 a year."

Louis had the phone propped between his ear and neck and with his two hands free, was winding a chartreuse shoelace round and round his left, middle finger, letting it dribble off, then rewinding again.

"Tell me about it."

"It's a silvery setting with a big diamond, rather old-fashioned. It's surrounded by little stones. I was thinking of selling the large diamond and keeping the setting, you know? I could maybe put a cheaper stone, a rhinestone, in where the big diamond was."

"But why Ginger? Is it an antique? Some of those old rings are just beautiful."

"See, I want to pay off my house. The ring belonged to my mother-in-law. We got along fine, but when Bill died I had to look around at my assets. I thought I could get some money out of that rock and I love it, but I'd still have the ring itself, only without the diamond. Maybe it's a stupid idea."

"No. I'll help you," he said suddenly. He drew forward in his chair, losing the shoelace to the floor in the process. "Why don't you send me the ring, insured special delivery. Get extra insurance, you know, for $10,000. I'm sure it will be safe."

Her package arrived two days later at the store, at ll:30. He'd been nervous, but he broke into the wrapping to reveal a little white box, the sight of which always pleased and calmed him. Inside, the ring beckoned. A real treasure: delicately set, charming, a grandmotherly feel. Louis was touched that his old friend trusted him with this. He tucked Ginger's box into his front coat pocket and called: "See you later, Otis. I'm out to lunch."

Wouldn't it be great if there were a whole neighborhood for precious stones? For jewelry and gem places? Not that he didn't appreciate drugstores and restaurants. But Aquamarine Street, Diamond Street, Pearl Street! And he'd love to name one thoroughfare in memory of his mother, Anna Clinton, whose birthstone had shone like blue flame from her ring finger: Sapphire Street.

He felt giddy and evasive as if he had a date with another woman. He glanced reflexively over his shoulder as he passed out of the front portal of Clinton's shoes. "This is silly," he argued aloud. "I'm not a criminal. Just helping a friend." He had a habit of talking to himself, while walking along a sidewalk. People often averted their eyes as they passed the conversational older gentleman, and once a bus driver became so absorbed watching Louis' mouth and lips conferring with nobody that he pressed the gas pedal with his loafer and bumped the truck in front of him.

He knew exactly where to go: three blocks along the street. Rudolpho buzzed him in.

"My friend! How nice to see you! I am wondering where are all the people who need jewelry today. How is the shoe trade?"

"Slow this week," replied Louis. "I have satin high heels that take any color dye sitting there, waiting for a prom. I've got new slipper shoes—the sock part at the top reaches to the knee, but they haven't sold. Maybe it's too hot in Texas for those. Maybe we need a sandal slipper."

Was he babbling? What would a sandal slipper be? Something "Roman" with straps holding your foot to a sole, and a sock-ish part hugging your calf?

"Louis," inquired Rudolpho. "Is everything well for you?"

"Yeah. Yes." he said. His mind had a way of wandering, he knew that. Violet certainly reminded him of it often enough.

"Listen, Rudolpho, I want to ask you a favor. I wonder if you could possibly, provided you had the time, appraise a ring for me. I need to insure it. It's an antique. I'll pay you, of course."

"Why certainly!"

"Or, I could offer you a pair of shoes in exchange. You know, merchant's courtesy."

"But, of course, my friend. What an enterprising idea! An appraisal for a pair of shoes. Show me your ring at once."

What class this guy has, thought Louis. What a beautiful suit. Light grey with pinstripes. Silk, no doubt, and the man was trim. Nothing to spare around the middle. Skin the color of coffee stirred with cream, the fingers slim, his nails cut evenly and no little lines of grime along the cuticle. Possibly even manicured. Rudolpho's hands were superbly enhanced by rings: a pinkie on his left, silvery and set in tiny blue chips of lapis. On his right ring finger was what looked like a handsome class ring, some kind of animal face with a deep maroon stone in the center. Rudolpho didn't overdo, the way Louis did. He could understate.

Rudolpho lifted the ring from the box, carefully positioned it under his eyepiece.

"Most unusual," he said. "Perhaps one hundred years old. From 1880 or 1870. You can tell by the setting, the way the miniature claws clasp the stone. Where did you find it?"

"I like jewelry. A friend asked me for my comments." Comments?

Rudolpho looked through his eyepiece again and turned the ring slightly to the left, to the right. "This is a one-and one-half carat diamond, with 18 facets. An expert cut the stone with utmost care. I believe it to be of European, likely Russian, design, very good quality. I would place its value at $10,000 except for one thing, amigo. There is a flaw in the center, which interrupts the flow, the shine."

Louis spirits ratcheted toward the floor, where his feet were. He'd had high hopes for the ring, which with his untrained naked eye he had observed to be quite gorgeous.

"The value in my opinion is in the splendid arrangement and setting, not so much in the diamond itself, large as it is. There are twelve small diamonds surrounding the mother stone, plus six emerald chips and six ruby chips. A beautiful design. I'd put the value at about $4,000."

Sapphire Street

"Four grand! Hell, that's a lot less than I thought. Say, Rudie, what do you think of the band? Pretty sturdy?" He loved the silver band. It reminded him of college dances, of *sail along silvery moon.*

"Of course. White gold. Very nice."

"Ginger," Louis crooned into the receiver, two hours later from his office. He'd pulled the shade over the glass window on the door before he dialed her Oklahoma City number.

"Louis!" she exclaimed. "How nice to hear from you. Did you get my package?"

"Yes, yes. Sure did. Wonderful antique. Ginger, I've examined your ring."

Of course that was true. He *had* examined her ring.

"Thanks. Thank you! And what do you think?"

"It's obviously about a hundred years old. Maybe 1870 or 1880. Can't tell for sure but those kinds of rings were made in Europe at that time."

"Europe!"

"Yes. And in Russia too. It has a dozen small diamonds surrounding the large one in the center, as I'm sure you know. Plus six emerald and six ruby chips. You can see them with a jeweler's eyepiece."

"Emeralds? Rubies? Is that why it glitters in the sun?"

"They're tiny. But very nice. A tiny rainbow."

"I'm so glad you think so."

"Yes. I do. Now, you should know that the large diamond in the center is lovely, but it has a flaw. Nothing that interferes with the beauty of the ring, but it means the value lies more in the whole setting, not in that one diamond."

"Are you saying I can't remove the diamond and sell it?"

"I'm afraid you'd get almost nothing for the big stone by itself. I'd put the value of the ring as a whole at about $4,500."

"Shoot. Jiminy Cricket. That's a letdown. I guess I'll have to figure another way to get that mortgage under control."

Words like "Jiminy Cricket" reminded Louis of his wife's square expressions and of how old they all were. He nudged the unpleasant feeling to the rear storage bins in the very back of his brain.

"Louis, thanks for your advice. I want to pay you."

Louis twitched for footing. He had an official appraisal of the ring, signed by Rudolpho and the uneasy feeling that he was a sort of thief.

"Actually, a friend who's more experienced than me provided the piece of paper you need for the insurance. I'll mail it to you. I sort of practice with him. I mean I tell him what I think of the piece, and he coaches me. He agreed completely with what I said. But you don't have to pay anything."

And she certainly shouldn't. Not to an old fart, who without exactly intending to, was in the final third of his life and buffing the truth, as if it needed extra shine.

Vibrations

One rainy Wednesday morning in late June, Louis glanced away from the hosiery rack and noticed a young woman sitting in one of the side chairs. Otis, on bended knee, was holding her stocking foot and turning it solicitously, to the right and to the left, with the "arches and stress sprains" expression on his face. Louis had trained him with a sales routine he could tailor to hippies or priests, doctors or basketball players. This customer seemed closest to the hippie category with straight blonde hair dripping to the middle of her back, granny glasses, hoop earrings, and a placid expression.

Young women like that were everywhere these days, mouthy and all-smiles, and their discourses about yoga, bean sprouts, and karma unnerved him. Shouldn't they be having families, arranging car payments, going to offices? Yet he was fascinated.

"My name is Abby," the girl announced. "I used to come here for all my shoes." A twist of dread and curiosity upwelled in Louis, and he leaned forward across the counter.

Sure enough, she was *that* Abby, his ex-daughter-in-law, whose diamond solitaire he'd been rotating on his pinkie a couple of Saturday mornings ago, right after swallowing his orange juice. She was probably the only person he knew, he realized suddenly, who wouldn't think he was off the page for wearing a woman's engagement ring. She caught his gaze, reeled him in.

"Hello Louis! I'm in town, needing shoes. Wanting shoes. No more barefoot afternoons for me." Lord. He edged over. He definitely wanted Otis to handle the sale, but he'd have to say something back.

"Hello! Well, hello! Abby! Damn. How long's it been? You know how the memory gets at my age. How are your folks?"

Abby's closet had not contained sharp heels or tight skirts, only lapdog clothes—cords and T-shirts. But today she was both hip and resplendent: black denim jeans and a silky maroon blouse with long sleeves and rhinestone buttons.

"I'll go get those boots," said Otis, and she shifted her thin legs slightly.

"My mother died last year and Dad's been keeping to himself, as much as he can. He's still in Washington, but you know he's not such a big shot any more and when Mom got sick he resigned from some of his committees. He keeps on getting elected, though."

"God, I'm sorry about Eva."

Vi and Louis, Eva and Scott had kept in touch at holidays after the divorce. Yes, it was true. Eva's Christmas cards had stopped coming year before last.

With tribal certainty, the three Clintons had blamed Abby absolutely for the demise of the marriage. Of course when they were talking with the Prestons on the phone, Vi and Louis had tried to sound philosophical: young couples didn't stay together the way their parents did. Good thing they were still so young. The times were strange. But also, Eva Preston once interjected, Abby's a little wild.

"I'll tell you what, it's been six years hasn't it? Where are you living, Abby?"

"Hot Springs. I have a shop in Hot Springs, Arkansas."

A shop? Louis was astounded.

"We sell rocks and minerals. It's a crystal shop. Yukon geodes. Polished nuggets of the most beautiful Brazilian agates. Lourdes crystal. Smoky rose quartz. Healers come in and show me how to position a sliver of chalcedony on my forehead to keep my energies together. I listen; they're my customers."

Some hippie thing. Well, that was Abby. Yet Louis was excited. Agates? Quartz? Did Tom know about all this? Louis doubted she was defrauding the people of Arkansas on purpose, but there itched in him a scepticism that reminded him of Violet. He flicked it away, determined not to be dismissive like his wife.

"Hot Springs? Vi and I went there in the forties a couple of times. Terrible roads. Arkansas never did build highways until twenty years after everybody else and instead of being embarrassed at how slow they were, they were proud of it—sent an exhibit on the highway system to San Antonio in 1968. Other states are bragging about nuclear power plants and skyscrapers. The razorbacks showed brand new paved roads snaking through the hillbilly mountains to those pretty, bubbling springs. Horse races, too, and gambling, dances at night. Those baths get your skin good and hot—make you feel young!"

"Louis, I had to do something. I was wiped out from drugs, ripped up. They were nice to me there, and I stayed a few months. A friend got me a job in her store. She gave me the first shift, so I had to get up in the morning to unlock and open the place. She basically saved my life."

Louis was sitting next to Abby, as if he too were a customer, bewildered by the profusion of low-topped suede bedroom slippers. He didn't want to be curious, didn't want her brazenly in his store. Questions rippled up from inside him yet he wanted to keep his distance. In a way, nothing had changed: Abby had always been a force, even when she wasn't in the room.

"Abby," he said, "we never imagined you in Arkansas."

Her name was really Susan Alison Preston, but sometime in the early 1970s she revised it to Abigail Moonspinner. She had her reasons. "Susan" was boring and Preston definitely boring, and besides it was her father's name and therefore she wished to be away from it. "Moonspinner" zoomed into her brain without warning like a gift from god; there wasn't any controversy in her mind on that point. But she pondered her first name at length. She knew that if you were going for the sound alone, the music of your name, you'd want three syllables, so as to harmonize with "moonspinner." Since she, Susan Alison Preston, was keynoting a new beginning by the very act of changing her name; since she was at square one, so to speak, that first name must start with the letter "A." She rejected her actual middle name, "Alison," because it reminded her of Yankee girls' school students.

She selected Abigail because it had three syllables, because the nickname Abby invoked the radical Abraham "Abbie" Hoffman, because she liked being called the same word you use to signify a convent. She claimed that with her name and therefore her soul she aspired to embody something radical—peace—and a goal, spirituality.

Louis remembered the blistering hot afternoon when, over ice-cold Cokes sprigged with mint leaves, Tom Clinton and his girlfriend had explained her naming strategy at length. They were sitting on the Clintons' easygoing porch in the shade of the green-and-white striped awning, a rotating electric fan whirling short blasts of hot air at them. The rendering of each detail elicited from the tall, sweet young man and the petite, strong-minded young woman great rushes of laughter. Years later, Tom told his parents that day after day, hour upon hour, would go by while she figured out convoluted justifications like that, and therefore she didn't have time to study. The heat also interfered with her college career. Whenever the city was muggy and sweltering, she puffed on San Antone gold—just about every afternoon, March to November.

At the time, Tom seemed delighted to call her Abby; in fact sometimes he positively murmured the word *Abby Abby Abby.* Vi and Louis complied but in more matter-of-fact tones of voice. That afternoon, drinking those same Cokes, Tom and Abby revealed the virtues of nude volleyball, played in a swimming pool for modesty. Or was it to keep cool? To get wet? All three? More peals of laughter. Vi and Louis were reminded for the thousandth time that they couldn't possibly understand all that much about their son's generation.

Abby, born Susan, grew up in Philadelphia, the daughter of a politician and his no-nonsense wife, Eva, who came from Lancaster, Pennsylvania. Eva matriculated at Dickinson College in Carlisle, a magnet for ham radio operators in the 1930s. There she met her husband, a history major and president of the student body, class of 1939. Elected to Congress after the war, when he was a young father, Scott Preston shuttled between Philadelphia and Washington and nurtured in his children the pleasures of social studies class and civic-mindedness. Radio waves were a mystery that aroused lifelong enthusiasm in Eva, and she had a collection of vintage components. Her radio experience had enabled her to contact Japanese hams, and she had an abiding interest in the Pacific. She encouraged her daughters to not only learn the history of Pennsylvania in school, but also that of Asia. Southeast Asia. Abby listened.

By the time Abby was sixteen, she was demonstrating against the Vietnam war and for civil rights, women's liberation, sexual freedom. Like thousands of other distressed families, the Prestons engaged in frequent debates on these subjects over dinner that blazed into shouting battles. But unlike most other dads, Scott Preston was actually *writing* the laws, thus giving his firstborn hope that she could talk him out of more troop deployments. Eva usually sided with her kids, but would exit the room as soon as her husband and daughter raised their voices, so she rarely got to finish dessert. Night after night, the claw feet of her mahogany dining room chair scraped against the oak floorboards as she pushed impatiently away from the table. The scratches could not be waxed off. Everybody dreaded mealtime.

In 1968 the Preston family—Eva, Scotty ("Great Scott"), and daughters Susan, Louise, and Natalie—made plans to attend the Democratic National Convention. By early summer, loopy radicals as well as hard-headed moderates knew they would be assembling in the streets of Chicago to serve notice to the party of Roosevelt that the war was intolerable. But Scott Preston forbade his daughter from participating in any way, for he was by then the Speaker of the House of Representatives.

For appearance's sake, Scott needed his family in Chicago. He wanted his gals available to appear on stage the final evening at the convention to peck the Democratic nominee for president on the cheek. His wife and younger daughters didn't mind, and often enjoyed, chatting with delegates and looking well-groomed for the cameras. But Susan refused. She flew to Chicago determined to escape the hotel and take to the streets. Scott hired security guards to make sure she didn't. That August week every word Susan threw at her father was sharp and white-hot. Her aim was Olympian, her javelin swift. Whenever he stepped into an elevator with her, he involuntarily cringed against the opposite wall. He recoiled from eating with the family, not even a sandwich. By day, he shook hands with lobbyists, hailed the Pennsylvania delegation, the Senate majority leader, and the President, and expressed dismay at the unkempt students in the streets, inexplicably hurling bags of human excrement at authority figures. But Susan's anger had penetrated into his very nerves. He was shaken by the police-thugs, bashing well-meaning citizens, children similar to his daughter, even scuffling with reporters like Dan Rather.

After the day's caucuses, rallies, and bad news, Scott would steal back to the hotel long after midnight, hoping to avoid his girl, only to find her waiting up for him. She was like a vitriolic journalist, filing reports of moral transgressions, despairing of the country's future, interrogating him. That was the problem. She thought he could end global conflict all by himself. He knew the Vietnam war was a mistake, but she simply would not listen when he explained how military obligations develop and errors occur. She seemed to care more for Vietnamese villagers than for her own home state. With the streets of Chicago an armed camp, now there was the future of the Democratic Party to worry about, not to mention Congress. Not only did he have to answer to the voters of Pennsylvania, to steel workers, teachers, and ethnic groups; to the President, to Walter Cronkite. But *she* would happily roast him alive, no matter how late the hour. It was, without a trace of doubt, the worst week of his life.

A year later, after an exhausting senior year of high school, Speaker and Mrs. Preston removed their daughter to Texas, thinking it was a faraway place that didn't put up with backtalk. There was a private university in Houston that was supposed to have a conservative faculty and high academic standards. Abby was accepted and she enrolled, but didn't hint at her father's identity to anyone—Mr. Speaker, *the* Speaker of the House, his hand at the throttle of the United States war machine.

Tom Clinton was her math tutor. In the study rooms at the library, they held hands while he told her about disappearing equations. The Prestons had been relieved when she fell in love with a soft-spoken math whiz who got along with his parents, a Texas shoe salesman and a nurse. Abby didn't tell Tom who her father was until after their first weekend together in Galveston. It was time for decisions to be made about the draft, and Tom was reviewing his choices. Under the influence of lysergic acid diethylamide—LSD—

using oyster shells, they drew a line in the beach sand representing the long border between Canada and the United States. They marked exit points with driftwood, rocked back on their heels, and toasted the gods with cantaloupe shakes from the cooler.

At nineteen, Abby had been generically agitated, like a locomotive gasping for a way out of the station. Now, this morning trying on tan suede boots, she seemed possessed of an almost maddening calm. She described for Louis the open pit mines near Hot Springs, home of the richest deposits of quartz in the United States and a haven for sick people, anticipating the healing power of ancient crystal energy.

"People are camped around the periphery of the mine, in a state of perpetual worship. I persuaded my friend Jillian to switch from jewelry to quartz because I thought the crystal freaks'd go for our stuff. I bought my share of the shop with money my mother left me. She owned a little piece of the radio business and had her profits tucked away—did she ever tell you? Plus I have stock in the quartz mine. Don't look away like that."

Louis must have averted his eyes without realizing.

"A really hip geologist told me the Earth contains shining lattices of light. Just look at agate and you can feel its sacred qualities. The rock emanates. It glows. I don't take drugs any more because I suck a piece of amethyst every morning. I actually have a decent amount of money, Louis. I give most of it to Arab-American organizations. Listen, how are you and Vi?"

He didn't believe her. She could never, no possible way, handle the inventory, displays, accounting, insurance, buying schedules, the cranky customers. Clipping flowers maybe, but a stock portfolio? No. She must be exaggerating. She was probably a clerk, selling jewelry part-time. Well, said a tiny voice off to the side of his consciousness, you don't always offer the purest version of truth yourself.

"Violet's fine. Busy at the hospital and the house is spic and span, as you can imagine. Still snipping her chives and giving them to the whole neighborhood," answered Louis carefully. He felt skittish; he wished she hadn't stopped in.

"Since my mom died, I've thought about Violet a lot. Like one time when I told her I felt sick. My parents usually suspected me when I didn't feel good—thought I was faking it or stoned. It was 100 degrees outside. Violet said anybody would feel sick in that heat. She gave me a Coke to settle my stomach. It was ice cold and it tingled all the way down. No bullshit. No lectures. A Coca-Cola. I felt better right away, not like a freak everybody was mad at."

Abby decided on a pair of pricey sea green leather boots. She paid $119 with a credit card and alerted Louis she'd be back in a couple of months for a special occasion. Wired through her earlobes were silver hoops strung with turquoise corn kernels, and she wore several carved silver rings set with intriguing stones. She seemed to like pretty things, as he did, and yet she also held firm beliefs, though she could be opinionated and obnoxious.

Louis watched Abby leave confidently, and he actually envied her for an instant. Then he remembered his son. Six years ago, Abby was too mixed up for anybody to cope with. She had finished three years of college and then dropped out. She was stoned half the time. She couldn't keep a job. She wanted a divorce because Tom had doubts about evading the draft. Louis and Vi both thought the war was serving no good purpose, didn't want him killed, were ready to consider anything. But Tom wasn't sure about becoming a conscientious objector or a draft dodger, leaving for Canada and never coming back. He finally decided to serve as a private like everybody else. He believed in equality, in walking shoulder to shoulder with the next guy. But once enlisted, he was quickly spotted and ordered to use his math to decode enemy messages. Tom was sickened by American killing in Vietnam, but his interceptions brought the crimes of the Viet Cong into his consciousness. For a while he hated Americans and Vietnamese alike.

Abby couldn't realize what he'd gone through. She thought anybody who went to the war was corrupt, even the medics. She was bored by his math. She wanted to learn Arabic and live on the West Bank with the Palestinians. She waited until Tom was discharged and then, like a perturbed hawk, swooped at him with the news that the marriage was over. What awful times those had been! And here she was now cruising the Montrose shops for business—for her alleged quartz mine.

Not Oatmeal

"She's just growing up," nodded Vi as they ate dinner on the porch that evening. "These kids. On the loose."

"She's coming back here in the fall. Not sure why," Louis commented.

"Do you think she's telling the truth about that mine?" Violet asked.

"No," answered Louis. "I don't."

Violet's knees jumped inexplicably, and her plate of spaghetti jumped also. She had to spring forward to the rescue. Why was she so nervous, discussing Abby?

"Really? You think Abby would lie about her mine?"

"*Her mine?* How did you get the idea it was hers? I think she wants to sound rich and smart, but there's no way."

"Didn't she say she owned part of it? I'd like to believe her, Louis. She didn't used to be a liar—high strung maybe—but she's no riddle. Her judgment wasn't the best, but you could see straight into her. Whatever was on her mind, she broadcast loud and clear."

The next day at noon, Louis was arranging Ginger's "pine trees in mist" series of get-well cards in his storefront window. Cognizant of color combinations, he devised a "forest of cards" among a selection of hiking boots to give people the subconscious idea that his shoes would walk them reliably, comfortably, through the woods. He and Otis were busy, kneeling inside the window seat, when

Violet pushed through the front door, sturdy in her white hospital shoes and white hose. "Hi honey," she called, a little too gaily. "Got any high heels? What're those?"

"Note cards by Ginger Knickerson. Remember I told you we talked on the phone and well, she said she was painting these, in retirement, you know, for fun, and next thing I know she sent them to me. Nice, don't you think?"

"Yes," said Vi. They were sort of her style, Louis thought grudgingly. "Did you say her husband was dead?"

"Yeah. Passed away two years ago. Remember Bill?"

"Not really. But can she make a living painting these cards?"

"What's the difference? She enjoys doing it."

It irked him that Violet could never accept that some human activity is simply pleasurable. She always had to examine everything like it was laundry, for wrinkles and stains.

"So why are her cards finding their way into our store window? Shouldn't we show socks and shoe polish? Aren't we in the shoe business?"

Louis shifted his weight from one knee to the other, surveyed his display, and swung himself out of the window well and back onto the carpet.

"Come on, Violet. We want a classy clientele. I've always sold supplementary items! This is an experiment. If people like looking at cards while they're waiting for Otis to find their shoes, great. I'll mail the proceeds to Oklahoma." What was her problem? Was she jealous? He was trying to decorate, get hikers in, that was all.

"You take the forty percent off the top, though. Don't you forget! Are you adopting old Oklahoma ladies, Louie? How about me? Could I have some service?" She laughed and rubbed the back of her hand over her forehead in a mock gesture of pain.

Old Oklahoma ladies? Why didn't she go back to the hospital where she belonged—with sick people! She was the one who was old.

"Don't get in a twitch about Ginger because she paints pretty pictures. That's all I'm saying." Then, just to tilt her noggin, for pure push-'em-back meanness, he kept on: "Last Saturday while you were in emergency, I called around town for prices on birthstones. I'm going to dribble away $2,000 on pearls, peridots, aquamarines, and rubies. Then I'm going to put them in an expensive little velvet pouch, so I can empty the stones into my hand to look, whenever I want. I'm going to a lecture on gems, too."

Like revelations of sin, his plans spewed forth. Did he really have those plans? He'd seen a notice about the lecture, but couldn't remember what day it was supposed to take place. He *had* made two calls about emerald prices last Saturday.

He *would* go to the lecture.

"Waste of time and money," Violet was chuckling. "Hey Louie Fourteenth. Your jewelry thing again?"

When he and Violet were together in a room with brooches, bracelets, and surgical gauze, he beat a path to the shiny objects and she to the bandages. So should he be fixing the gutters or volunteering at the League of Women Voters, instead of swooning over bits of rock? And when she said you had to cut corners, eat the scraps, wear out the old suit, there was no way to answer back. She was always right. Was he acting so weird because he expected her to disapprove? Did he have the spine to oppose her?

Feeling lonely, apprehensive, and old, Louis walked away from his wife, wheeling around a display of foot powder. Violet's forehead crinkled in alarm. She brushed off her white, uniformed shoulders one at a time, her way when she was worried. It wasn't like him to turn on his heels like that.

Louis was usually so solicitous, and she took it for granted. In 1936 when Louis met Violet in New Orleans, she was working as a typist half-days and taking care of her younger sisters and her ailing mama. She didn't have anything. Her father had died a drunk in the Catholic home, and she'd almost abandoned her ambition to be a nurse. Louis encouraged her to follow her dream. But she didn't help him one bit when he was longing for something better! Anything he did that wasn't immediately, obviously practical, she viewed as extravagance, as if she were still the girl on Bernadette Street during the Depresion, subsisting on the home vegetable garden.

Violet's attitude made him touchy. He wondered if his moral fibers were shredding. Well okay, he admitted to a *lust for shiny objects!* Did that mean he and Ginger (and Abby?) were small? Had no principles?

Violet anxiously followed him to his office and once inside, she closed the door and tried to soothe him.

"Honey, I'm thinking about retirement, you know. I want us to be able to put crawfish on the table. Or oatmeal, at least."

"Think about something besides money!" Louis' voice rose, as he scrambled for courage. "I'm thinking too. In fact I'm thinking about the rest of my life and how I want to spend my time. I like precious stones. I like *rocks*! That's it. I'm going to fritter away hours fondling them, while you tape broken wrists back together and count pennies."

He had an impulse to corral change and shove it at her, across the desk. His hand had crept into his pants pocket. He clamped a fist over the coins and kept it there. Anything to stop that jingling.

A Life

Fifty miles' journey from Houston by road and ferry, Galveston Island stretches along the coast of the Gulf of Mexico, an independent wing of sand. It was perhaps its separation from the mainland that lured merchants and industrialists, itinerants and swimmers, bodybuilders and the bishop, to expect from that resort and port town steady prosperity and exemption from the hazard and whine of other cities.

Louis Clinton was born in Galveston in 1915 to Howard and

Sapphire Street

Anna Clinton, long natives of that island, and not people to take anything for granted, for Anna had survived the terrible hurricane of 1900. Her parents' house collapsed in the gale, and they lost all their possessions. After the catastrophe, which killed six thousand people, the city constructed a seawall to resist storm surges, an immense civic project that attracted hundreds of workers; Howard came from New Orleans to join the crews. By cooking and serving meals to the men who built the seawall, Anna slowly regained her bearings, and she and Howard met at the site. Daughter Lucy was born in 1905; there followed three miscarriages, and in 1915, brother Louis came along. Both children were curious, stubborn, and friendly.

Anna Clinton ran a bakery from her kitchen. She liked drizzling pink and yellow sugar icing over chocolate cake at Easter, and she enjoyed crafting brides and grooms for four-tiered wedding cakes. She gained a reputation for ginger snaps and pecan sandies, angel cake with strawberry sauce, blackberry pie, pecan torte. Ultimately, weddings by Anna were sought after by wealthy locals and by winter Texans, temporary residents from up north. Meanwhile, Howard worked hard as a partner in a luxury automobile dealership, and people rich as cream ventured from Houston, Beaumont, San Antonio, and Austin to test drive his Packards and Cadillacs.

Because of the kind of customers their parents had, the children, Lucy and Louis, were exposed when very young to people who had leisure time and were jovial about life. Howard and Anna Clinton's economic trajectory was skyward, as they catered to nouveau oil riche, cotton shippers, and restaurateurs, and in 1928 they bought a handsome house off Broadway, the main boulevard. Through the teens and twenties, Howard used to tweak her buttocks, calling them his "wedding cakes." When he sang out "How's my cakes?" to Anna, the children knew he was in a happy frame of mind.

One fall day in 1929, however, the stock market crashed, and soon demand for luxury cars and fancy wedding cakes crashed with it. Anna and Howard regrouped. They'd been fairly prudent for the preceding twenty years, and by drawing on savings, managed to keep a grip on their house, but Howard lost his partnership in the auto business. He had to look for a job in someone else's company. After many months out of work, he was relieved to be employed, and he put his outgoing nature to good use selling typewriters.

Anna now did a brisk business in casseroles and cookies for ordinary citizens. In the space of one year, her market of bankers, resort hotel owners, whiskey merchants, and real estate brokers spun around like the needle of a compass to sailors, fishermen, street cleaners, shopgirls. Some of them were the same people, just old clients forced to settle for new jobs. Her Depression-era customers—especially the oystermen—liked her spicy recipes. Half the time she gave away what she was cooking for there were hundreds of bankrupt men and women tossing bobbers and dead bait into the bays of the Texas coast trying to catch enough catfish and croakers to survive. During his last moments alive, a desperate black worker had chosen to feed one of Anna's pretty cakes to his son, and this made an impression. It taught Louis that a beautiful thing can provide solace and inspiration in times of suffering.

Within three years Howard was the top salesman for Williams Office Machines and was driving a Ford, his young son by his side, all over east Texas and Louisiana, persuading the residents of the amazing efficiency of his typewriters. In 1933, Louis enrolled in the University of Texas, but after two years of ancient history and chemistry quizzes, he went back on the road with his father. On a sales trip to New Orleans, Howard's home town, they stopped by Nat's Grocery and Tavern. There Louis met Nat's young employee Violet Lumiere, who needed a typewriter, and who as a result of Louis' increasingly frequent visits to New Orleans, succumbed to his loquacious charm. They were married in 1937.

Louis didn't stick with typewriters; he and his father didn't own the business anyway, and Louis wanted to be his own boss. He couldn't really say the shoe business was his dream, but once the Second World War ended, he determined to get work that would continue to be in demand. He knew he could sell just about anything and decided to pick something practical, a product that people would always need.

Louis was interested in style and color, in fashion and materials, but in the early years, he didn't yet have a solid line of bread and butter shoes. His shop in the Montrose area of Houston, near two colleges and a neighborhood of early-century mansions, drew established families as well as students wanting a bargain. He learned to stock lightweight rubber-soled shoes for the cafeteria, janitorial, hospital, and postal workers; lace-up oxfords and brown leather loafers for professors; canvas tennis shoes for students. In hot muggy Houston, a city where trucks spewing clouds of DDT cruised neighborhoods for mosquitoes; land of attic fans, sweatbands, and sleeveless T-shirts; the metropolis where all citizens—schoolteachers and toddlers, bus drivers and ad execs, veterinarians and mayors, refrigerator designers and rice farmers, nuns and wildcatters—all wished to be cool from the bottom up. So Louis made sandals his specialty. He applied himself to emphatic discussions with European, South American, and Asian distributors and collected a fabulous inventory: slip-on, slip-off, open-toed, open-heeled, low-slung, highbrow, fuchsia, peach, ivory. It was relatively easy to pursue the women's market, but to lasso men in macho Texas he had to be cagey. In catalogs, he found massive-looking, heavy-soled but lightweight sandals with handy straps that wouldn't come loose. He had photos taken of football stars sitting in big trucks, the driver's door flung open so the camera could zoom onto their sandals as they pressed on the gas pedals. He hired an advertising agency to incite a campaign, "Be Man-Sized & Cool," a slogan that dovetailed coincidentally with the onset of "cool" among teens, and by the end of the fifties, Louis could reach into his wallet and find several twenty dollar bills.

Clinton's Shoes was a discount house for sandals; he never charged full price. The business enlarged three times between 1954 and 1979, eventually occupying a half-block of space. Before X-Mart or Y-Mart there was Clinton's Shoes. He, Violet, and Tom prospered.

In the early years, Louis devoted long hours to every aspect of the business. In 1953 he took accounting classes. He studied clothing design in 1956 and '57 by checking books out of the library and sitting in on night classes at the University of Houston to get a feel for foot fashion. By the seventies, the style and color of shoes became secondary to comfort and health. He signed up for "orthopedic trends" at Vi's hospital where he questioned physical therapists about stress fractures and the hopelessness of flat feet.

When sales were slow, he promoted his product. In the sixties, if you purchased "Canyon" shoes, you got a free foot massage. In the seventies, organic foot powder with every pair of running shoes; in the early eighties, a certificate for a pedicure at Matt's Makeover. Later, Matt came to the store and performed on-the-spot pedicures. Louis carried ankle bracelets, hosiery, and socks. Socks with tassels, Valentine socks, ringing socks with actual bells that tinkled as you walked; socks with lights that flashed when you reached aerobic levels. Louis adapted to the times. He extended his stock to accommodate the eclectic population that gradually came to inhabit the area.

His parents and sister had stayed on in Galveston. One afternoon in 1947, Lucy had driven to Texas City to claim a set of cups and saucers, which she had ordered from the Wedgewood Company in England. She could save ten percent if she collected the package herself at the docks, instead of letting the importer hire a truck to deliver it to her front door in nearby Galveston, and who knew whether fragile cargo would make it intact anyway? During the hour when she was locating the warehouse, handing cash to the broker, and loading the china into her car, a ship carrying fertilizer caught fire and the flames vaulted to shore, where there were dozens of refineries. The harbor and docks blew up, the glow of Texas City could be seen all the way from Houston, forty miles away, and Lucy was killed from inhaling toxic fumes.

Anna died in 1960, by which time Howard had long been gone, and Lucy's death was thirteen years past. Anna had carefully considered how to disperse her personal treasures. She left the house and savings to her son Louis. Since her daughter had passed away, she specified that her few pieces of jewelry were to go to him too, and her baking pans to her daughter-in-law. There was a chance that Violet might use the cookware and even appreciate it, but her aversion to finery was a family fact and Anna saw no reason to bequeath pins, watches, and her great-grandmother's antique pearls to someone who might feature them in a garage sale or worse yet, give them away to a sick stranger at the hospital.

Her judgment in this matter was sound. In the very metal and rock of her adornments, Louis found and kept alive his mother. He especially loved her sapphire ring, a birthstone signifying clarity of mind, which she had found on the beach in the debris of the great hurricane, and this he had held high in his right hand at dawn, noon, midafternoon, and dusk, turning it toward the sun and away, for the sheer pleasure of watching changes in its luminous blue aura. When he was two or three years old, she had teased him to find the star inside. The two would hold the ring under a reading lamp, and she would turn it until the lacy white cross—the star—floated up from the deep blue. How often he had seen that ring circling her finger, dusted over by flour! How frequently her right hand had crimped around a funnel of sugar icing, as she dotted a cake in roses! The small stone set in silver had endured hurricanes, heat, sand, and thousands of hours in the kitchen. Whenever he touched it, he felt her industrious good nature and rapport with beauty.

Tiara in August

Lecturing at the Museum of Natural Science was a young geologist named Arthur Bright, originally from Seattle, a place where mist glinted in the high branches of Ponderosa pines. He'd attended Rice University in Houston where he learned to analyze multicolored shale strata for traces of oil that in turn led to gushers. He earned his living as part-time professor of precious minerals and as consultant for oil companies, locating and testing the rock formations that sheltered black gold. Though he preferred the harmonies of Mozart to all other sounds, he'd learned to appreciate the whine of oil rigs pumping crude because that minor key heralded an accompanying leap in his bank balance. He adored jade.

The summer had passed into August, and the weather was hot enough to fry something in. But the air conditioning was way too high. Louis sat in the lecture hall shivering but transfixed by this young man. Professor Bright explained that rock formations, in fact rock itself, came into being because of millions of years of pressure under the surface of the globe. Minerals beloved by humans emerged from the sizzling core of the planet and jutted into mountainsides and canyons as deposits of emeralds or rubies or diamonds. Louis was fascinated by Professor Bright's slides. First, there were charts showing the strata of the earth, followed by close-up photographs of hexagonal purple amethyst prisms from Mexico and pale yellow Brazilian chalcedony, shaped like brain coral. Although there were industrial uses for quartz, such as in radio crystals, and for diamonds, which are harder than any other known material, Arthur Bright said that the *sheer beauty* of these minerals was the main reason people searched for them. The human spirit craved the shining pieces of rock from the heart of Mother Earth. The pursuit of beauty was like the need for religion, love, or food—part of human nature. Unlike much of modern art, for example, even the most ordinary person could enjoy a solitaire diamond or a jade pendant without knowing one thing about its chemical composition. To the accompaniment of the Pachelbel Canon, he ended his presentation with a ceiling-high projection of a diamond, sapphire, and emerald tiara created for Catherine the Great.

Louis was dazed. He felt as if he had finally, in this auditorium, found his people, a village populated by ancient kin with whom understanding ran deep and unfettered in the bloodstream. For some ten minutes, he kept his seat as though hypnotized, then slowly stood to exit the auditorium.

He spied Rudolpho Martine in the lobby.

"Rudolpho! Great to see you here!" said Louis.

"Why yes, what a pleasant lecture," replied Rudolpho.

"You study geology in Mexico?"

"Not so much. More on jewelry design. But I like a refresher on the origins of my stones. How is your friend with the ring?"

"I talked to Ginger on Monday," Louis said. They'd spoken every week right through June and July. Last Monday he'd telephoned her at noon, just before his ham sandwich. His memory of the phone call with Ginger, his pleasure at the lecture and admiration for Rudolpho, the thought of Saturday morning when he would be alone and free to admire his rings, all alloyed to put a spring in Louis' step.

"You know, Rudolpho, she wasn't sure what to do with your appraisal. She did insure the ring of course. She's wearing it more, I think. Liked knowing the background on it."

Louis slipped out into the muggy heat; the crickets and frogs were roaring from the oleander hedges that lined the brick path at the front of the museum. He loved the idea that he and Rudolpho independently selected the same evening's entertainment.

He sat in his parked car for a few minutes, thinking back to the conversation with Ginger from last Monday, replaying parts of it in his mind. With her, he could freely impersonate a real gemologist, and she, incidentally, seemed to need him a little bit.

"Ginger! It's Louis, your diamond man."

"Hello Louie. You okay?"

"Yeah, fine. You?"

"Good. Tired but that's the golden years."

"Don't I know. New cards this weekend?"

"Yes, one kind of nice one of pine trees, with flags and bunting in the branches. I'm inspired by the Fourth."

"Do it from the roof?"

"I did, yes I did. It's quiet there, and I can spread out."

"Three of your other ones sold last week. The ducks, the lakeside with the rowboat, and the Indian paintbrushes."

"Isn't that a thing. Would you believe?"

Ginger was troubled because she had lent $20 to her grandson, against the wishes of her son and daughter-in-law. They said the kid wouldn't pay it back, was taking advantage of her, needed to be told no.

Louis wasn't sure what she should do. Vi would've known what to say.

"Ginger, maybe you should tell him to pay you $2 a week. Something he can handle."

"I might do that. He worries me. Cocky. Listen, why don't you and Violet come visit me? We'd barbecue and you could meet my kids."

Louis didn't want Violet involved in a rendezvous with Ginger.

"We're always so busy with the store and her with the hospital. Maybe sometime."

"Think about it," she said. "Did I tell you I've ordered a shredder?"

"No. What for?"

"I think people should destroy their old papers."

What could she have that needed to be shredded? She was spending too much time alone, worrying.

"What papers? Shredders are for the CIA."

"Your old checks. Credit card records. Bank statements."

"How old?"

"I saved them since 1958."

"Just throw them away. Don't worry about it."

"People go through your garbage. They write down your financial information."

"But Ginger, account numbers from twenty years ago don't matter."

"You can't be too careful."

"You ought to toss the stuff. Tear the papers in half if you want. Into the trash. Watch them haul it away and look forward to the extra closet space."

"Louie, are you too trusting? You concern me. Want to borrow my shredder?"

"No. No, I don't. Thanks anyway," he chuckled.

"I'd better go; the doorbell is going. I like your calls so much."

"You're one sweet lady, Ginger. Goodbye for now."

No one but Louis would think this was a remotely compelling conversation. But he'd enjoyed those few minutes. After all Ginger had her family and neighbors, but maybe she was ashamed to tell them exactly what frightened her. Maybe she needed his advice.

And his mind veered also to his visit, two weeks earlier, to Martine's. He had been thinking that if Tom didn't want it, he might bequeath his mother's sapphire ring to old friends from Galveston, someone in the Wilkens family. Probably Charlotte, who as a small girl had been fascinated by the star. "I don't want an appraisal, exactly," he told Rudolpho. "But this ring belonged to my mother. I wanted to show you."

"Of course!" responded Rudolpho, who immediately centered the ring beneath his magnifier.

"Amigo, you have a prize here. The setting is delicate, feminine, and crafted with interesting flaws, rather than being highly professional. I can see the marks where the silver was hammered, evidence of an artisan's work, not the work of a couture jeweler. It is undoubtedly handmade by a local artist, perhaps a hundred years ago. To tell you the truth, overall it has the feel of Central America to me. But even more intriguing is the stone. And the lovely star. A type we see in Asia, in Sri Lanka. As to how the stone and the silver came together, I couldn't say."

Louis was thrilled to hear Rudolpho's assessment. And he was dazzled by Arthur Bright. His passion was shared by an oil man, a geologist, a hard scientist whose bank account must be swollen from consulting fees. Someone who indulged his lust for crown jewels and also was perfectly solvent, both conditions flowing from the same inspiration—rocks! Who cared why you liked pretty stones? It was part of the species plan. No wonder Louis didn't want to sell them to get cash for his car payments! He felt like he was in a jet plane: no need to understand how the fuel system works; just fly through the pure blue sky on a wing and a prayer.

A Fresh Rain

Not the usual heat sink of a Monday, this morning came on with a billowy rain, a dawn rain, like Easter, meant to resurrect the soul. So buoyed was Louis that he didn't even switch on his wipers during the short drive to work. Each droplet brimmed with sunlight, and a rainbow hovered over the freeway.

After his ten o'clock doughnut, he sorted the mail, fussed over the slipper displays, and glanced at rival newspaper ads. With his coffee steaming beside him, he prepared to call Ginger at the usual time. He itched to tell her about the lecture, about Arthur Bright, and the plan forming in his mind to work at the store part-time and to concentrate on selling birthstones.

The phone rang seven times. Louis redialed. He waited through ten, eleven, fifteen rings, thinking, well she's not home. I guess we really didn't have a routine, after all. I don't know why I think she's always going to be at the phone, waiting for me.

But he felt disappointed, almost morose, and marched gruffly out the back door to get a taco.

At two p.m. he telephoned again. After three rings, an unfamiliar voice answered "hello," a voice so dull, so flat, he couldn't tell if it was a man or a woman.

"Hi. This is Louis Clinton, a friend of Ginger Knickerson's. Wondering if I could speak to her?"

"Oh hello, Mr. Clinton. I'm her daughter Sharon. Yes, she's mentioned you. In Houston? From college?"

"That's right. Good to talk to you Sharon."

"Mr. Clinton, I'm sorry to have to tell you but my mother died last week. She had a stroke Tuesday and died in the hospital Wednesday." Her voice broke.

"No. Good god. That's terrible. God."

"We can't believe she's gone. I can't sleep or eat and my kids look awful. My sister cries constantly. I don't know what we'll do."

"She told me what a loving family you are and how proud she was of you." Louis was losing his voice.

"Did you ever see her cards?"

"Yes, I've seen a few. She sent them to me. Some were on display in my store window."

"She was spending all her time on the cards lately, to the point that we were a little worried. She was obsessed. She wanted to do stars and planets. She'd climb to the roof so she could do treetops. We teased her about it. Told her to go play golf and relax. I wish we hadn't bugged her."

"You were trying to help!"

"I'd better go," said Sharon.

"I'm sorry. Listen, I'd like to call you in a few weeks, when things are quieter—maybe if there's an extra card there you don't want…"

"Well, sure. Mom would love to think someone wanted her cards. But you'd better send me an envelope. I won't remember otherwise."

Louis didn't want to let go of Sharon, but the blaring dial tone forced him. The click of the receiver shot through his stomach like a cramp. He swiveled to the side and around, to the side and around, in his chair, and then took himself out the back for the second time that day.

He felt numb and stirred up, all at once. He wanted some air, time to picture Ginger and what had happened. But somehow her voice, her cards, and Sharon floated away as he walked. He became absorbed in his own street, Mariella Street, its doorsteps compelling him, as if it was his last day there. Three doors away was the Firenze Deli, sausages hanging from the rafters, along with mesh baskets overflowing with garlic and pretty red peppers. An Italian thing. Truthfully, there was so much more to look at now. In 1946 there were just a few houses and boxy office buildings.

Everything was realigning in increments, as if there had been a series of earthquakes too small to register, but still causing cracks beneath the surface. Now he looked around and noticed the sum of the tiny tremors: the neighborhood had done a somersault.

There had always been Mexican joints, Tex-Mex places, tamale bars. Go in, sling down a beer, crunch nachos. In the old days, the only vegetable was refried beans, maybe guacamole. Now it was like California had invented it and was making you eat a lot of extra vegetables with your Mexican food. Maria's Fiesta Grande was a new generation. More Mexico, too, less Texas. Looked like a plaza in Oaxaca. The menu included dusky sauces ground from pumpkin seeds and papaya desserts. Now Tom made really great refritos, and he didn't use lard. Amazing. Just a pinch of bacon. Cilantro. He learned how in Arizona and Colorado. Everything was all mixed up. What if his son would come home, open a restaurant? Amita's Sari Emporium. Who knew in the 1950s what a sari was? Six yards of silk, dancing away from a woman, a butterfly among cowboys. Sonny Page's Grits and Groceries crowded with black and white students, a checkerboard, some of them holding hands with each other, people wanting a stomach full of soft, warm, cheap lunch and not ashamed of country food. First Baptist Church. Vi had grown

Sapphire Street

up disdaining hard-shell Baptists—New Orleans Catholics carried that prejudice close to their chests—and Violet, even with her stricter ways, still enjoyed her glasses of wine. But this afternoon Louis saw the frame building and simple white steeple with affection, for it was part of his landscape. They were corseted, straight-laced, sure, but basically just trying to get it right.

How to get it right? There wasn't much time. Two gay bars, next door to one another, like brothers. As long as you didn't ambush anyone else, why not? Because it was the middle of the afternoon and he was alone, and because in the face of death, be it slow or sudden, anything you might want to do seemed suddenly perfectly acceptable to Louis, he stepped into one of the bars, Ask a Marine, where Marine Corps paraphernalia crammed every surface and regaled every wall. Floor-to-ceiling posters of advertisements for the corps, the recruits clean shaven and spit polished, decked out in white, very white, uniforms. Batons, American flags, hats. Medals. Boots? How many actual Marines walked in here?

Louis had no desire to be driving along. He wanted to feel Mariella Street through the bottom of his feet. He was wearing Docksiders, made of canvas, with thin soles, that anchored you and were sturdy, in touch with the ground.

Behind Martine's Jewelry, in the window of Elsa's Antiques, he saw a "pillow" from Vietnam. But small and hard, not bosomy and soft. It was a ceramic turtle, the shell carved in wobbly squares to look like a real turtle. The creature's head stretched from the shell, quizzically eyeing a curved shelf upon its back. The curved shelf must be the "pillow" part, a device for holding something, and it couldn't be for your head. For your hand? For your wrist? A fork? Or would it be chopsticks? Pillow. One word for him, another meaning altogether on the other side of the world. Some Vietnamese family was letting this treasure go, to net some extra cash. He whispered aloud to his reflection: "I could display a necklace on that ceramic pillow," but interrupted himself and stopped when the lady in high heels, standing next to him, turned to stare at him. He thought of Mr. Dao's missing foot.

The actual fact of Ginger's death had drifted from his mind but that fact had affected him as if his main circuit breaker had been off but was now thrown on, so that current was animating him from within. He was absorbed without distraction in the most familiar and ordinary sights, which seemed vulnerable, precious, aglow.

But now Louis wanted to get home. He hurried past Martine's Jewelry, its shimmering bracelets and rings a sharp reminder of Ginger. He wanted to tell his wife about things. He wanted to be with Violet. She shouldn't expose herself the way she did in that hospital. It was crazy to confront viruses and open wounds day after day after day. He walked faster.

He had to cross Montrose Boulevard, which was jammed with trucks, buses, motorcycles, taxis, Fords, Toyotas huffing in an endless stream, waiting for the traffic light to change. His mother Anna's cautions sidled onto his lips: look both ways, no, look carefully to the right, then look very carefully to the left and make sure no one's moving. Don't go until you're sure the cars are all stopped. *They're not looking out for little boys! You have to do the watching!*

Just across Montrose and up two blocks was Lincoln Street, where the pavement was completely empty. And then he was walking along his own street, his own realm, not moving in quicktime as he usually did, but proceeding steadily, straight and true. Louis headed toward his house, another three blocks in, now under the protection of the massive live oaks that lined both sides of the street. Their branches lilted toward the sky and arched over him, creating a tunnel of sun-dimpled shade.

Louis turned into his sidewalk, aware of the clear, washed air, and hungrily took in the front porch. Maybe he'd water Violet's banana tree, still thriving in a pot against all reason. He'd sit in his sling chair all afternoon, waiting for his wife to get home, eager to hear about her day. He'd help her unlace her white hospital shoes, lift her tired feet into his lap, so she could rest, so he could really look at her.

Flawless

According to the *Houston Chronicle*, rockhounds, aesthetes, healers, fortune tellers, miners, scientists, and schoolchildren were *all* eagerly anticipating the exhibition in the Houston Museum of Natural Science of a flawless, 107-pound crystal ball, honed from virgin Burmese quartz into a wondrous and powerful globe.

The splendid 242,320-carat crystal, bigger than a basketball, was to be on loan from the Smithsonian Institution's Museum of Natural History for thirty days, when it would go back to Washington, D.C., perhaps of its own volition. Why Houston had been chosen for this honor was a subject of speculation, but a gentleman known as Arthur Bright was evidently the linchpin. For a certain stratum of the city, a substantial segment of which lived in the Montrose area zip code, the event was the undisputed herald of a new age. Furthermore, the crystal ball would be displayed out of the case, leaving it to shimmer unimpeded toward the souls of rapt visitors.

In the way that sticky hot weather ate into you, plagued your skin from without and infected your mood from within, Louis had been enervated since the phone conversation with Sharon. He had mailed her a self-addressed manila envelope and enclosed his business card, a card he'd only given out once—to Ginger—with a note of sympathy and the wish that Sharon might find a few minutes to send him one of her mother's get-well cards. But you couldn't tell, he knew that. People had a way of clutching in the face of death, and every shred of Ginger, all her smallest possessions, would be poignant and precious to her children. Louis could only hope.

But news of the crystal ball had lifted his spirits. Whereas earlier in the summer he would've told Ginger about the great globe, giving the impression that he would go see it, now she was gone, he had a new urge—to act on his impulses, not just pretend over the phone.

Louis watched clips of the arrival on the evening news. First there was dead quiet, as the lads in blue handled the cargo carefully, positioning it between them on a hand cart, wheeling it slowly into the terminal and out the entrance way, where a mass of people were exultantly waiting to greet the heavy safe. A swell of applause for the guards who lifted it into the armored truck.

Sandwich boards abounded. The Young Scientists Club, represented by two junior high school girls in mock-thick glasses and white lab coats, proclaimed:

> Quartz is a crystalline fusion of earth's two most common elements: oxygen, which contributes nearly half the weight of the Earth's crust, and silicon, which accounts for another quarter of it.

Astronaut colors flecked the crowd. An extremely thin woman, her onyx-black hair pulled back to a severe bun, rustled through, wearing a quilted-foil jumpsuit, her offer inked in red on her back: "Ask Gloria what's happening on Venus!" Manufacturers of soft felt showcased their neatly folded, rainbow-colored cloths on card tables. The sign said: "We polish for the gods." Gypsy women in kerchiefs, hoop earrings, and ankle-length black skirts decorated in red poppies, and their men in knickers and embroidered vests, spoke Eastern European languages and sat cross-legged on blankets, crystal balls in place, urging passersby to assess their futures. Spokesmen for a miner's union, dressed in overalls and headlamps, had apparently sped to Houston by bus from Utah.

There was the resemblance to a political rally, except the roar was gentle, and Louis felt a tenderness for this eclectic group of believers, each with different homage to pay.

He decided to go to the museum the day of the opening and

was thrilled by the huge banner proclaiming the exhibition and the long lines of people waiting to enter.

Inside, the introductory panel read:

> Quartz is harder than steel and for at least 30,000 years humans have fashioned it, in the form of flint and jasper, into weapons and tools: axheads, bowls, cups, bottles, beads, and rings.

He pictured the ancients in furs and beads, with few alternatives, so to speak, other than the gorgeous mineral. Of course, weren't they afraid of everything? Weren't those weird ceremonies to make up for abysmal conditions, starvation, storms? No matter. With a trill of envy, he realized they got to *worship* things; worship was part of their lives.

Louis wasn't religious. Except for Easter and Christmas, he hadn't been to church in years. Many of his Vietnamese customers were Buddhists; Mrs. Amita, of Amita's Saris, was Hindu; there were too many Christian sects to count and synagogues were a mystery. It was a muddle, and he didn't feel the need to sort it out. That people fought vicious wars over such things was one of the puzzles of existence. Tom knew how to sit in a yoga position, ankles crossed, feet tucked under his butt, eyes closed, reaching for stillness. But Louis could never concentrate enough to meditate. His mind jogged back and forth in time, from mockingbirds to dumping trash at the store to Abby's father in Congress, to peeling cucumbers—without pattern or purpose. He had the same problem when he tried to pray, which he almost never did. It didn't work on him. Sacred wasn't in his vocabulary. Until the crystal ball.

He circled the globe slowly, reluctant to water down the initial ecstatic shock. It was like experiencing his mother's beloved sapphire, to the power of a thousand. It glowed from way inside; was exquisitely clear, perfectly polished. He could see the person on the other side of the globe, directly opposite, as upside down, but whole, as if a mirror was tilting the world for him to study from a radical new perspective. He felt his own body, hair, eyes, mouth, shoulders, to be facets of a divine whole, a revelation of magnificent light.

He did not believe you could foretell the future, and the transcendent beauty of the crystal ball didn't shake that conviction. But now he knew deeply why people revered the polished shining crystal, a perfect emblem of god's creation, a journey to the center of the earth.

This was the singular event for which Abby had been planning to return to Houston. Now, as Louis stood spellbound, his eyes wet, Abby approached from behind, hooked her arm through his. "Louis, would you like to invest in my quartz mine?"

Refraction

After twirling in the Gulf of Mexico for two days, tropical storm Darlene had whacked Miami with gales and tidal surges, pelted Lake Pontchartrain with torrents of rain, sucking muddy waters onto Bourbon Street, and was now a mature hurricane roughing up her third major city in four days. Fifty miles inland and connected to the Gulf by a ship channel, Houston wouldn't suffer tidal waves, but the ditches, bayous, gullies, and swamps crisscrossing the sea-level sprawl were already brimming.

Like most citizens of the Gulf Coast, Louis and Violet had experienced many hurricanes and prided themselves on being ready. Still, you never knew—wind and water were dangerous, and their insurance wouldn't cover a really big loss. At the store, they stretched big X's of masking tape across the window panes to reduce the likelihood of shattering, and pushed dozens of shoe boxes into the centers of storerooms, stacking the boots, sandals, and high heels on shelves and tables, and covered the merchandise in plastic tarps in case a window blew out and rain barreled in. The alarm system would be disabled when power and phone lines tore down, so Vi and Louis chained the doors shut to deter vandals. Louis carried Ginger's get-well cards home. Since her death he'd attributed a healing effect to them, and he stored them with his gemstones and rings and Anna's sapphire inside his cherry wood jewelry box, which he wrapped in plastic and tucked under the eaves in the attic.

At home they filled the bathtub, prepared water bottles, tested batteries, loaded flashlights, and gathered matches and candles; Violet froze blocks of ice to use when the refrigerator lost power. When disaster was on the launch pad, Violet and Louis traditionally made a good cold lunch. Vi had seen so many families gulping Big Macs in the hospital waiting room. She believed it was much better to steady yourself with healthy home cooking that reminded you of better times. Therefore the meal should be thought of as a picnic and must have something special in it such as cold crab or pecan pie. For Darlene, she assembled oranges, bananas, deviled eggs, french bread, cheese, boiled shrimp, and her mama's remoulade sauce. The Clintons were thus sustained in front of the gloomy television after Kennedy was shot in Dallas, while waiting for the results of a loan-application hearing when the store needed remodeling, during Tom's pneumonia, and for several hurricane watches. There were times, especially in hospitals, when they didn't feel like eating anything and the spread lay untouched. But the cheerful snacks were there to soothe them, to suggest a road back.

Tom called to check on them, and Louis and Vi chatted with him, promising to be careful. Violet pulled in the potted begonias and her banana tree and protected the azaleas with burlap. Louis popped batteries into the portable radio. By nine on this Monday night, the weather reports on television were continuous—"Storm Watch Now!" Their weather lady Marcia was reporting from downtown Memorial Park, where the branches of pine trees were snapping off and scuttling across the golf course. She was wearing a green slicker with a hood and sheltering her mic in a plastic cover. Marcia's umbrella whirling away in the gale made great footage and was shown at least twenty times through the evening, the way advertisements were repeated insanely in case you didn't get it the first time. Marcia's hair, eyebrows, and nose were dripping.

"Why doesn't she get indoors? Ever since Dan Rather got soaked from Hurricane Carla they all have to go out in it," said Violet. "The wind is 100 miles an hour right where I'm standing," Marcia gasped. "Stay inside! Forget about running out for a gallon of milk! It's too late! This witch'll hover over Houston most of the night and then move inland and gradually lose force. We don't know how strong the winds'll be. Back to you, Curt."

They lost Marcia at ll:03 p.m. when the power blew, and they hurried upstairs into the bathroom, where the tile walls afforded extra strength and where they'd be one story above the street, now ten inches deep with god's rushing water. Often Houston only got the woolly edges of hurricanes, a few hours of high winds and rain, but Darlene was a direct hit.

From midnight until five a.m. Violet and Louis huddled on the floor in the bathroom on the yellow shag rug. The immense, terrifying noise of the wind and the battering rain made them afraid to sleep. Louis squirmed away from sitting cross-legged on pillows, back against the wall, to stretching his legs out straight, and so did Violet. They found a way to curl together, Louis' arms around his wife from behind. Later, they shifted and Violet leaned against his chest, her head just under his chin, and she settled her arm around his middle.

At three a.m. she tickled his ribs as if they were teenagers hiding for a smooch while their parents slept in another part of the house. She peeled an orange, producing a perfect intact spiral, something she did for her kids in the hospital, and they ate one section at a time, gaining energy from its defiant tartness. "Mmm," Louis whispered. "Mmm yourself," she answered.

The flames in two Mexican fiesta candles shuddered because of rogue drafts. Like a huge alien wolf, the wind howled without mercy. They heard something crack downstairs but didn't dare go look. They peered through the bathroom window and watched an oak tree next door crash into the street, hitting cars, but no houses. They didn't expect to drown or to lose the house. This wasn't war or apocalypse. But you couldn't be sure, and a person could go crazy from the sheer stubborn wailing of that wind.

"Maybe we should've gone to a shelter," Louis muttered to himself. But there was nothing to do but wait.

At first light, rain still gashed down in sheets, but the wind seemed to have diminished. Louis and Violet ventured from the bathroom to look from their bedroom window. Lincoln Street was a mad river; the water level at two feet was high enough to dislodge and turn a Harley, high enough to be flooding over thresholds and into living rooms. Oleander bushes, a toy truck, sofa cushions, and the body of a dachshund floated along the walk that led from the streaming road to their front porch. Lincoln was a magnolia- and oak-lined street, with palm trees parked liberally throughout. Now the graceful feathery fronds on the tops of the palms had been ripped away, so that only the trunks remained, forlorn sticks jutting into gray air.

Marcia had been replaced by Earl at "Stormwatch," who confirmed over the transistor radio that Darlene was crawling away from the city. People, he advised, should stay indoors until the hard rain subsided because of the danger of flying debris. But Louis and Vi tiptoed downstairs in the dim light. Yes, a window was broken but the masking tape held the pieces together. There were two inches of water throughout the living and dining rooms, the downstairs bedroom, but the kitchen was clear. They'd rolled up the carpets so damage to floors was the main problem. And they found only one snake: a slim, black, already dead three-footer, in a ceramic pot with the umbrella tree, next to the telephone table. Relieved, they nibbled on the picnic. Louis boiled water on the gas stove, and the coffee he made tasted warm and good all the way down to their stomachs.

By noon the rain lightened up, and people were drifting outside. The neighborhood looked like it had been mashed under a large malevolent heel. The main thing was the trees. Dozens of trees were down, and branches were strewn around like twigs. Streets were barely passable on foot, much less by car. But only one roof had been brushed by a crashing oak, and the house itself wasn't badly damaged.

"Jesus, Vi. Where's the car?"

"Oh my god," she said, "Could it have floated away?"

The Chevy had been on the street, but it had been lifted by water, turned sideways, and was comically stuck in the side of Fletcher and Rose's shed, three houses down. Would a tow truck come and pull it home? Could it be driven, after the brakes dried out? Louis felt curiously detached from the sorry spectacle. Because of the generally grim scene, the fate of the car just didn't bother him much.

The saddest sight was the animals—sparrows' heads packed down in mud, a Siamese cat caught in a gate.

They had to clean up during daylight, because power wouldn't be restored for a couple of days. Violet wanted to get to the hospital, sure that they'd need her to give tetanus shots and tend bruises and coughs, but there were no drownings, thank god, in her district. Both were anxious to get to the store.

They didn't set out until three in the afternoon, and they had to shuffle through mud, water, and debris to get to Clinton's Shoes. Fire ants were clinging together for survival in harried clumps, dangerous islands floating on the surface of the muddy waters. Maria's kelpie was barking, but a forlorn, whimpering effort, and Maria herself was sitting on her stoop, petting the confused animal, up to his paws in muddy water. Martine's Jewelry was still boarded up— it looked all right, really. But the normally festive restaurants and grocery stores seemed numb, cardboard boxes and vegetable scraps washed up against their closed front doors.

Except that there were no displays in them, the Clintons' shop windows appeared normal—no broken glass, no standing water inside the wells. On the floor there were two or three inches of water, which seemed curiously propelled by a slight current, but otherwise the showroom was as they'd left it: chairs stacked in corners away from the doors and windows, area rugs rolled and steady on top of counters; display tables in place. Louis and Violet stood in the middle of the family business holding hands, heartened by the relatively good condition of the store after the depressing mess in the streets. They unlocked the offices and the main inventory storeroom.

Shoe boxes had tumbled to the floor. The tarps and plastic didn't hold uniformly—lids had slipped off boxes, and shoes shimmied out into six inches of standing water. A soggy pile of red, navy, black, and white leather and cardboard smelled of mud, as if water had rushed through, knocking things around at random. The shoe box edifices hadn't been stable enough.

"Oh honey, what went wrong?"

"God, I don't know. Where'd the water come from?" Louis pulled up the tops of his rubber boots and walked to the mass of shoes.

"Maybe with the power out...I can't think. What a mess. I hate mud." Violet's eyes were shiny. She was close to crying.

"The pump back here didn't work. Water leaked in."

"We better get after this mud. I don't mind the work, but the inventory! We'll lose a bunch won't we? Wind got in here somehow."

"We got hit," said Louis. "Whipped by big bad Darlene."

Vi started to cry. Must've been way too much, thought Louis, staying up all night, mud in the house, mud in the store, dead squirrels in the yard.

"Don't worry, sweetheart! This isn't that bad. Probably just lost two or three hundred pairs. Not the end of the world. Just so damn much mud." He reached the chaos of shoes. "Let's donate the damaged shoes to the hospital and we'll get the display of half-pairs going again for our one-legged friends. Hell, it'll be good for business."

"Louis, you think I'm boring!"

I could use boring, he thought. Way too much excitement lately.

"No way," he answered. "Practical. Smart. Pretty. Not boring. You're my best friend! My friends aren't boring." He took her hand.

There was nothing to lean on that wasn't damp and no place to sit down. They were standing in the muddy, ankle-deep water, flashlights on the wreckage.

"I should've stayed practical!" she wailed. "I know what to do but I don't do it."

"Vi, this isn't your fault. We tried to get ready for Lady Darlene. We did the best we could. Look outside—sausages from the deli scattered over the sidewalk; boxes of taco shells from Maria's; we can handle this. Everybody's got trouble."

"I don't know if we can."

"What are you talking about? Let's get out of this smelly room."

She almost never asked his advice; she seemed to know what to do about everything. He led her by the hand, out to the front of the store, and resolutely placed two folding chairs side by side near the center island display. They sat down. She pushed her chair as close to his as it could get.

"Louis, I did something."

"What?"

"I'm not sure how bad it is."

"You couldn't do anything that bad. Hurricanes are bad. You're not bad. Those wonderful shrimp! Mama's remoulade sauce. We should be celebrating that we're healthy."

"That's right. We're okay." She was sobbing.

"Vi? What's the matter?"

"Well, we don't have that much flood insurance, and we're going to need cash. But I took half the savings account and spent it without telling you."

This was not at all like Violet. She hated spending money, and she was completely forthright. She never hid her actions from him. Of course the savings account was technically half hers. But to dip in without consulting him?"

"I've been corresponding with Abby."

"What? Corresponding? Letters? Why didn't you tell me? I told *you* when she came to the store. Why didn't you tell me then?" Louis was amazed. "What about Tom?"

"She and Tom are finished. It's in the past; no point dwelling on it. When my son was hurting so bad from her, I wanted to hurt her back. But when Eva died, Abby wrote me a letter. She asked me not to tell you because you're so sensitive about anything to do with Tom."

"And you kept a secret. For Abby? What got into you? Abby was a zombie. She didn't know the truth from a hole in the ground. The other day at the museum she asked me to invest in a quartz mine and I said no. No! One syllable."

"She's changed. She's like a lot of teenagers, frayed at the edges until they find their way. I'm not saying I trust her exactly."

"Vi, the savings?"

She swallowed and pulled her chair away from him, slightly.

"Louis, we need the money now to buy more shoes! But I invested it in Abby's quartz mine! Remember? She owns a quartz mine?"

"She said that. But I didn't believe her. How could she?"

"She bought a partnership with money her mother left her. She thought quartz would be dandy for crystal vibrations and energy healing. But they use that same quartz for radio crystals. Apollo. The space shuttle. Big business. She's making a fortune."

"How do you know? How could you know that? You don't know anything about mining! Quartz! Arkansas!"

"I called a stockbroker. He suggested that I invest in electronics; it's up and coming. Quartz wafers in clocks and televisions and pretty soon he thinks there will be more computers. Such as one on every desk in every office in America and why didn't I consider investing in components. You, Louis, will have a computer instead of a cash register. Some people already do. I was afraid of making a mistake but I got excited talking to him. And I said what would be the source for components? Is that mining sometimes and he said yes. I said is it quartz mines and he said yes, it could be, and he'd call me back. I guess I thought I could be a big daddy or something. He called with the names of four hot corporations, and Abby's was one of them. She's already a supplier for an up-and-coming company named after a fruit—I forget—that makes personal computers. I want to save the income for Tom. It's the least that girl can do for him."

Violet started heaving again and wiping her face on her sleeve. The indignity of Vi's eyes and nose running free made Louis feel slightly dizzy. His head wanted to fall against something. But he produced for his wife a big square handkerchief, embroidered in black with the letter "L," which happened to be in his pocket.

"After you said you were spending $2,000 on emeralds, I was mad. I thought you were going to waste our money. You think I'm so boring when I'm just trying to take care of us and I don't want to waste our hard work."

"Not emeralds. Aquamarines. But Violet I didn't really spend that money on aquamarines."

"But you're going to. You were rehearsing for the day you will do it. I know you are. We've got to find a way to pay for all that."

We?

"See, the mine could be a source of gemstones for you, if you must play with rocks. *Stockholders get discounts!*"

"Discounts? Discounts? I need a discount for new brakes, hell, not for quartz crystals! For running shoes. Medium-heeled prom shoes. For fixing buckled wood on my living room floor—no *replacing* it! For hauling great big palm trees out of my driveway. Does Abby give discounts for that? For something practical? Why in hell did you get involved with that girl? A stockbroker? Computers? People like me will never use a computer. *Computers? You have lost your mind* and I've got to scrape mud off sixty-five pairs of Italian sandals!"

She sucked in her breath, hard.

"Honey, there's one more thing. They said it's better if you hang on to the stock, ride out the ups and downs in the market, so I agreed not to touch the money for two years." She slumped forward, her face in her hands, her feet settled miserably in a puddle. Her sobs were even louder than his semi-shrieked observations about computers. Louis had jerked his chair away from hers and stood up; now he was pacing the room where he'd spent most of his waking hours for more than thirty years and running his fingers through his thin hair. Every step he took caused a minor splash and squishing noise, very like the noises Violet was emitting through her cupped hands.

Like a baby getting her bearings after a huge cry, Violet finally started catching her breath; her gasping subsided into a round of sniffles, punctuated by long, loud nose blowing.

"Could you work part-time in the store? You're getting older, you know. You should take time for your rubies if you want."

He'd been thinking of a birthstone business. But Louis was tired, really tired. He'd been awake all night, listening to roaring wind and satanic rain. His living room and kitchen were submerged in several inches of water. His car had floated away and was beached somewhere, the upholstery no doubt already rotting. His life's work had been funneled by the years into a foul-smelling tangle of slippers and pumps and loafers—now littered before him, under a luminous sheen of mud.

Wasn't Darlene the disaster Violet had always been preparing for? Hadn't she actually been right? Yet now when he needed his surefooted healer, he had a sobbing, confused—and *maybe broke*—woman with damp ankles, just as lost as he was.

The squeak of Louis' boots pacing through water was interrupted by the occasional honking of Vi blowing her nose. At the same instant, the sounds struck both of them as funny and both were hit by quakes of laughter.

Louis' dismay at the dispersion of the savings account was becoming interlaced with a new fascination for his wife. His mind and heart were on ricochet, and now he wanted to grab her and run out into the awful street.

"What the hell," he said. "I'm starting a birthstone business. Emeralds, Inc. Peridots. Sapphires."

The word *aquamarine* sounded good, too.

Looking Good

Houston 1980s

Certain things about his father hovered in Bobby's memory like stale air in a shut room. For example, he had spoken often about gaining strength for his shoulders, arms, and hands through yardwork and finger exercises. He had extolled the value of a tenacious grip and calloused palms, had a habit of leading with his right as he disciplined his children.

When at eighty-seven years of age, a stroke left Richard Zimmer speechless and paralyzed, it was his right side that was affected. To no one's dismay, he fell into a coma. A week passed, then two. People sent lilies. Gwen called Bobby at the salon.

"Bobby, do you think you could go to the hospital and give your father a haircut? He wouldn't want to look like a slob."

"I'm pretty busy all week, Mom. A lot of new clients."

"Look, honey, he's lying there with his eyes closed, breathing funny. I've been going in the mornings, and I water the flowers in case he wakes up. But they say he won't be waking up. I know you're busy but this is still a little scary, you know, and—if he wakes up or even if he doesn't, you want him to look okay, right? You don't want him worried he's been left with bad hair? Well, could you? And will you do mine for the funeral?"

Gwen was only seventy and a pretty woman. Her children were hoping she'd buy a Wonderbra and tango off to Cancun as soon as the old man went to hell. Bobby imagined her directing funeral arrangements, head cocked, wedging the phone against her shoulder while she flipped through Victoria's Secret promos. He could almost hear the rustle of catalog pages.

"Okay, I'll do you both. Why not. How about I do him day after tomorrow, on Saturday, at the hospital?"

Bobby had long ago grasped that his father was a competent engineer, a decent yard man, good at softball, but fundamentally and irrevocably ill-tempered. There was nothing anyone could do about it. His malevolence was a fact of life, like mudslides. Better to face reality and avoid the endangered area. Bobby and his sisters knew that whether sprinkle or cloudburst, Richard's spite came out of the overarching blue. That it wasn't really all that personal.

Still, not long ago, Richard had once again managed to shake him all through. Bobby had stopped at his parents' house for lunch and had enjoyed a turkey sandwich—the best kind, made from his mother's leftovers. Gwen then left for an afternoon of shopping; Richard was rearranging some boxes, and Bobby paid no particular attention.

In fact, Richard had been straightening the hall closet and came upon the box of photographs. To him it was a jumble, a mess, weeds. Sure, he'd seen Gwen pull out her family pictures numerous times through the years, and although one pile was marked "Mother and Daddy" and another "high school," most were without labels of any kind. So, he would always say, what good were they, crammed together in a box? He for one might like to know who these people were. Like the child with the plump little belly, short pants, and suspenders, pretty-boy tie. Snug between his papa in pinstripes and his mama in feathers. That floral sofa. Was it a birthday party, a wedding, Sunday dinner, what? Bobby didn't want to listen to it. He wanted to finish his dish of ice cream and leave. Which he did.

But to Bobby and his sisters growing up, the giant box had been utterly irresistible, like a great green canyon rich with switchbacks and secret passages. Stories about their mother's life before them, stories that were also theirs. The children asked a million questions and Gwen loved it—here were Aunt Doris and Uncle Charlie as teenagers at a dance; Grandpa and Grandma slim and tan at the beach; Great-Grandmother in a jumper at school—when they were *young*, not gray haired and slow like now. Gwen made Bobby stand at the mirror while she held an old picture of Great Uncle Herbert (who died of flu in 1924) next to his face because everybody said he looked like Uncle Herbert, and you could immediately see the blazing resemblance, and the wonders of ancestry and influence unfurled before the children. Bobby had cried a little when his sisters asked: What if you were adopted? And didn't know where you came from?

Gwen had said she'd organize her photos when she retired and now she was retired, and she still hadn't gotten around to it. But the pictures—six or seven hundred of them—remained luminous, waiting to be mined, *uranium*.

After Bobby left the house, Richard had yanked the box full of people he didn't know, people who had advantages his family did not have, and yet still didn't manage to label anything. He opened the flaps and grabbed a fistful, the top fifty photos, which he shoved into a large brown envelope. Then he carried the box, with the rest of the pictures still in it, to the curb, adding frayed envelopes and dead magazines, orange peels and defunct bicycle tires, until the box was overflowing. Next to it, he put the main trash cans. The garbage truck rolled by Friday at ten, as usual, and took it all away.

About two weeks later, Gwen discovered what had happened because a local newspaper was soliciting childhood photos. She opened the hall closet to rummage for the one of her four-year-old-self on the sailboat. Instead of her box, she found an eleven-by-seventeen-inch accordion envelope containing a fraction of the extant total. When she asked her husband about it, he shot off his theory about how if you don't sort and label your property, you must not really care much, how he needed storage space, and so on.

This event, despite dozens of previous minor and medium-sized cruelties, was the one that broke her. She shouted for him from the kitchen. "Watch!" she screamed. "Watch!" She tried to force her wedding ring, which was set in five small diamonds, down the garbage disposal where, during a grinding racket, it was hacked at but survived. Then she had waited on the curb in a terry cloth robe, her knees tucked beneath her, for the trash man. But for reasons she did not understand, she failed to throw her wedding ring onto the truck.

She Fed-Exed the ring to Bobby. She couldn't stand the sight of it. She did not consider herself married any longer. But she did not leave Richard. Since she did not leave him, Helen, Denise, Katie, and Bobby concluded that she was in for the duration. Either she actually loved him or she had consigned his meanness to a far corner of her mind, where it nevertheless irradiated like a bad star.

Bobby tried to remember Richard tossing him a softball or assembling a model train when he was small. But he couldn't picture those times any more; those moments had been torn away by the years that followed. Anyway, he had a life.

Bobby loved the beauty salon, where he could be both relaxed and meticulous. Men appreciated his straightforward but smart work. Women lounged in the styling chair, closed their eyes, and stretched out their stocking feet while he massaged cucumber shampoo into their tired scalps. Though he often heard "I want to look like Cher" or Madonna or Princess Diana, when a client whispered: *Venus*, he knew life was really good. They talked and he talked, too. About spit curls and gray hair. About neighborhoods, his garden, baseball, the public schools. He liked the good will, the simplicity of

Looking Good

the conversation, and he enjoyed his clients. Like Marvin, a Republican speech writer who just as Bobby commenced shaving the back of his neck tended to deliver delicious intelligence about various public servants. Roberta, physical therapist to the national gymnastics champion; tennis bums; astronauts; secretaries. "Zookeepers tell me things about each other that make me blush all over," he was fond of saying. But he didn't pass tales—in addition to being unsavory, gossip was definitely bad for business. He received substantial tips. He liked making people look good.

Bobby sometimes had women lovers, sometimes men, but he'd never settled down with anybody. He adored his three sisters. In summer, his back door was open every weekend. Neighbors, nieces, nephews, and buddies trafficked in and out, watching baseball on his thirty-inch television and splashing around his lap pool. He took pleasure in flipping burgers or crafting pad Thai, depending on who was over. When his childhood friend Dolly was pregnant but single, he assisted at the birth of her twins. But he preferred to live alone, to go home at night and choose whom to spend time with.

Denise, Katie, and Helen had a Saturday morning date at his house every two months. The girls, all in their thirties, cooked breakfast—French toast or waffles or omelets—and Bobby did everybody's hair. Along the way there were shaggy dog stories, stock tips, recipes. News about offices, marriages, kids. The parents. Yards.

"So, you think pine bark or oak chips?"

"I think grass clippings."

"No. Pine needles. They're soft."

"Can't keep the kids out of it. They like to roll around."

"You're not supposed to collect grass clippings. Let the mower spew them over the lawn."

"Yeah, it's good for lawn."

"Fax the department of horticulture. They'll tell you."

"Faxes are driving me crazy. I hate it. Too much junk."

"Handy, though."

"But you think you have to read it all."

"I don't. Jesus, the stuff I get. Bracelet lost in restroom. Package missing."

Last time they got together, Helen made a spinach soufflé; Denise brought croissants. They pestered Katie about her current shade of blonde. Twice divorced, Katie had her hair colored at Andre's, as Bobby didn't use chemicals on his sisters—dyes and perms were too complicated for home. Only cuts and styling. For Katie over the years he'd provided bangs, center parts, side parts, layering. He'd given her stark and straight, curly and provocative. Now she had a close-cropped, no-hair, I-am-not-a-girl look. An investment counselor by day, Katie owned two leather garter belts for evening. The short-short hair was part of a new year's resolution to get a grip on her libido but she soon discovered that such hair could in a heartbeat be gelled and spiked, reminding everybody of leather and blue shooters all over again. Accompanied by the merry, high-pitched snip-snip of Bobby's styling scissors, Katie updated her family on the state of the Dow, interspersing her advice with vignettes about a guy named Todd, who had endeared himself to her during *Love Videos by Tanya*. Bobby started with her, since it was a matter of tidying the head, nothing that required tremendous concentration.

Taking her chin in his hands and rotating her head to the right and to the left for a final check, he finished and offered her a large hand mirror, so she could inspect the back. They all paused for a swallow of o.j. and champagne. Denise slid into the styling chair the girls had given to Bobby when he graduated from beauty school. She swiveled around to face the mirror, her brother standing behind. This was an image dear to all the sisters—Bobby up tall behind that chair, faces of a sister and brother framed in the mirror, Bobby's above; Bobby fingering, combing, brushing.

"Bobby, I want something new. I'm tired of all this hair."

"Like...?"

"I don't know."

She let him brush her exuberant auburn hair, in slow strokes. He loved the health and shine of Denise's hair, for she used conditioners and was careful in the sun. Katie plugged in the coffee pot; Helen had turned from the stove to listen.

"Maybe really really short."

"You won't like it," Bobby said.

"You won't like it," agreed Katie.

"You'll hate it," nodded Helen.

"Why not? The kids pull my hair, and I'm always tying it back to get it out of the way."

"But you've had long hair for twelve years. You'll miss it. It's you." Helen sounded alarmed.

No one wanted to bring up the bad day when their father had dragged Denise to a beauty shop. She was sixteen, and he'd stood there, bellowing to the stylist like an ape.

"She's too vain about her hair. She can't handle the boys as it is. Give her something short. Clip it so it just covers her ears. Go on."

Richard had offered Sylvia four times her usual rate, if she would handle his stubborn daughter. But at the first crack of the shears, when six inches of curls hit the floor, Denise let out a wail that caused the other customers to jump; there were swishes as *Redbook* magazines pitched off their laps to the floor. She cried through the whole ordeal, and Sylvia, though she accepted the money, told Mr. Richard Zimmer to never come back. She was not interested in family fights. Denise moved out of her parents' house at seventeen, with Helen's help.

"You sure, Denise?"

"Come on. Dad butchered me a long time ago. Time to get over it. I'm thirty. I want to try something new. Anyway, it's my idea, not his. It's okay."

"I don't want to be the one," said Bobby. He felt depressed.

"Come on. It has to be you."

Bobby made Katie take a dumb picture of him poised with

the scissors, Denise encouraging him. Then he patted her head and washed the lovely tresses using his best shampoo and conditioner. He untangled it expertly, a few strands at a time, chattering away about the yellow and maroon primroses in his garden, the new taco place near work, his box seats at the ball game, as if she were a child boarding a plane, in need of distraction before vaulting into the blue for her first real ride away from home.

He stopped snipping when her hair was three inches below shoulder length. "Next time," Bobby advised. "More later if you want. But not yet."

He unclasped the cape, shook it off her shoulders, gave her his hand as she left the chair. The girls gathered around, whistling. Denise looked smashing. Bobby's new style suited the soft lines of her mouth and her round face perfectly. And it was still pretty long. He had a policy of never regretting hair that had already been chopped, but he was thinking: who had beautiful long hair any more that he could brush and brush?

"Helen, hon, you're next."

Helen worked in production for a recording company and wore jeans to the office. She had three kids and two goldens, and her husband Del spent two weeks out of four on the road for AT&T. There was no time for nonsense. Bobby trimmed the split ends and repaired her bangs and that was that. By the time he'd gotten to Helen, his sisters had given him a gleaming kitchen and polished furniture, as well as a major breakfast. They didn't talk about their father much when they were together. Because they'd all had enough. Yes, really enough.

In the lobby at Mercy Hospital Bobby stumbled slightly, undone by a wave of fatigue. He sank into a soft corduroy armchair and paged through *Esquire*. He read the first page of an article on sports agents, losing himself in it, forgetting his surroundings totally, thinking only about basketball stars and endorsement deals. When a large, oval

Looking Good

nurse strolled by, keys clattering on her belt, he was jerked back to the hospital, but without enthusiasm, without sadness, just a tremendous lethargy. Earlier, he'd phoned his mother.

"Mom, I'm on my way over."

"Oh, honey, thanks. That'll be so nice. Are you all right?"

"Yes. Fine. You?"

"Good. Really. I'll be at the grocery store for a while."

"You coming today?"

"No, I'll leave you to it. I'll stop by later. This evening, I think."

He stepped onto the elevator for the ride up, the ride toward his old father. Bobby had twice before visited while Gwen was there. Katie and Denise stopped in the day after the stroke. Del wasn't coming because he was busy and couldn't bear his father-in-law who was anyway unconscious, but Helen and her kids came, since the old man had always been pleasant to his grandchildren. En route to the room, Bobby did not dwell on the times when as a teenager he had shouted at the walls: *Dad, go away. Leave me alone. Couldn't you just forget it? Dad, shut up.* Nor did he ponder the years of keeping his distance, denying any similarities between himself and his father, evading the influence. Instead he took note of the other passenger in the small elevator. A young woman with fabulous layered red hair, hoop earrings, and amazing breasts—the word "*jugs*" popped into his mind—tumbling over the brink of her turquoise neckline. She smelled of fruit—banana oil?—and was quite tanned, Bahamas tanned. She was like a ticket out of there, and Bobby grinned to himself.

He exited the elevator on the third floor and walked to 303, a private room with an enormous sunny window overlooking a pond and a golf course. Bobby scanned the green, appreciating the vista of well-groomed recreation before he made himself tiptoe to the bedside.

The old man didn't exactly look asleep. His eyelids were fluttering, and the breaths were odd—gurgling and loud; the I.V.

and monitors were hovering overhead like mechanical handlers, except this was Richard, his father, on the verge of disappearing forever. Bobby felt nothing. Not relief, not anger, not anything at all. Well, I guess I grew out of him long ago, he thought. But he was mesmerized by the sight of the man silenced and diminished, no longer a force, as if none of it had ever happened. Should he wash his hands? Before? After?

He thought: Good-bye, you bastard. I'll spruce you up and then why don't you just get on with it?

His body was immobile. His arms appeared to have been arranged sensibly, perhaps by a nurse, so they wouldn't get caught in the tubes, but they didn't form a gesture that would be Richard's, for the palms lay open, the fingers pliant. *He was ten years old and left his bike on the front porch for the second time and his father in a rage. That fist barreling down to the glass table, the cracking.* Every infraction aggrandized; nothing could be simple or ordinary.

Richard wore a loose-fitting white hospital gown, and he was so much thinner. The image of the big bad father being bathed, toweled, and dressed by a matriarchal nurse outweighing the man by forty pounds made Bobby set his jaw and stare harder at what was left of him.

Richard's hair was unkempt, like a refugee's—he'd been in bed for seventeen days. It was clean but too long and there were mashed places; clumps were divided stupidly, crushed feathers. Richard Zimmer smelled of perspiring flesh and lemon aftershave, likely due to misalignments by a well-meaning nurse, since he hated lemon and didn't mind sweat. Bobby felt a spurt of regret, remembering things in snapshots: his father fishing on a sunny pier, sweeping the front sidewalk, hoeing his azaleas. Saying it was fine to get dirt on you, fine to sweat, it was a sign of good workman's labor, of being alive, outdoors in the green world.

Bobby opened his shoulder bag, rummaged for a comb, barber scissors, mousse. He felt a strong aversion to touching his father. The sputtery breaths were unnerving.

He recoiled. Backed away toward the window. Looked outside. Golfers taking swings. White balls, high arcs, a glorious deep blue sky.

Richard had allowed Bobby to cut his hair only once, the year he graduated from beauty school. Gwen asked, in his father's presence, what he wanted for Christmas? And Bobby, only twenty-three years old, still thinking he could impress his father, turned toward Richard and replied: *I want to give you a haircut. I want to be your barber for the holidays. Just relax. I'll take care of it.* His father had disliked the whole experience; a son who was a "hair designer" was totally suspect, an alien, a fag. He was annoyed at having to sit still in his own home, and he criticized the results—too short in the back, too messy on the sides. Bobby didn't try it again. He stayed clear.

But now, he draped a lightweight cape over his father's shoulders and across his chest, to capture the clipped hair. Taking Richard's chin in hand, he shifted his face to the left. He dipped a comb into water and ran it through the hair to see its condition. This was awkward because he had to move the heavy head, lifting it slightly from the pillow, so he could see how long the hair was getting in back. Well, it was shaggy, stark white, dry, dull. He ran his palm over it. Rough. "Use a conditioner," he advised, aloud. A few hairs stuck to the comb. He went to the bathroom sink and rinsed it, the sound of the gushing tap a welcome interruption in the peculiar silence.

He stepped back and assessed the square jaw, rough skin, thin eyebrows, lids closed down over the gray eyes. The mouth turned under, like a frown asleep. This haircut should be something the old man would have liked—something from the forties or fifties, his era? Bobby's vintage hairdos were in demand. Or should it be the neat and distinguished senior citizen, conservative but current? The latter, he thought. He picked up the scissors. From somewhere far away, he heard his own voice: *Sure I can deal with the bald spot. I'll just move the part over; I'll make you look good. Let's see....* He hummed a Frank

Sinatra tune, "Nice and Easy." *So, you still busy with your yard? Yeah, I get the urge now and then. Tomatoes. Parsley. You have to have plenty of sun. I can never get dill to grow. What about your grandchildren? Your granddaughter won a prize? Math? Wow. Wait a second. Hold on while I clip this. You're worried about your daughter... Look, everybody gets divorced. You're retired? Used to build bridges? That's great. Vacation? Me? I think I'll get away in the fall. You know I love California.*

He kept his voice low, soft, working all the time. He needed room to maneuver. His father was dead weight; if Bobby let the head go, it rolled sideways, so he had to take care with the pillows and be alert to every shift.

With premium scissors he carefully trimmed an inch around the ears. He manipulated the hair on top of his father's head in sections, thinning and shaping, letting it fall back to the scalp in layers—the whisk whisk of the scissors, a pleasant, tender sound, the only sound. This he did slowly, wanting to do a good job worthy of respect. He styled the old hair, front and back and sides, holding the head up, turning the face as needed, and then combed through, perfecting a side part, patting down stray wisps. Mousse? No. Maybe for the funeral. Pulling Richard's head forward toward his own chest, Bobby neatened the neckline. He could see that his father needed a shave. He didn't have a razor, but he could clean up the whiskers. Bobby opened the scissors and arrested the blades on his father's exposed cheek. He intended to clip close. In a split second, his hand jerked. He jabbed the skin, and his own heartbeat roared forth, so loud the other patients must have heard it. Blood surfaced, trickled; a tiny stream traveled down to his father's chin, along his neck, under the sheet.

"Mr. Zimmer?" A nurse had materialized in the doorway. Her name tag read *Violet Clinton*. "I heard voices in here and came to see if Mr. Zimmer had regained consciousness." She paused. "Look at that. His hair. You did a beautiful job on his hair. Beautiful. He'd be so pleased. So sweet of you."

"Oh hello. Well thanks. I'm his son."

It was just a nick, and the trickle stopped, leaving a red trail. There was no change in expression, except for a twitch in the forehead. Bobby rinsed the scissors and comb and put them back in his shoulder bag. With a hand towel, he dabbed away the red trail. He washed his hands in warm, soapy water, taking his time. His father's breath was still scattered, rattly.

Will you take a picture. Of me and my father.

Sure, why of course.

He showed her how to touch the red button, just lightly. She accepted the camera, first cranking the bed so Richard was more upright, half-sitting. They braced his head with pillows so it wouldn't droop to the side, and Bobby sat beside him, on the edge. He put his arm around the faltered shoulders, pulling close to steady his body, took hold of his limp left hand.

Dad. Dad? It's Bobby. Squeeze my hand if you can hear me.

There was a squeeze. The flash fired, filling the room with dazzling light.

Letters Home

Saigon 1970

Stepping off the air-conditioned Pan Am flight, Charlotte Wilkens was roasted by heat, swollen heat from hell, as bad as Galveston in high August. Still, she managed better than her comrades from Connecticut and Michigan who nearly staggered down the portable stairs into the alien air. And there was a resounding smell—was it rotting garbage? Sewers? Dead fish?

"Welcome to Saigon. Come this way," the security officer grinned.

Charlotte wished for a shower and a nap, but she couldn't have them yet. She straightened her shirttail, loosened her belt to dry out her sweaty waistband, clipped her frizzed hair back with barrettes. Charlotte Wilkens, from Galveston, and lately the Bay Area; James Lightner, trained for intelligence, from Hartford; and Marie Olsen, nurse, from Dearborn, Michigan, were chauffeured by Phan Van Giau in a vintage Citroen over a pocked road, through masses of people on motorbikes, on foot, on bicycles, past enormous green fronds on ravishing trees to a concrete block building near central

Saigon. After a blur of banana leaves and yellow pumpkin blossoms, they were inside. A black army sergeant offered his hand; Charlotte was glad to see him.

"Hello! Miss Wilkens? Private Olsen? My name is Randall, and I'm here to orient you and give you background on your new jobs. I know you're tired, so we'll keep it brief for today. Hello Corporal Lightner."

"Thanks, sergeant," the three replied.

"Iced coffee?"

That sounded good; everyone nodded yes.

"How do you deal with the heat?" Marie asked.

"Fans, shorts, siestas, wait for the sun to go down," he answered. "I'd expect Miss Wilkens would have less trouble with it than some. Texas, isn't it?"

"Yes sir, Galveston. It's hot but it's an island and we have breezes off the gulf. However, I've lived in cool northern California for many years."

"We've been needing a language specialist; we'll try not to overwhelm you with requests at first."

January 10, 1970
Dear Mama,
Here's hoping you're okay. How's that parakeet? Everybody's been so good about writing to me; I get a bunch of mail about once a week and then I take a shower, get a lemonade, and sit down to read and to sweat. It's about 85 degrees and just so humid here that it feels hotter. Then I take another shower. I keep a wet cloth on my night stand to keep my forehead fresh.

Still wondering exactly what all I'm going to be doing here. There are many Chinese in Saigon so I expect to use my Chinese, and there are Cambodians, so I'm studying Khmer. But they also need translators for interceptions from tribal and rural areas in the north. So I study a lot. And my Vietnamese is improving daily. They say it's pretty safe; there's good security for us, so don't worry.

Love, Charlotte

She was ready to start, glad to be away from Berkeley where she'd been feeling useless. She was just divorced and had wanted out of her life in California, thought that in Asia she could parlay her ease with languages to some purpose. She did not support the war in Vietnam, which at best seemed a conflict mishandled by stupid Americans, but she was not political, not pro-communist. She was studious and kept a low profile, already anomalous as a black woman, a black professor. But she knew of so many black boys drafted, injured, killed, and thought vaguely that maybe she could help mitigate the trouble. (A week after she arrived in Southeast Asia, she knew that idea was totally delusional.) She had also hoped to practice her craft. She loved to study literary texts, had a doctorate in comparative literature, the comparisons being Chinese, French, and Spanish. After she taught herself Spanish as a child in Texas, French came easy as did Italian, but it was Chinese that thrilled her—she delighted in deciphering the characters, in mastering tonal changes, in the grace and wit of the calligraphy. After that, Vietnamese hummed like a small orchestra in her head: Quoc-ngu, the national script, was rendered in roman letters with the diacritics marking pronunciation as well as variations in pitch that signaled different meanings to the same syllable. Right up her alley.

Charlotte's path to Vietnam had been twisted, full of brambles. After Martin left her, after the shock, after she had been stung and distraught for months, there came fatigue, anomie. She suffered from a dread of waking up and a longing for the fog in the morning. Shades of gray had pleased her; she hated the sunny, perfect Berkeley afternoons.

Letters Home

Making decisions was torture. She would turn the big pages of the newspaper for an hour and then abandon trying to find a movie or a TV show to watch. She couldn't concentrate, couldn't get through two paragraphs of news. She liked horoscopes and gossip and advice, felt lost when she finished "Dear Abby." Opening her modest closet, she was overwhelmed by the choices of slacks, shirts, dresses. So this is why people end up in pajamas day after day, she thought. There was no way she could focus enough to read a magazine. Her bookshelves bowed with the weight of her dictionaries, with French lit in French, Chinese poetry in Chinese. Looking at her library was exhausting. Loved books by Jean Toomer, Langston Hughes, and Conan Doyle left her listless. One night she came home, and the entryway light would not turn on. She felt her way to the kitchen, bathroom, bedroom, flicking the switches to no avail, finally found the phone. "You pay, you get juice," scolded the guy at the power company. Bills lay in piles she forgot to look through; sometimes she didn't get around to feeding Brenda, her Dalmatian, who, pacing and bewildered, would bark and nip at her.

One day when she had slept late for a Tuesday—until nine— she dawdled for two hours in her kitchen, cooking sausage, eggs with jalapenos and cheese, tortillas, grilled tomatoes, custard, and coffee; when she was depressed she ate big. As this mound of breakfast was making even her pj's feel too tight, the phone rang.

"Charlotte, why are you home?" Her mama dived right in.

"No classes today."

"Are you dressed yet?"

"Well...."

"What are you wearing?"

"Mama, please! Give me a break."

"I want to picture you looking sharp and sitting down to work."

"I know. Well, I'm pulling on my jeans but I still look pretty sharp. Except they're too tight."

"You should wear a nice pair of slacks."

"Right."

"What are you doing for the rest of the day?"

"I'm not sure yet."

"It's eleven o'clock. Why not go out for a walk, get some exercise?"

"Maybe I'll window shop."

"That does not sound like you, but all right, just get out of the house. Put on some earrings. Don't waste too much time on him."

Her mama had been mostly silent when Charlotte first told her about the split. She'd counted on more grandchildren, and Martin was a catch, a man with a future. Patty had raised six children alone, and divorce did not sit well with her.

"Hey, aren't you still mad at me about Martin?"

"What do you mean?"

"Oh you know. You were so proud of me for being married and now I'm not."

"I'm over that. You don't need a cheater. You hear me?"

"Yes ma'am, yes, I hear you. "

"Love you, sugar."

"Love you too."

Charlotte was the youngest of her six and the brainiest, and Patty Wilkens was not going to let her slide.

Charlotte put on a skirt and a fresh white blouse, big earrings and sandals with heels, but still good for walking. She was despondent, but without the cargo of a husband, little by little—sometimes—intriguingly free. Now after her mother's call, suddenly, she stepped off her porch that morning with the dog, and she felt looser, almost double-jointed, taking the hills in her neighborhood with an easy gait.

In town she glanced at window displays—menus, kitchen gadgets, shoes, and outside an Indochina aid office she drifted toward the door, found herself inside the place. She saw application forms and next thing she knew, was flipping through. While she filled them out, a bad humor gripped her again, so she pulled out her tape player and earphones and popped in a Marvin Gaye cassette. She slouched in her chair, really didn't care what they thought.

A week later, she was sitting across a desk from Mr. Lacey, who had a crew cut and large, black-rimmed glasses. Brenda had curled herself on the floor against Charlotte's chair.

"Hello Miss Wilkens. I won't waste any time. I see that you claim to be an instructor on the Berkeley campus. Is that correct?"

"Yes, I claim that."

"There is a section of this application that asks about your knowledge of foreign languages. You have checked Chinese, Spanish, French, and Italian. Under 'passing familiarity' you checked Japanese."

He switched suddenly to Italian. *"Questo è la verità?"* Are you telling the truth?

Charlotte replied in Italian: "*Sì, è vero.* I have a good ear and a photographic memory. I was born that way. I have no other explanation for it." She assumed that he was itching to say: *And I see that you are a black woman. I wonder how is this possible?*

"Someone remembered that you were listening to music or maybe it was the news in the lobby. While you filled out the application. Plus you brought that dog in here. My coworkers and I passed this form around and made jokes. Decided it was a kid screwing with us." Still in Italian.

Charlotte replied in English: "No, I'm not a kid."

"Ever been arrested?" He coughed, switching to English.

"I spent the night in jail in 1966 because I joined a protest against the police in Galveston. There was a riot and someone died, but I was already in jail when it happened. Otherwise, just one other time, for DWI."

"Why the DWI arrest?"

"My husband left me and I was a mess."

"Your colleagues at Berkeley let it go?"

"Are you kidding? It's Berkeley. Professors have been picked up for drugs, tax evasion, antiwar stuff, you name it. I haven't."

"Why is that?" Coughing and a sneeze.

"I've always liked poetry better than crowds. The kind I can read in a library, usually written in characters. Gesundheit."

"Thank you. I am allergic to dogs and cats." Charlotte noticed one cat on Mr. Lacey's windowsill and another on top of his file cabinet. "So do you think you could learn Vietnamese?"

"Yes, I think I could."

"Quickly, I suppose?"

"Yeah, ah suppose," she answered, in the heaviest, slangiest southern black English she could muster. Mr. Lacey smiled at her.

In the Saigon office, they sipped their bland, watery coffees.

"Mr. Lightner, how are you?"

"Apart from dehydration, fine," answered James. He was a tall, cheerful, blue-eyed kid, self-possessed, though only twenty years old. He'd enlisted in the service to avoid being drafted, so he could choose his fate. Charlotte felt protective toward him, wondered about his family. Were there brothers and sisters? Was he ever in college?

"We'd like to talk to you alone, if you don't mind. For just a little while."

"Sure." James had mentioned on the plane that intelligence officers might be briefed immediately. He descended stairs into a basement and did not rejoin them that afternoon. Marie stayed behind to fill out forms, while Charlotte was invited to a different room, down a long hallway. There were no windows, only a table and four chairs, and even though she was not in the army, she found herself being introduced to an army major. He struck her as preoccupied and tense. He tried to smile.

"Good morning, Miss Wilkens. How was your trip?"

"Fine," she replied. "Long ride, but I like to fly."

"Good. Please, sit down and take it easy. You must be ready for some rest."

"You're right about that. I'm looking forward to a shower and a nap."

"I won't keep you too long. You are reported to have great potential in intelligence. Your test scores are very high, and I hear you have a way with people." Test scores, thought Charlotte. I can give you test scores. People, I am not so sure.

"We need undercover officers to infiltrate left-wing Vietnamese political groups, and we're asking American soldiers to help with that."

"I am not in the military," she interrupted. "I work for an aid group."

"Of course, I understand. But we are asking for your assistance."

"You have South Vietnamese agents for that job, I'd presume," said Charlotte. "An American black person wouldn't exactly blend into the Southeast Asian jungle."

He scowled at her forthrightness. "You would be an idealistic young teacher, helping children with English."

"Not that young," she pointed out. The major paced and didn't smile. He was short of breath in his excitement about this assignment.

"We know that they are indoctrinating young black soldiers, filling their minds with communist propaganda so they'll subvert the war effort."

"Are you sure about that? How could they?"

"Our soldiers are discharged and return to the West Coast; they have expertise with munitions and knowledge of politics and they join the Black Panthers. They instigate riots; they are dissatisfied with American society."

That's preposterous, Charlotte thought. You are paranoid and suspicious. She answered:

"Sir, the danger you are describing sounds highly improbable and the mission very dangerous. I would prefer not to take it on."

"That is your right. You don't have to accept. Let me know if you change your mind, and keep this conversation to yourself."

"I won't be changing my mind," Charlotte shook her head.

She returned to the front office, where she and Marie finished the paperwork. Then, Phan Van Giau, whom they learned to call Chu Giau (Uncle Giau) or Chu (Uncle), drove them to quarters on a pleasant street with shops and green corners.

"Be very careful on the street," he cautioned. "There are snipers and spies, and you'd best keep yourselves armed. Even women."

Marie Olsen, from Michigan, was of Swedish ancestry, large-boned and strong, with straight blonde hair cut like Buster Brown, a loud step and straightforward manner. Charlotte, who was accustomed to the held voices in art galleries and libraries, wondered how they'd get along in their apartment. But Marie's farmhand quality endeared her to Charlotte, who had been lately bored by academics dressed in corduroy jackets with patches at the elbows and nuanced opinions on everything. Marie's parents were veterans of the Ford assembly line and had died when she was in high school. She found a job as a secretary at seventeen and was enrolled in nursing classes at a community college when her younger brother was drafted; she enlisted to be near him, to personally make sure he came back. Charlotte's father had cleaned fish for a living near the beaches in Galveston; after he died, her mother raised six children on her own during the Depression and war. Charlotte respected Marie's long haul and felt her abiding grace; they liked each other.

After two days in Saigon neither Charlotte nor Marie noticed the smell anymore, and the heat became just another hazard. Charlotte had a prickly rash on the insides of her elbows, so she constantly wanted to scratch. In her bedroom, inside her mosquito net, she was relatively protected from insects, but not necessarily from rodents and reptiles, and there was the sound of mysterious scampering as well as the whine of mosquitoes. She grew fond of the goofy lizards, small geckos, that ran overhead, their tiny feet grasping the ceiling so they didn't thump to the floor. The bedrooms had rafters with nets spread across, and the women wondered uneasily about the strength of the nets. When, one night, a thick-necked reptilian creature with bug eyes and vicious-looking shark teeth lumbered along a small beam, hollering *GECK—O, GECK—O,* Charlotte yelled and Marie came running to save her life if need be. He scooted out of sight, and next day the landlord assured them that the creatures ate insects. "They are okay, okay. Good neighbors, really," adding that, if they wished, he could unleash a cat to go after the gecko. Imagining the yowls, screeches, and bloodshed that would ensue, Charlotte and Marie declined the offer. As it turned out, their big gecko only appeared occasionally, apparently busy with other matters.

On noisy nights, bad dreams invaded: she was barefoot on her mother's porch counting ticks emerging from floorboards. Or: a six-fold screen painted in bird and flower, the swan half-eaten, the bamboo mangled—closing around her, suffocating her. So she acquired earplugs.

She would position her pistol on the night stand, fix the netting, and read herself to sleep. She tried to concentrate on Indochinese history and liked *The Story of Kieu,* the Vietnamese national poem, but also reached for murder mysteries, Sherlock Holmes. Or she tuned in the shortwave. She liked the foreign broadcasts—All-India Radio, Radio Moscow, the BBC. She liked fiddling with the dials and antenna and didn't mind the static, which reminded her of old movies, a shipwrecked crew trying to get help with only a radio. For the Vietnamese locals who wished to practice English, the Voice of America provided programs in "special English"—very slow broadcasts recounting forestry methods in the American northwest or supplying polka music with genial commentary, prompting Charlotte to wonder who listened. For she had not noticed any giant sequoias or dirndl skirts in Saigon. She kept her bedroom door locked, as she and Marie did not want to shoot each other accidentally.

> January 21
> *Dear Mama,*
> Your package arrived. Since you sent it to the office, the security people had to open it, and the whole staff gobbled up your lemon sugar cookies. What a treat!
>
> I am working more or less nine to five and try to go for a walk early in the morning when it's cooler. The apartment is five miles from the office building and a driver—we call him Uncle Giau—picks me up around eight. This is one of the ways they keep us safe, so you can ease your mind. The apartment is a basic kitchenette-sitting room, bathroom, and two bedrooms. I am sharing with Marie Olsen. We met on the plane coming over and she's a good one, a nurse. We're lucky to have two bedrooms and that suits me fine. I'm too old to share a room with a strange woman, especially after being married for ten years. I had imagined something on stilts in a wet rice field, banana trees waving in the wind, thatch roof. But we're in an ordinary rooming house; it has eight units and is owned by a French guy who has spent his whole life here. Marie and I went to a movie—*A Hard Day's Night*, with subtitles in Vietnamese. We sang "I Should've Known Better" all the way home.
>
> Love you,
> Charlotte

Charlotte and Martin had been talking about having a baby. But Martin owned a hip African art gallery in San Francisco, and his hours became more and more erratic. Then one night at a gallery reception, he invited Charlotte with big whispers behind a folding screen pasted over with collage-y blowups of Jimi Hendrix and announced he was in love with another woman—Mandy, a twenty-one-year-old South African, who was positive she was gonna have a hit record any day now.

She translated reports—what had gone wrong with a delivery of electric fans; how defoliated areas would sprout up again in no time—from Vietnamese to English, for American officials: How many windshields were blown out last month; why hundreds of thousands more dollars would be needed for weapons and jeeps. Thus she learned that the helicopters at Hue were short of spark plugs and a mechanic was sick with dengue fever. She translated and relayed the harebrained suggestion, from a grocer, that the Vietnamese love for mangos could possibly be exploited if American guards would withhold, and then grant, mangos to prisoners; maybe that would disorient them, make them cooperate. She was on call for soft talk and safe questions. When a senator visited, there was pressure to produce reports that colored the war effort, but no one cooperated except the major.

One morning, an old woman and her conical hat were cleared by security and invited to the basement questioning room. The woman's cheek was bruised, and her blouse was dirty. She talked very fast, then tears. Everyone was a potential recruit, a prop for democracy against the Viet Cong, especially someone that upset.

"Now don't worry," the major soothed, in English, patting her shoulder. "What's wrong?"

Charlotte translated, resisting an impulse to mime the patronizing pat.

"Oh, mister, I have two sons in the government army, stationed near Hue. I worry about them all the time."

"Ma'am, we are doing our best. The South Vietnamese army will be in charge of things before long."

"But it is very dangerous, very dangerous where they are."

"Yes, Mrs. Anh, maybe, but I am sure they're brave young men. Smart young men."

Charlotte translated into Vietnamese, adding: "I hope you don't mind if I ask you what happened to your face? Did you fall?" Mrs. Anh dabbed at her eyes.

"Yes, yes, my boys are brave and handsome. I miss them very much. My husband, he gets drunk and has bad dreams, too. He worries about our boys."

"And does he sometimes forget himself and hit you a little?" prompted Charlotte.

"Yes, miss. Sometimes. He is a good man, but he behaves better when my boys are here." Tears rushed down the crevices and puffy places under her eyes, down her cheeks, splattering on the table.

"What are you talking about, Charlotte? Translate what I say and what she says. Don't interfere," the major hissed.

"Sorry, sir. She says her husband hits her, and the sons evidently put a stop to it when they are home."

Randall, the sergeant, offered Mrs. Anh a cup of tea. The major shook his combed head, adjusted his buttons. "I don't have time for this."

The word "sir" stuck in Charlotte's throat, for this person was acting like an asshole, but she persisted. "Sir, is it all right if I check with her about cooking for a minute, and then send her home?"

"O.K. O.K. Remember that this one is pathetic, but the next one—the one you meet on the street—is carrying a grenade in her cleavage. I'm going back to my desk. Enough time wasted with these idiots."

Charlotte asked Mrs. Anh if mangos could really pacify the population and for advice on grilling fish, after which she exited, dabbing her eyes, into the afternoon heat.

February 18
Dear Mama,
Work is getting more intense. The boss can be difficult, and I am seeing some things I don't like happening, but noth-

ing unmanageable. At least it's still the dry season. They say when the rains come later in the summer, you are wet all the time, period. Anyway, I took a plane ride southeast, to the beach. With Marie and her brother and another friend from work. We stayed in a hotel that has a porch overlooking the surf. My god. Palm trees, like on a postcard. Straight and tall right by green water; mynah birds in the bushes. I haven't seen a flame tree yet but I hear they're gorgeous. The head waiter gave us free drinks after we had gone swimming. He said it would help us relax, being in the war and so on. I love the women's straight, shiny black hair. I've watched them washing it in the river. Wouldn't that be a pleasure? Maybe I will try it, when nobody's looking.

Tet, the Vietnamese New Year celebration, is just over. People have been out buying gifts, food, and small orange trees, loaded with fruit, and there's a festive feeling. Because of the Tet attacks two years ago by the north, firecrackers are banned. They sound too much like gunfire. Otherwise, it's been a holiday as usual, but they say it's more subdued than in years past.

Don't work too hard yourself. You sounded a little tired in your last letter. Don't keep anything from me, ok? I want to stay close.

Love, Charlotte

Marie had planned to join her brother Steve at the beach for the weekend, just northeast of the Mekong Delta. They wanted to see mangroves. Uncle Giau tried to describe them. "A swamp forest. The roots are not hidden in the earth. Instead, the trees seem to be standing on wiry claws, their roots bulging above the soil and water. Like a bad dream," he added helpfully.

Marie had invited Charlotte and James to come along. They couldn't drive because the road was too dangerous, but managed to catch a flight. Charlotte liked the little brother, who was huge, hefty enough to bash the communists. He seemed tired, a network of fine lines imprinted his face so distinctly that Charlotte imagined tracing over them with her fingers, smoothing his eyes and cheeks back to some calm. But he beamed at Marie, and when he clutched her around the waist and swung her around, they were like two bears dancing.

James organized a picnic on the beach with cold beers, and they floated on rafts in the surf, avoiding dangerous currents. When Steve spotted a turtle or a crane, he would yodel. They made an easy foursome; being Americans in a war zone in Asia trumped all other differences.

Charlotte had lived her childhood on the beaches in Galveston. She was a fair swimmer, no expert, but she loved to wade in and let the warm tides soften her and soak her scalp, especially now that she kept her hair natural, a cropped Afro. She pictured the breakers on this Asian coast bringing waters to her from home, perhaps from the sandbar where her mother was standing knee deep. She was enchanted by the palms along the shore, felt happy there.

James bobbed along in waist-high surf. He preferred adventure on dry land, was spooked by the whole idea of being in the South China sea. He wasn't a particularly wholesome guy, but now he longed for a small river, with old oak trees rooted on the banks, his uncle's dock and rowboats, girlfriends, sandwiches, Cokes—mangroves were massive, terrifying, crazy, and he was sure, snake infested.

James teased Charlotte at dinner. He pointed his radio at her, making Star Trek bleeping noises.

"Say something in Italian."
"Grazie."
"Chinese."
"Xie xie."
"French."

"Merci."
"Vietnamese."
"Cam on."
"Our universal translator."

"She reads weird poetry, too," offered Marie. Charlotte smiled at her.

After the beach weekend, Charlotte, Marie, James, and sometimes Randall hit the streets for dinner together a couple of times a week; they liked to venture away from places that catered to soldiers, though sometimes it was good to be surrounded by American English. They liked the sprawling, cacophonous vegetable and fish markets where you could park yourself by a stall and order big bowls of *pho*—noodles in beef broth, piled high with fresh greens—and where Charlotte could query the locals on their behalf. It was a relief to be surrounded by oblivious normality, people just talking—news of the street corner, news of the kitchen—their senses brightened by the tang of ginger, the aroma of lemongrass, the sparkling edge of a beer. One Friday evening between spoonfuls of soup, Randall turned to Charlotte.

"How old are you, Charlotte?" he asked.

"Thirty-eight."

"Wow, almost fifteen years older than me. But you're pretty hot stuff for an old lady."

"I'm hot all the time, here in Vietnam."

"No, I mean it. You're a babe. Unfortunately, I'm not available. Got a girl back home."

"What's got into you? You are some sassy black kid!"

"Yes, ma'am!" Randall picked up a straw, poked a spit wad into one end, and pointed it toward a gecko racing across the ceiling.

"Hey, lay off!" James swiped the straw away.

A babe, Charlotte thought. I am a scholar babe. On her thirty-sixth birthday, her mother had been insistent: "Charlotte, listen to me. You always were kind of a nice-looking little girl, but so serious, so maybe that right there is the explanation. Always considering something or other, always with a book. Frumpy, to be frank. But I sure do believe you are becoming prettier every year. Your face is beautiful!"

She was a professor and linguist, more at home in libraries than at parties, but she had rich brown eyes that caught you, that missed nothing but did not threaten people. A smooth forehead and a softness to her mouth. Her clothes were comfortable, not flashy, but she liked great glasses and shiny rings. Her sisters liked to tease about her nice rear end, had taught her that the test of a new dress was how her hips looked in it. She kept in shape, and her legs and stomach were well toned. Before the disaster with Martin had derailed her, she would fast walk and speed up to a jog for an hour a day, singing her mother's favorite gospel songs between gasps— "Joshua fit the battle of Jericho...."

She was embarrassed at how much she liked her own breasts. For now, she was the only one enjoying them, but in the shower she liked to smooth warm soap over and under them with her palms; she would cup both at once with two hands and stupid phrases would skip into her mind: ripe melons, no, ripe peaches, no, bigger than peaches but smaller than melons, thank god.

"Amazing, I think Miss Charlotte is blushing," interrupted Marie. "James, more spring rolls, how about it?"

March 5

Dear Mama,

Monday was a first. I was actually given a shoebox full of pieces of paper to work on. Usually it's been government documents or memos. Sometimes they want to know more about a particular person. They go through suspect neighborhoods and overturn trash cans. So I get laundry receipts, school exercises and homework, grocery lists: aspirin, toothpaste, batteries, Oreos, lemons. Duck feet. Rice, rice, rice.

There are eight thousand strains of rice in the world and several thousand in Vietnam, in case you were wondering. A bill for fixing a toilet (I translated it as "plumbing bill"); a receipt for a bike repair. I have to translate every word, in case there's a code embedded.

I was going nuts with these scraps of paper, so I translated a grocery list as: fried chicken, hush puppies, biscuits, honey, greens, gravy. Just to see if anybody would notice. Sure enough, no one has mentioned a thing.

The roaches here drive you insane, just like at home. Only they are bigger here and they fly at you in the dark some times. Uggggh.

I've met a young black guy, a sergeant. His name is Randall. I like seeing him around, and he helps me learn the ropes. Black soldiers are the shoulders of the military; make sure you know that.

Love, Charlotte

One Sunday morning, Charlotte was sampling fresh mango nectar on the terrace of the Palace Hotel, adjoining a plaza in central Saigon. The place had the feel of a tropical resort: rattan chairs, purple bougainvillea, waiters in starched white, iced pineapple drinks sprigged with mint and lemon.

A slender Vietnamese man, dressed in khakis and a linen shirt, paused on the street in front, passing his canvas briefcase from right hand to left, wiping his forehead with a handkerchief. He watched Charlotte for a few minutes.

"Miss?" he inquired in English. "Are you alone this morning?"

Instantly wary, Charlotte answered. "Just watching the city wake up."

"Have you been long in Saigon?"

"A few months. And you?"

"I was born in Cambodia, but I've been here all my life. Been busy surviving all these wars."

His wire rim glasses glinted in the sun, and his longish dark hair shone.

"You seem to be in a hurry. Are you usually busy on Sundays?"

"Yes, but you looked interesting."

What the hell. "Would you like to sit down for a minute?" she asked.

"Of course, thank you."

An architect working in Saigon, Tran Tien had plans to visit his mother's village in Cambodia in the next year, "if it hasn't been napalmed by then."

"What is your job here in Saigon? You're not a native."

She responded in Vietnamese. "I'm a translator."

The lines around his eyes and mouth suggested deep empathy and humor. He replied in French. "So you help the soldiers with their shopping? How to ask for the best baguettes? *Non, non, non,* you say to the grocer. We must have fresh, baked within the hour."

She answered in Chinese. "No, we spend our time looking for Peking duck and moo shi pork and Buddhist monks. As you may know, Americans are a very spiritual people."

He kept up, in perfect Mandarin. "The monks are one thing. But watch out for Chinese businessmen. They are better capitalists than you Americans, and they know how to invest their money in this forsaken country. They are much better chefs than the French. Try mapo dofu."

She came back in Spanish. "The real problem is finding a good taco in this town."

"No habla Espagnol." He continued, in Hong Kong English: "No way you will find a good taco in Saigon."

After several pitchers of delicious orange and papaya juice, and many morsels of crunchy spring rolls, they rambled for a couple of hours through markets, along the riverfront. At the Prosperity, a recently redone Chinese place, they tackled spicy fish and noodles, and Tien promised he would some time tell her a story about the Prosperity. When they parted, Charlotte was startled and touched to see his tender expression. They met for dinner the following evening, and again two nights later.

Through a fortuitous liaison with a Chinese businessman, he had studied architecture in Hong Kong where he'd preened his English and Chinese until they were both just slightly, elegantly accented. His great-grandfather was French, his mother was Cambodian, and his father Vietnamese; Tien and Charlotte compared their arms. His skin was a shade darker than most Vietnamese, close in color to hers, and Charlotte liked that.

With his two assistants, Tien had constructed schools, office buildings, restaurants, homes. His central telephone company had been blown up, a month after the opening banquet. "Part of doing business in occupied Saigon," he said, pointing out a shoe store he had designed, gutted by a bomb just after the first sale on tennis shoes. He seemed to love looking at her, and his admiration made her feel like a beautiful woman. Maybe it wasn't only her mother who thought so. He wanted to know about California, whose surfers and rock stars he'd seen in the movies, and about her family in Texas. Was it true that black people in America were not allowed to vote? Why were there riots in Detroit? She asked him about Cambodia, about Buddhism, about his mother, and she also really wanted to pull his hair back into a pony tail and play with it.

He liked rocks and minerals, and she admitted a taste for jewelry, but as a poor kid from southeast Texas and then as a professor in a milieu of students in faded jeans, she had not indulged it. Now, with Tien, jewelry shops became a destination on their walks. They would examine rubies, sapphires, and pearls and joke about a future in the Burma gem trade. They remarked about how nice it was to be making new friends.

Mr. Dinh Cao Khanh had entered Tien's office one morning in

1967, closing the door behind him and brushing a bit of dust from his trousers, all in one graceful motion. He wore a light shirt, his hair appeared coiffed, his shoes buffed. His ring was a discreet sapphire held in gold prongs.

Seeing this polished gentleman, Tien's assistant straightened himself in the splitting-vinyl chair by his typewriter and rose to greet the visitor.

"I would like to see Tran Tien. I have a project to discuss with him. He comes highly recommended."

"Certainly," said Le Van Thu. "Please sit down. Some tea?"

"Yes, thank you,"

A half hour passed while Tien and Khanh sipped tea and discussed the humidity, road repairs downtown, the pomegranate crop, boat races. Tien had learned not to count on anything; he was patient.

Finally, Khanh crossed his legs and sat back. "I am a banker, particularly experienced in the international arena. I have done business with the Japanese, the Chinese, the Americans, the French, the Thai, the Australians. I try to avoid the Burmese, Laotians, and Cambodians, as their countries are too impoverished, rules of engagement too loose, the black market too sturdy. Also, people there are not necessarily so schooled in the ways of the global marketplace.

"At any rate, I am now sixty and ready to retire. I see no sign of the Americans leaving any time soon, and I have decided to pursue a lifelong dream. I have always wanted to build and run a restaurant. I would like a place that serves all my favorite local dishes, plus an international selection. And let's face it, with so many foreigners in Saigon, this could be a very successful business venture."

Tien nodded. "An intriguing idea. It would be a nice challenge to build a new structure for a restaurant, rather than renovating an old one."

"Exactly, and as you have obviously surmised, that's why I have come to an architect. I have seen your work—a house just east, a postal office, renovations of the Starlight Hotel and the German consulate in Hue, which you have executed quietly and expertly."

"Thank you for your kind words. I try. I enjoy my projects."

That was not strictly true. He disliked the renovations; they were bread and butter for the little company, but trying to refit a decrepit hotel was time consuming and expensive.

"Good. May I show you the block, which I have purchased for this purpose?"

"Of course. When shall we go?"

"How about tomorrow, at lunchtime? We can discuss my ideas over a nice meal."

Khanh wanted expansive pavilions with classic "but friendly" steps down to a lotus pool and garden. He wanted fish, butterflies, frangipani, jasmine, frogs. He wanted a Japanese-style room with shoji doors, low tables, lanterns, tatami mats, a tokonoma alcove displaying ikebana. But the main part of the restaurant would be Southeast Asian in decor and atmosphere: bamboo, tile floors, louvers, raking shadows. His property was on the riverfront, promising wonderful possibilities for harmonies of light and water.

He explained that when customers entered, fretful and tired from a difficult day—at bank or store or school—he wanted them instantly soothed by the surroundings. Once the diners relaxed, the menus would entice them to gratifying gastronomic experiences. At tables of happiness, mergers and acquisitions would germinate; romances would effervesce.

Tien took no notes at the first meeting. He liked to listen with total absorption, then return to his office and write in a notebook. He prided himself on capturing the feeling behind what a client wanted.

"I am a Buddhist and this will be a vegetarian restaurant," said Khanh. Tien was unsure how to reflect this in the interiors.

"Just design a place that's both up to date and peaceful. The chef will be Mr. Shah, from Bangalore, and he has drafted a menu already that includes curries, soups, ginger salads, and for fun, a few South Indian dishes."

"How wonderful!" agreed Tien, feeling hungry.

"And one more thing: no living creature may be harmed during construction."

After a few months of fine dinners in rival restaurants, design sessions, drawings, plans, hiring suppliers, and many pots of tea, construction began. When a worker forgot his orders and whapped a fly, he was put on probation. When a week later, he squashed a spider, Khanh demanded his dismissal.

Tien objected. "Couldn't we warn him one more time? He has a family to support, and he is one of our best carpenters."

"One more chance," said Khanh. Mr. Khanh had assistants stationed around the site, watching the progress, and the workers learned to avoid their gaze.

One afternoon, a laborer was ready to stack his lumber near the concrete foundation, which had been poured the week before. It was now curing, almost ready for the frame to be erected on the surface. Today he would set up the scaffolding, on which the workers would balance as the building took shape. He went to the open truck where the bamboo poles waited. He pushed at the poles, causing them to shift and roll and rattle. From among the poles, something moved toward him. A snake, looking sleepy and sick, was creeping about in the pile. He recognized it at once as a bamboo viper, quite poisonous and known for being irritable. He didn't want to lose his job, so instead of hacking it to pieces, he clapped a plastic bucket over it and carried it to the river. He could not, however, justify releasing a poisonous animal into the water, so he surreptitiously smothered the snake. He got away with it because the assistants had not followed him. There were other lapses.

"Ok to slap at mosquitoes, as long as you miss!" instructed Tien. Around dusk, after Khanh's assistants had gone home, you could see a dozen men slapping at mosquitoes, and missing.

Dinh Cao Khanh's Prosperity restaurant opened during the celebration of the New Year in Vietnam. Khanh hoped that people would be in a holiday mood; he decorated with delightful miniature orange trees and red and gold banners, and he offered free lunches the first day. The food was superb, and at three p.m. Mr. Shah, the chef, was toasted by fifty-three happy customers. The dining room filled again in the evening, and people idled until closing at ten.

Prosperity served its first fine meals January 30, 1968. At three a.m. January 31, the National Liberation Front, also called the Viet Cong, and the People's Army of North Vietnam, launched countrywide attacks against the South Vietnamese and American forces, known as the Tet offensive. In Saigon, a band of commandos invaded the American embassy, sabotaged the radio station, and hit numerous other targets. Despite warnings to stay home and keep safe, Khanh decided to check Prosperity and make sure everything was all right. When he arrived at nine in the morning, he saw a heap of elegant rubble; the place had been bombed. A teenage boy, who apparently broke into the kitchen after hours looking for scraps, was killed. Fortunately, there were no other casualties.

Khanh's pain was profound, and he was ashamed of his suffering.

"I am crying for my restaurant," he spoke softly to Tien. "I wanted a place of beauty; I wanted to defy the war, and look, I've been punished. A flame of loveliness against an ashen sky when the only true sanctuary is the heart."

Tien could not speak at first. Prosperity had been luminous, one of his most treasured commissions. A peculiar feeling washed over him, like a desire unrequited, that he wished he'd seen the explosion that destroyed Prosperity. Out walking one day, he was blown down to the ground when a grenade struck a stationery shop near him. His hands, arms, and neck were nicked by wood splinters and glass; a young woman tore out of the front door yelling for help, as sheets of rose, yellow, and pale green paper fluttered over the heads of panicked bystanders. The shop blazed for half an hour, into a ruin of smoldering pastels. Despite rivulets of blood on his elbows, Tien stood fascinated, gazing at the walls and door frames as they burned, shifted, and burned some more, as if an ordinary fire in someone's stove had swelled larger than life before crumbling to embers.

He would find himself at a news stand or pharmacy or tea stall, wandering in a daydream of racket and flames. Riding a bus, he would be watching the scene outside his window and then he would no longer see the street rolling by, but smoke and ash. He wondered who threw the bomb into Prosperity's main dining room, where the bomber ran to, where he was now.

Tien pictures a grenade the size of a grapefruit—not rich, promising, and yellow, but rough and dusty, and of course not at all like a fragrant fruit, which, if flying, would be tumbling from the branches of its tree, or perhaps tossed by a child to her mother, or a mother to her child, but rather, a rabid, dark projectile, hurled by a terrified boy through the window of his restaurant, blitzing the glass, thudding to the new tile floor, zigzagging like a bloated pinball among the legs of the teak tables and bamboo chairs, brushing the immense porcelain flowerpot by the bar, finally wobbling, and pausing, ready at last to leap apart: poised at the tokonoma, the alcove with its pristine ikebana—a single star orchid, a rare shade of blue, bits of moss draped about the root.

At the moment the grenade is pausing, the boy bomber is escaping the blast, is running, panting and exhausted and by then is a dozen blocks away, in the dark of the city. Later, in New York and Washington, London, Tel Aviv, Bali, Casablanca, and in the Iraq wars, bombers stay for their bombings, linger to be part of the detonation. But three decades earlier, in Saigon, this boy throws the bomb and runs for his life. He believes he is sending the bomb so he can find a future, so he can have a wife and children and farm in the kind of country he wishes for; he does not want to die. So now, deep in the alleyways of the city, this one is thrilled by the embrace of his comrades, who in their anger and exultation lift him to their shoulders. He is sixteen, crying with relief and pride. There are many explosions that night but this one is *his*, and it will be two decades before he learns that someone inside the building was killed, before he feels even a whisper of regret.

Tien also came to feel it was *his* explosion, and so also did Khanh. But since none had actually witnessed it, all three could only imagine it, over and over again in their minds. The young bomber, ravenous at his bowl of rice, sees only distant beautiful fires and rich smoke. Tien, in line at a poultry market, conjures the immense roar, bottles of chili sauce and spoons gusting into mid-air, napkins ripped to dust, lanterns smashing to bits. Khanh, in his favorite chair at home, weeps for the golden fish in the garden pool blinded by the flash, and for the menus with their harmonious lettering.

And there was a fourth person who knew the explosion, another boy, a dead boy, who, like the bomber, had waited forever that night in the dark with the trash—he had come late and hungry into the black kitchen, and so the bomb, in addition to bolstering the cause, also stopped a thief, that boy who had lived with his small grandmother, the boy who had stuffed his cheeks with stolen melon and rice.

March 16
Dear Mama,
Great to hear about your tomatoes. Those church judges can be tough sometimes. Amazing. Well, I'm not surprised. Your tomatoes are so sweet and you do tend them carefully, like you used to tend us. Like you still do.

My job changes all the time! I am now being included sometimes as an interpreter during conversations with Vietnamese. I'm told that my Vietnamese is getting better, but I do struggle for words, often. These are routine conversations, nothing high security. Like talking to the man who delivers lunch or clarifying questions from the electrician.

    Love, Charlotte

Security had towed a man about thirty-five years old and dressed in a clean blue shirt and dark trousers into the office for interrogation, not small talk about groceries. Charlotte was asked to interpret. The major seemed relaxed. He began.

"What is your name?"

"Nguyen Ngoc Dieu."

"What is your business?"

"I sell vegetables. At a vegetable market."

"I'll bet you work long hours."

"Yes, I do. I start before dawn and work through dinnertime."

"But you were not at your market last Thursday morning."

"No, I was sick."

"You are well dressed for a vegetable seller."

"When you picked me up I was preparing to visit my priest."

"Are you Catholic?"

"Yes."

"Did he expect you?"

"I hadn't told him I was coming."

"Why were you going to see your priest?"

"That is rather personal, sir."

"Has to do with sins, does it?" laughed the major.

"A little bit, yes, it does."

"You are Catholic?"

"Yes. I am."

"How many children do you have?"

"I have been blessed with five children. May I ask why are you questioning me? My wife will be concerned."

The major was smelling a good get. His nostrils distended. To

Charlotte, he spit out: "This a lying bastard."

"What kind of sin, Mr. Dieu?"

"That is my own business. That is between myself and the priest."

The major hauled back and slapped the fellow hard across the face. Jabbed his stomach with his fist. Charlotte recoiled at Dieu's low moan.

"You had better answer me, Mr. Dieu, if you want to see that priest of yours again. You had better tell me about your sins. You approached an Afro-American soldier?"

Dieu was hugging himself, sweating, and looking confused, so the major became helpful. "Black, Negro, like Miss Wilkens here."

"You have many black soldiers in Vietnam. We talk sometimes."

"What do you talk about?"

"Rain. Sun. Where to buy dragonfruit. Just talk."

"Do you talk about Bobby Seale? Martin Luther King? Do you talk about black communists in California?"

Charlotte lost control of her eyes, and they rolled heavenward. She whispered to the major: "What does a black radical have to do with him?"

"Charlotte, you are the interpreter. You have no thoughts on the matter. Leave this to me!" He was yelling.

"Major," she smiled, politely. "I have been living in California. What in the hell are you talking about?"

"The VC recruits black soldiers here, lures them to the north with drugs, indoctrinates them, and then sends them back to the U.S. to infiltrate black churches."

"*Lures them? Up north?* How could a black soldier hide out in the Vietnamese jungle? Sends them back? Where? To Kansas City? *Churches?* You are losing your mind."

The major was in a red fury. She pictured him slapping her too; slapping Randall, the sergeant; slapping the table. The major had smoked way too much hash, or else his scenario was correct, and the

VC were the ones who had smoked too much.

Dieu was terrified.

"You will be in prison for years if you don't talk to me. You'll be beaten in the stomach until you can't stand up."

Charlotte translated, then added in Vietnamese, "Tell the truth and I'll help you."

"Trust you?" Dieu shivered.

"I am not the major," she said. "I am different."

To the major, she spoke in English, as if translating: "What are the charges? I can't be sent to prison for nothing, nothing at all!"

"Why were you talking to Private Mullens last Tuesday at four p.m.?"

"He passes by my house sometimes. We were talking about the heat. About fishing. About Little Richard. He has learned some Vietnamese and I wanted to encourage him."

"That was all? Were you selling him heroin?"

"No, sir."

"Were you inviting him to be a spy?"

"No sir."

"Were you selling him hashish?"

"No."

"Opium?"

"No."

"Were you inviting him to be a spy?"

"No! I was not!"

"Are you a Catholic?"

"Yes!"

"What sin, Mr. Dieu?"

Mr. Dieu turned to Charlotte: "Please. I am so ashamed. I can't tell you what my sin is, but it has nothing to do with the U.S. army, nothing to do with black soldiers or drugs."

She reported to the major: "He says he's too ashamed to tell us."

Letters Home

"What sin?" screamed the major.

They had nothing on him, except secretive behavior and conversing on the street with a black soldier. They let him go, but James was told to have the guy followed. Mr. Dieu was observed for several weeks, and he had indeed been lying. He didn't get up at dawn and he wasn't a vegetable vendor. He arose at seven or eight or nine. He was a Catholic, but never entered a church and didn't confide in priests. He did have five children and he did keep a routine: after breakfast, he kissed his wife, who provided a lunch of rice and vegetables. Three mornings a week he marched straight to the Sunshine Appliance Store; the other two days, he strolled first to a lady friend's house, where he had gleeful sex for two hours, after which he resumed selling refrigerators and blenders.

April 4

Dear Mama,

Did I tell you that locals call the soldiers *Joe?*—"Hey Joe." People are used to black American soldiers, not so used to civilian black women. When I chat with passersby, I amuse myself by saying in Vietnamese words like "onyx, ink, coal." Then I tell them I'm not actually "black," but really I'm more like coffee, chocolate, tea, mahogany, teak. Or when children stare, I trot out the word and point to the skin on my arm. Or my cheek. Sometimes I say: "café au lait," and they smile. Lots of people are wasted—frightened, sick, grieving, but you can still joke around with them. They assume I'm a nurse and run up, asking for medicine: "My mother has bad headache!" Or: "My arm! My arm!" and I get a look at an infection. Children beg for pocket knives, sweets. Most of us carry Band-Aids, alcohol, aspirin, and hard candies to give out.

Speaking of which, I get the idea from your letters that your headaches are back? Let me know, ok?

Sometimes people shout: "Hey lady! where do you come from?" In English. Or French. And I answer in Vietnamese: "I come from Texas." They are startled by that. "Is Texas in New York?" "No, on the southern coast of the United States. It's hot, like here. Bugs, like here. Here it's more beautiful." And really, Mama, the country is beautiful: mountains and pretty lakes with boats, a long coastline. I saw a bit, flying in. I don't want them to think Americans are just colonizing, not bothering to learn the local language or customs, but that happens a lot. Some American soldiers are terrible racists, even though the South Vietnamese are our allies.

Now you've got to write and tell me about church. How do you like the reverend? & keep me updated on that bird. And don't fret about me. Martin has someone else and that's that. I am making new friends and keep very busy.

Love, Charlotte

"My mother and father live south of here," Tien had told Charlotte, "on a riverbank. It's not so safe to travel there right now. My two young sisters are at home. I worry." She loved to hear about his family and pressed him for pictures.

They had met half a dozen times—three times the first week, and then as if to brake themselves, twice the second week, and now he was having her to dinner. He invited her to his house, with his aunt, with Le Van Thu, his assistant from the office, and Thu's wife and two daughters. His home was surprisingly ramshackle, needed paint inside, and had barely any furniture.

"I have chosen a soft sofa with big flat cushions, bamboo and wood chairs, and a new table," he explained. "But I've been so busy I haven't even picked them up." Incense and candles were arranged on a low table, with pillows on the floor, in the living area; there was a small kitchen, empty birdcages, and two more small rooms. The second floor was accessible by a stairway outside, and a rickety balcony extended the width of the front. Upstairs was one large room, where Tien slept. His clothes were folded neatly, but placed around the perimeter in stacks on the floor, not hung in closets. It reminded Charlotte of grad student housing.

He told her his plans for moving walls, installing cabinets, wrapping the upstairs balcony around the entire house, extending the front porch.

"Do you mind living alone?" she asked him.

"I'm not alone much. I have a sister who comes over, and my aunt and uncle, and their children. In Vietnam, if you have space and no children, you expect relatives to stay often, and they do, sometimes for weeks or months. I don't mind having the house to myself once in a while."

He hesitated. "My aunt is cooking tonight because she wants to meet you. She's a good and generous soul and she's fond of me. I am so embarrassed to say it, but there are those in my family who wouldn't approve of our friendship. My parents are tolerant, but some of my Vietnamese cousins see Africans at the lower rungs; some of them wouldn't accept my mother because she's Cambodian and her skin is darker. But the fact that you're educated and obviously cultured would move you up the ladder in their estimation. And you come from a big and powerful country. But I hate talking about social classes. Rungs! Ladders are for bigots and morons!"

Nevermind. In parts of the USA, she was viewed as barely a notch above sharecropper. Who knew what her own family would think about Tien?

Tien loved to fashion a client's unformed desires into a tangible structure to live or work or rest in. It was fascinating to blend specifications and aesthetics. Wiring, plaster, and wood intrigued him; color, light, and space inspired and delighted him. But after the bombing of Prosperity, the bonds between his heart and his creations loosened and frayed. He was still committed to realizing his clients' purposes but he came to prefer the more practical, less artistic projects such as prudent rearrangement of storage spaces in an office building and better aligning of corridors in a school. He had lost clients when he insisted to the point of anger on more expensive, bomb-resistant materials. He became expert with supplies that could withstand fire, such as four-hour gypsum.

He arrived at his rented office each morning feeling lucky. He liked to roll his stool to his drafting table, enjoying the sound of the wheels rumbling over the floor. Above the table were shelves, crammed with file boxes. The files held sheafs of drawings, legal pads scribbled with his notes about client wishes, site details, contractors' bids. He had a library of books about Brunelleschi and the Renaissance masters of domes and colonnades, about newcomers such as I. M. Pei, a young Chinese American who deployed hard edges, steel, glass, as well as archaeologists' reports and pictures of the Buddhist temples at Pagan, by anonymous artists lost to time in Burma.

Tien had quickly introduced Charlotte to his office and proudly took her to his warehouse. The warehouse was a capacious square structure packed with lumber, tiles, windows, pipes, and bags of concrete flanked by a warren of small rooms and closets containing wood samples, light fixtures, suppliers' catalogs, manuals. He stopped there almost daily to direct the work and bargain with dealers. Even more than the office, the warehouse bespoke an amalgam of art, engineering, and satisfying practicalities.

Tien particularly liked a nearby house he had designed for a wealthy general. He and Charlotte visited the man, who was pleased to let them tour its cool porches, modern kitchen, and teak-lined living and dining rooms.

In contrast, Charlotte couldn't demonstrate her work, which she increasingly despised; she sometimes wished she could show Tien her classrooms in California. She had to report the creepy

Mr. Dieu's statements, inhaling phrases in Vietnamese and exhaling them in English. And to interpret his evasions and furtive looks. That was her work in this war zone.

She had come to heartily dislike the major, who despite his sometimes pleasant Oregon manner had the will of a B-52. James told her he was skimming the accounts, that he disbursed the money to gemstone dealers. They would joke about the little bag of sapphires and rubies he must have hidden somewhere, and how he'd smuggle it out one of these days. He didn't care who got killed, as long as they weren't Americans.

After a few weeks in Saigon, among the memos and reports, Charlotte began to find Vietnamese soldiers' notebooks on her desk in the morning. She asked who the men were and how did this office get hold of the notebooks and was told to mind her own business. But she quickly realized that the stuff belonged to captured or dead enemy troops. From what she could tell, the papers of these ordinary soldiers held nothing of strategic interest; some had been fighting for fifteen years, some were still boys.

Inside the notebooks were sketches of the geography in the countryside, lists of duties, medical reports, family photographs, poems from friends. Often there was poetry written by the dead soldier himself. She had wanted to escape the insular world of academia, change her life, contribute something. She had been trained quickly, recently, to speak Vietnamese, had much to learn, but she approached these verses as she would any piece of literature.

"Why does it take two days to translate a few lines?" badgered the major. He demanded summaries. Okay, for the major, a clumsy paraphrase would do. But some of the poems she encountered were so beautiful, she wanted to perfect and share them.

> When I got back to base
> I sensed something had happened.
> They said you went to hospital

and my heart was torn and sad.
I always think of you...
Your life runs out like a red silk banner.
Your many friends are waiting,
anxious for news about you.
Dear brother, my feelings well up
and I wish so much to see you....

She decided to show the poetry to Tien.

One morning Uncle Giau was driving Charlotte to the office through streets mobbed with pedestrians, vendors, scooters, cyclos, trucks. Charlotte was paging through a newspaper in the back seat when a firecracker noise tore through the racket. The car lurched, and Uncle Giau thumped forward against the steering wheel, causing the horn to honk, to blare. The car careened onto a sidewalk, and Charlotte jumped out the back door and threw herself into the front seat, pounding the brake. She managed to halt the vehicle as it bashed into a vendor's cart loaded with melons.

A bullet had hit him, dear Uncle Giau, her steady source of tips and good cheer, in the upper shoulder, throttling him, but not fatally. Weeping almost imperceptibly from the pain, he was cared for at a hospital emergency room, but it was afternoon before Charlotte could stop shaking.

Charlotte had deeply alarmed everyone by considering Vietnam in the first place. Her phone shook with calls from her mother, brothers, and sisters, caught between their basic approval of "serving your country" and fear for her safety. Friends had been frantic, tried to talk her out of it.

Now she was stunned to be coexisting with snipers and corrupt Americans. She had been glad to escape California where, she now brutally understood, she'd been dwelling in a world overgrown with subtle calligraphy and small, cerebral challenges, leached through

Letters Home

by despair over Martin. Americans were losing the war in Southeast Asia; were being crushed inside a civil war they did not belong to. She absolutely did not want her mother to know how dangerous it was. The U.S. was withdrawing, so troops were exposed for no military reason. The word was that a third of the soldiers had tried heroin.

May 3

Dear Mama,

Loved your letter about crabbing with the kids. And about your dinner with corn and garlic bread. Food here is spicy, which I like, but nothing beats your dirty rice. Here the rice really is dirty. You find dead ants and bits of the road in it.

Been busy at work and getting to know the city a little more. I enjoy the noodle shops in the market and all the wonderful fruits I don't get in California. Mangosteens, in particular. They are like tangerines, except the sections are white and they taste sweet, not quite like citrus. Nice.

You keep asking what exactly I am translating. Mostly inventories and memos: the height of water towers or the price of pork. A far cry from Chinese poetry! But yesterday, I was given a bag of material taken from the pockets of a dead VC soldier, including a love letter. The letter was two pages, handwritten; it had been damp and the ink was smeared. I spread it over the desk, with my pen and dictionaries. Just a low-level guy, at least they think so, despised by the South Vietnamese, but loved like mad by somebody named Van (Cloud). I had to look up a few words—they didn't spend much time on romance at the language school. She tells about her vegetable garden and her studies and how she misses him. It's sad; they were just a young couple.

Everybody is marking time until they can leave here. But there is a lot to observe and enjoy. I'm safe and healthy.

Love, Charlotte

She almost wrote: "I am safe and healthy, but today I hate it"—but as usual, she didn't, so her mother wouldn't worry.

Darling husband, I love you. I miss you like crazy. I do not sleep very well, but don't worry. Nothing is wrong, except that you are not here. I would give the sun and moon and stars to touch you right now, to hold your hand for a few minutes. I am not telling you to make you anxious, only so you won't be lonely and so you will know how much we want you back. I hope you sleep well; I hope you dream of me. I will see you three Saturdays from now at my mother's house. Love, Van

There was an envelope, with "For Van" written on the outside, and a romantic name, the endearment *Em*, "little sister." *Remember this poem that I sang to you, Em, just before I left:*

THE KING STAR

The King Star trails nine lesser stars.
I loved you since your mother gave you birth.
The King Star trails nine opposing stars.
I loved you since your mother carried you.
The King Star trails nine stars, side by side.
I loved you since your mother met your father.

They believed he was a courier for a communist group in the north; his neck pouch had an "expedite" sticker on it. The little bag was stitched of battered cloth and cardboard. Inside, a pocket watch pushed under the flap. Receipts for typhoid and tetanus vaccine. Coins. The letter from Van. A picture of a baby. Good god.

She now saw her old life bursting with gifts and luck, slightly nicked by manageable disadvantages and small losses. She had signed on to a rogue universe. Charlotte began to fully comprehend where she was. As if the atmosphere she'd been breathing was finally revealed to her, with its poisons visible as snow. She absorbed the thought that she was not going to survive a year in Saigon. She wrote it out in several languages: *I could die here.*

"Do you sketch it first? Dream about it?" Over dinner at Tien's place one evening Charlotte asked him to tell about how he made a building. He would converse with clients, drink tea. "In Vietnam, men think they run things and try to tell women what to do." Tien wanted to impress Charlotte, so he added, "But I like to talk to the women." He prepared four drawings early—no detailed plans in advance—then inhabited the site, adding numerous clarification sketches each day. He lifted the spoon from his soup and waved it like a wand, then placed it in the center of the table. His face was warm and bright as a vocalist's, approaching the piano.

"You start small, like an oyster and its grain of sand. You imagine a spoon, a bowl to accompany the spoon, the wine glass, the water glass. A vase. Irises. Lilies. You think of a table, a tablecloth, chairs. A ceiling, windows." He wanted to tell everything to her, pull her face to his shoulder. He paused, singing inside.

"You think of how the light could wash over pale walls at dusk or pour in at noon. The room is a pearl that fattens, layer by layer. The floor—ebony or bleached pine or stone—must enhance the table. From outside, the roofline, the entrance, what kind of welcome does it offer. Inside out."

They were sitting, legs tucked under, on his floor. Charlotte listened, watching his hands rise and fall and jump, like a maestro, in time with his voice. His eyes and mouth, his linen shirt. His hair, which she had not yet touched. Now his hands rested across from her on the low table. She put her right hand over his left, her left over his right, leaned across, and kissed him.

She called him Tien, his given name. He called her "Sweet." Tien was fascinated by the texture of her hair, its rough strength. When they made love, he held her head with one hand, slipping it under.

Charlotte had always liked to feel smaller than a man and had preferred a stout presence, robust shoulders, big chest. But Tien's lean body pleased her unimaginably. "Swing low, sweet chariot," she would whisper to him. They created profound disarray in the mosquito netting. In bed their sounds were like people on roller coaster rides, Space Mountain. She amazed herself by yelping with pleasure which in turn caused Tien great amusement. They figured they blended just fine with the magnificent bedlam of frogs and crickets at night.

She taught him slang: *I'm outta here. Put it there, brother. No way. It's my party.* He would make her speak a Texas drawl, which he claimed caused him to lose his mind with desire.

"Say *taco*," he would beg, getting naked. "Say *you all*."

One Sunday in June, cloaked in the raucous sound of monsoon rains drenching the city, they were dozing in her bed. Tien propped himself on one elbow, stroking her under the chin with his other hand. She slid against him, and he kissed her.

"I love you. Already."

"And I love you," she said. She didn't have to think for the words.

"We grew up in a shotgun house close to the beach. I'm the youngest and my brothers and sisters, especially my sister Beverly, took me swimming every day in summer and we loved to dive into the waves. When we got older, we mostly waded and splashed so we could keep our hair right."

They were in Tien's office, listening to the tap, tap of raindrops; he had moved a potted banana tree just under a leak. Near the window was a bamboo and mother-of-pearl cage, sheltering Tien's precious songbird, an oriole. He told her that the oriole requires sugar water for nourishment, as well as crickets, or it will not sing. "Or it sings off-key," Tien smiled.

Tien was sitting at his drafting table; Charlotte stood beside him, her hand resting on his shoulder.

"What do you need most to do your work?" she asked.

"A pencil, eraser. Charcoal. A brush."

"What for?"

"For sweeping eraser debris away."

"What else?"

"Tape to keep drawings in place. Light." He swiveled, adjusted his desk lamp so a circle lit on her face, then he moved it up and down her body, until she pushed it away, shy and laughing.

"T square. Parallel rule. Paper. What about your desk?" he asked.

"Nothing to see: My glasses. A pencil, pen. Dictionaries. Lined pad of paper."

"That all?"

"*Ca-phe da.* Filtered coffee."

In folders, he kept templates used for illustrating plans—you could outline a miniature sofa, lamp, toilet, or bed onto a blueprint, to show how your design might work, or suggest bamboo, mango trees, pools, walkways. They sat then and sketched her apartment, so Charlotte could mail the likeness home to her mother. Together they rendered a kitchen alcove, a stove and refrigerator, a bed in her room, a bed in Marie's; a table, a chair. Even with the template, she was hopeless and made smudges, while Tien produced refined shading and precise tracery.

The truth was, she'd taken many photos, but hadn't mailed them. Now, caught in a curl of love for Tien, she wanted everything to be composed with a delicate pencil, by a fine hand. They made two drawings, one for her mother. In the other, he drew two people, resembling himself and Charlotte, drinking coffee on the couch, even managed tiny glasses and a filter. He shaded her skin darker than his. He added a poem in ink—one, he said, that "everybody knows."

The stream runs clear to its stones.
The fish swim in sharp outline.
Girl, turn your face so I may draw it.
Tomorrow, if we should drift apart,
I will find you by this picture.

June 19
Dear Mama,
It's hot and wet! Reminds me of home, but wetter! Umbrellas don't help. Raincoats don't help.

Your last letter ended in the middle of a sentence, not like you. Are you sick and not telling me? Please let me know. I've been thinking about your dining area. Maybe you could get rid of the wall in the kitchen and put a counter there instead? It would make it all seem bigger. I have a friend here who has some ideas. We made a drawing of my apartment, and I am sending it to you. I haven't taken pictures yet; I never seem to have the flash ready, but I'll do it soon.

How's young Claudia? Edward and Carla? What about the piano lessons? I want to hear all your news. Been busy lately, but I am happy.

More soon.
Love, Charlotte

Charlotte and Tien were at his house, sipping red wine.
"I'm quitting the major."
"What will you do? Sweet Charlotte, don't leave yet!" He looked stricken.
"Not yet, no, I don't want to leave you. I can translate for someone else."
She kissed him, and they drew closer together. They loved each other's touch and quickly interlaced on the floor, dozing among pil-

lows for a while. Later, there was a knock on the front door. Tien let her go, but slowly, and stood, yawning pleasantly, for they soothed and quieted each other, instinctively.

Tien stepped out, and she could hear the voice of Thu, the assistant. Curiously they were speaking Khmer, the language of Cambodia and much of the south. Charlotte had never mentioned to Tien that she could follow Khmer, though she was not fluent.

Thu said: "Everything has been locked away in the warehouse. No one will find it."

"You know Charlotte is here. I'd better go. See you later."

He returned to the cushions on the floor.

"Tien, what language were you speaking out there?"

"Oh that's Khmer. I know some because of my mother."

"Why speak it to Thu? He's Vietnamese."

"He has problems to go over and didn't want you to listen."

"I see." She rotated her glass so the wine circled and jumped. "What's hidden in the warehouse?"

He shook his head. "I should've known you would know Khmer. How stupid of me."

"Just don't tell me you're VC, okay. I couldn't stand to be used like that."

"I'm too healthy to be VC. You can spot them because of their pallor. They're sick, not well fed. No, sweet one, not VC. Vietnamese spiced with Khmer. But I do have a job on the side, besides architecture."

"Are you going to tell me about it? Do I want to know?"

He walked the room in his bare feet. Pushed his hair back with both hands, adjusted his glasses. Took her beautiful face in his hands. He loved her accent, which was unlike any English he'd ever heard; he supposed the gentle notes in her voice were southern. Her Chinese was very good and her Vietnamese improving. She had such an ear for languages, like having a gift for music, and he longed to sing to her, that was how crazy he was getting. As she confronted him, he was astonished at how fear of losing her chopped at the pit of his stomach. He was accustomed to being self-sufficient, to being the center of his world. Now she was fast becoming his center.

"All right. I am helping to hide food and medicine for some families in the Mekong Delta. I have nothing to do with delivery; I just store it. But we are in need of better transport. I don't see why the mothers and sisters and children should starve or die from diarrhea because their men are in combat."

"What about the Saigon government soldiers? What about their families?"

"I know. I do care about them. But these people are relatives of my mother."

"What kind of combat? They're NLF, right? Same as Viet Cong, VC?"

"They're innocent people who need supplies. I have a good income, no children, and a warehouse."

"The warehouse with the lumber and concrete and nails in it?"

"Yes, and bags of rice, pain killers, water purification tablets. You know there's huge traffic between the city and rural NLF areas in the Mekong Delta."

She knew. She'd translated the memos.

"Drugs?"

"No."

"You must know a lot of communists."

"Of course. From the north and south. But I don't subscribe to the ideologues 'fight and talk, talk and fight.' They are too patient for me. I've learned to pick tiny battles and stay away from soldiers."

"Are you spying for the VC?"

"No," Tien answered. "I'm distributing rice and medicine. You mustn't tell anyone about this."

Charlotte had come to Vietnam for her own reasons. She was both ordinary and exceptional at home: jilted and lost but rather attractive; from a large black family with a widowed mother, but educated and multilingual. Now she was again reminded that she was a total outsider here, a foreigner in the midst of a wild civil war, that everyone concealed something, every person had an angle, a crime, a cause. Here, her own boss was a conniver and bully, alien to her. Here, the scholar's talent was wasted on memos and matériel. Here, the architect's proud rooms were created, raised, and destroyed. A woman's leg would be shot, repaired by the good nurse, shot again; the Buddhist monk was compelled from his altars to immolation.

Charlotte kissed him. She slid to the floor, the pillows, more in love than she'd been ten minutes earlier.

"I'll keep quiet."

July 28

Dear Mama,

Hey, don't censor Claudia's letters to me. I look forward to her little poems and pictures. You ask who "we" is. Well, it's often Marie and/or James and Randall. And we have a couple of new Vietnamese friends, and an architect I know, a nice man. I've had dinner at his house. In the USA, you would not be inviting foreign strangers home for dinner very much. Well, maybe you would. You've always had a big heart and you're a great cook, so why not. I love you very much, never forget that.

I have a few days off soon, and we're planning another beach trip. We're going together with James, Marie, and her brother Steve. I can't wait to relax on the sand, like when I was little. I never get tired of it. Love to swim, not hard, just gently.

I am considering a change of job, here in Saigon, and I might take some time off. More on this soon. Don't worry. And take your medicine.

Love you,
Charlotte

The beach near Vung Tau, southeast of Saigon, called Plages Aux Vents by the French, could be extremely windy and was known for a vicious riptide. But the little band of friends hoped to be lucky and resolved to stay close to shore. They had reservations at the Bon Matin, a hotel overlooking the beach and frequented, even during this war, by French tourists who, according to Uncle Giau, set sail for Vietnam to recapture that old colonial feeling. In the lobby Marie and Charlotte noticed a mademoiselle in a broad sun hat trimmed with pumpkin blossoms and a yellow silk off-the-shoulder dress, tiptoeing in spike-heeled sandals. Having just lived through the sixties in Berkeley, Charlotte had never encountered such a woman except in movies. "Oh yeah. You see people like that in bad bars in Detroit," grinned Marie.

Charlotte loved the seashore. She had great tenderness for her warm Gulf of Mexico where she'd grown up, and she was also awestruck by cliffs soaring above the Pacific Ocean, in California where she had lived for so many years. The clear water of the South China Sea, the white sand, the palms towering into blue sky, welcomed her with a strange familiarity, like a twisty dream of home. She lured Marie into the surf, and they swam backstrokes through the waves. They flung towels on the sand and napped, read magazines, drank beer, and swam some more. The men romped on floats; somebody found a volleyball, and they played without a net, their fists happy to be whacking something. Everything seemed quiet and easy, and it was heavenly to be able to stroll back to their rooms, shower, rest, and then convene for a breezy sunset. The second evening, over gin and tonics, on the hotel veranda, James eyed Charlotte.

"So, you're hanging out with Tien, basically all the time, right?"

"I love Tien. Miss him every minute we're not together."

"Makes me jealous. Makes me lonely for a woman."

Charlotte opened a tissue-filled box, lifted out the magnificent brush that she'd found for Tien—for sweeping a table free of dust or clearing eraser debris from drawings and plans, as you shaded and perfected. It was shaped like a miniature harp, with a grip polished to a muted glow. The wood was ebony, the bristles red sable, inlaid with a tiny likeness of a temple; you could even see the steps leading to a shrine inside. She had given it to him the night before, and now they wanted to show their friends this small work of art that would bring extra pleasure to the pursuit of architecture.

Tien had been deeply touched by her gift; after prolonged admiration, he insisted on brushing her skin with it. The feathery bristles felt like soft air, and then she brushed him too: forehead, lips, neck, shoulders, teasing and laughing, and then more quietly, as he fell into sleep.

Tien, just out of the shower, joined them, wearing a pressed white shirt with embroidery on the front panels, his hair still wet and combed back. He reached for her hand.

"The brush is beautiful, isn't it? For clearing my drawings. For sweeping away bad dreams."

A waiter in a white vest supplied grilled skewers of chicken.

"You still haven't ever really told us what you do all day, Mr. Intelligence," Marie pointed out to James, suddenly. "Spy business?"

"Hey, call me a recruiter."

"Recruiting what? For who?"

Charlotte knew that James was on the verge of requesting leave, that he hated the war, but now wasn't the time to go into that.

"I talk to people who may help us. Charlotte here helped us translate sometimes."

"Help us do what?" asked Steve.

"Help us find Viet Cong enclaves, or caches of guns, help us search out a route to a camp somewhere. Then we try to protect local people so they're not VC targets."

"You mean they're seen as informers."

"They *are* informers," nodded James. "It's dangerous for them."

"A lot of the roads in the north are terrible. Potholes, mud," Steve added.

"Tell them what words I need to know," interrupted Charlotte.

"Oh you know—where are they, how many, are you crazy, no thanks, no way, take your hands off me. Mango. Philanderer. But maybe we don't want to bother Tien with this stuff."

"I haven't seen any vehicles," continued Marie's brother. "People on bicycles, though. Once I was patrolling on top of a hill and below me were maybe thirty bicycles, carrying bags of something. Slowly sidewinding through the jungle."

"Did you do anything?" Marie looked worried.

"I radioed my commander, but those little guys on bikes were out of sight and into the jungle so fast, we never found them. Besides, if it was rice, I don't know what's wrong with that. They gotta eat."

"Don't you want the enemy to starve?"

"Not their kids. But yeah, I hate being shot at. If they're hungry, their aim isn't as good." He was getting uneasy about the subject. The conversation shifted.

Marie and Steve told about beaches on Lake Michigan; no, there weren't palm trees or hibiscus but there were gigantic sand dunes. Can't be true! James and Charlotte protested—not dunes! The waiter refreshed their drinks and provided spring rolls. An orange sun hung in the sky, then dissolved all at once into the drift of the green sea, and the wind picked up. They could hear French chatter at the next table.

Later, Charlotte would remember that she was the first to feel it because there was a small rush of air under her right ear. Her earring, a dangling bead and hoop, tossed around. A ping. A firecracker noise. Then one more.

Marie's eyes shot wide open, in shock and astonishment. Blood spewed from her neck, onto Charlotte's cheek, over the spring rolls. James' gin and tonic swirled pink.

Steve grabbed his sister's shoulders, pulled her against his chest, and threw himself and Marie down to the floor; Charlotte and James dove under the table, and dozens of diners were scrambling and shrieking amid crashing dishes. Steve was crying and yelling for help and kissing Marie's forehead: "Don't worry sweetie, you're going to be fine, we'll make you fine. Stay still, I'll take care of you." James and Charlotte frantically tore James' shirt into a bandage and tried to slow the bleeding, while they were jammed under the table.

Tien had slumped backwards in his chair, his head tottering over his left shoulder. A cloud of red widened over his left shirt pocket. A few seconds passed before Charlotte saw, before she screamed, kissed his hands like mad.

No more bullets came. An ambulance raced to the front door, almost immediately—the maître d' was familiar with guerilla warfare and knew whom to call. Although wire mesh was nailed in place to prevent grenades from reaching the veranda, it was useless against a sniper. While they were bundling Marie and Tien on stretchers, the owner strode among the overturned chairs and tables.

"Ladies and gentlemen, the gunman is in custody. We hope you'll go back to your places. We'll seat everybody inside and we will be serving complimentary drinks."

Ten minutes later they reached the hospital three blocks away, and Marie was in emergency and Tien on his way to a trauma unit. The waiter in the white vest found Steve, James, and Charlotte in the waiting room, and gave them a small bottle of Irish whiskey and more spring rolls "to help you calm down." He also brought Tien's ebony brush.

Marie's collarbone was shattered, but the bullet had missed her artery. She was fitted with a neck brace and helicoptered to a military hospital in Saigon, where Steve hovered with orchids every day. She'd been expecting orders for Danang, but the army wasn't sure any more. Soon after she returned to the apartment, they told her they didn't like two members of the same family being in combat zones, especially when one had already almost been killed. No sniper was ever arrested; the owner of the Bon Matin had just said that to quiet the customers.

After the shooting, on Sunday, Monday, Tuesday, Wednesday, Thursday, and Friday nights, in several hospitals, Charlotte lived on pallets by Tien's bed. His parents knew her from Tien's letters and sobbed with her as his body went limp and his breathing slowed. He died on Saturday.

August 15
Dear Mama,
The monsoon was pitiless; I used to like storms but this is too much for me. I am ready for a calm climate.

I've resigned my position here, before my term is up, and I'll be returning in a week. That will give me time to shut down my apartment, clean out my desk.

Mama, I have had a man since I've been here, a Vietnamese. We were in love, and I am pregnant. The baby's father was killed by a sniper. We don't know who did it, but Tien was sending food to peasants south of here, and we think that is why he was shot. Or there was no reason at all, just like there's no reason for anything.

I am going to keep the baby and move back to California. I know this isn't how you would like it to happen, but that's what I want. But first I'm coming home. I'm a mess, and I need you.

Love, Charlotte

Night Work

Washington, D.C. 1990s

Serena Arborvitae Wilkens pressed "60 seconds" on the microwave keypad, swiveled on her stool, and waited for the fried chicken to heat up. She knew the thigh and wings would splatter right through the wax paper, that fried was bad for her, that her supper imparted an aroma inappropriate for an art museum. But the drag of guarding an unused entrance all night long was driving her to it.

Her post was nicely equipped with monitors for checking galleries and other entrances, two security phones, portable refrigerator, coffeepot, and TV, but after six p.m., the sign-in record yawned with blank spaces. Once, stranded in a zone of blind boredom, she actually read the daytime "official visitors" log, discovering that once or twice a week, persons such as Francis Sinatra, Confucius, V. Mary, Bud Da, and Eleanor Roosevelt were stopping by for art appreciation. Since everyone who signed in had to produce identification, the perpetrator must be somebody teasing the security guards. Serena chuckled at the joke, laughed, and then laughed some more—beyond reason—sucking, in between laughs, at threads of chicken from her bones. That was what the long nights were doing to her.

But tonight promised delectable variation from the routine of dead quiet. A reception was to mark the opening of *West and East: The Folding Picture,* and already caterers were sweeping past her importantly, arranging white wine, asparagus spears, mineral water, and radish roses for the guests. Serena was to work an extended evening shift, eight p.m. to six a.m. On such special occasions, Serena and the other guards wore navy dress uniforms with gold braid dripping from the shoulders, brass badges, and white gloves. For the opening of *Folding Picture,* a show of screens from Japan, China, Paris, and New York, they were expecting quite the visitations: the just-retired Speaker of the House of Representatives; Ambassadors LeComte and Kato; donors, collectors, architects.

Sergeant Wilkens' dark skin gave her cover, was an advantage after sunset. She was proficient in marksmanship and had excellent night vision. When she was discovered to be left-handed, her first-grade teacher had slapped her into using her right hand anyway. The result was that she was ambidextrous, a trait that, combined with natural agility, gave her an edge in self-defense exercises.

Except at staff meetings, she'd only encountered the director once, a Tuesday evening around eleven p.m. Serena had wadded up the greasy paper plate from supper and was perfecting her underhand toss to the trash can when he knocked. Dr. Masters was a rather severe gentleman, pale, tall, and terribly busy, even when he was standing still. That night Serena finally understood the phrase "hand wringing," for Dr. Masters was squeezing one whole hand with his other whole hand, then tugging at the thumb, index, middle, ring, and pinky finger of his left, each in turn, with his right; and then he switched hands and did it all over again. She pondered the idea of employing those capable hands to direct a laundry service.

"Hello, officer. How are things?" he inquired, tweaking his thumb.

"Fine, Dr. Masters, just fine. Quiet, but I guess that's good."

Night Work

"What about that woman outside the door, with the blankets and shopping cart? She's always there, every time I come in here."

"I'll watch her."

"I suppose people give her money."

"I don't know—could be." Did the muttering young woman realize who had been leaving chicken wings and biscuits for her in little plastic bags?

"They use our restrooms, don't they?"

"I think so, yes, sometimes."

"Would we have grounds for preventing those people from coming in?"

"Nothing illegal about it, sir."

"Make sure she doesn't scare anyone or bring her cart in here. She might be drunk. Do some damage."

"Yes sir. I'll keep an eye on her."

"And how are you tonight? Anything going on?"

"A visitor mentioned a silverfish crawling across a picture of St. Sebastian. Gallery Four."

"As careful as we are?"

He inspected the galleries every morning at seven a.m., and if he discovered an unpolished bodhisattva or Virgin Mary off-perpendicular, memos were issued and declarations of policy made. Correcting details like that, he was quoted as saying, ensured the difference between the harmonies in his museum and the mess at Natural History.

"Also, somebody asked me why Krishna has a blue face."

"Krishna is a god," Dr. Masters answered, "a blue one. A Hindu god. I'm in baroque, you know. Here, take one of these brochures. *Six Questions about India.* See what it says. I'm going to my office to get some papers. Be back in about a half hour."

Striding out of the gloom of the office corridor later, he told her to unlock the side door so he could get to his Saab more quickly, and she accompanied him through the darkened corridors. She had heard that he lived alone except for his goldfish and observed that there were bags under his eyes, despite a full staff of assistants, an elegant office, a pressed white shirt.

"Are you tired, sir?" she inquired.

"I had to come get the fundraising file," he complained. "I was in storage with my Berninis today. I forgot about everything else." He hadn't spoken to a soul in fifteen hours and now he held forth: he was scheduled to lobby on the Hill for donor tax breaks tomorrow, and there were three donor dinners this week. Yes, he was tired.

In fact Serena knew a lot about Dora, the young woman with the shopping cart who resided in the cypress hedges along the museum's pebbled drive. As a security officer, it was her job to know. Dora was short for "Adora," which referred to "adore." "Adoration is to Christians what nirvana is to Muslims," Dora had explained, getting her religious practices slightly confused. "I changed my name so I would never forget." Dora dwelled inside sandwich boards that proclaimed "I adore Jesus." With her shopping cart set on brake, she usually sat peaceably on the curb in an Amish-style long dark dress, her blonde hair tucked into a white cap, legs stretched out before her, one stiff sign at her back and one at her front. When she dozed, her head would flop to her shoulder, her legs bend sharply at the knees; the sandwich boards skewed on their cords, so she looked like a discarded puppet.

One evening around ten p.m., Serena went into the ladies' room to wash her hands and was joined at the next sink by Dora, also washing her hands.

"Nice weather we're having, isn't it?" Serena remarked.

"Oh yes," answered Dora. "I do thank the Lord for that. God bless you, Serena." And she pushed through the swinging restroom door into the corridor. Serena blended into the shadows and followed, wondering how Dora had managed to remain inside the museum after hours—maybe she had a hiding place. So instead of immediately urging her into the deep night, where the dregs of Washington, D.C., were wide awake and looking for trouble, Serena acted as if Dora were just another student of sculpture. Praying the flapping sandwich boards would not thump any exhibit cases, Serena observed Dora trundle confidently through the dim galleries, like a duck familiar with her nesting area—and into Gallery Seven. She paused before a six-foot bronze statue of Shiva, laced her hands together, and chanted: "Here's the church and here's the steeple, open the doors and see the people," wagging her fingers in the child's game. Then she stepped closer and began, it seemed, counting and as she spoke each number, she pointed toward the statue, *one, two, three, four.*

"I keep counting four arms—is that right? Sometimes I don't see things quite truly. Lord Jesus doesn't have four arms, does he?"

Serena called from the doorway. "That ain't Jesus, honey. That's Shiva."

"But isn't he our Lord?"

"Yes ma'am. Lord Shiva. From India. Not Jesus. This one has four arms."

Dora resumed counting and sure enough, kept getting four, kept being confused. Serena flicked on her flashlight. "Why don't I take you to a picture of Jesus? There are a few of those in here, too." So they walked along together to *Art of the Renaissance*, site of an imposing, gilded sixteenth-century statue of Lord Jesus, properly fitted with but two arms and two legs, before whom both bowed their heads in the quiet darkness, before Serena helped Dora to the exit.

Former Speaker of the House of Representatives Scott Preston, a new museum trustee, also known as "Great Scott," "Scotty," and "Scott's Honor," didn't carry a wine glass around, a habit from party fundraisers when you need your grip free for shaking hands. He arrived late at the reception, and guests were dispersing, but he strolled toward the immaculate courtyard.

Scotty stepped past someone from Horticulture. "That Japanese anemone is quite a rare variety," she commented gaily. "And healthy, too. How delightful!" Brilliant red blossoms dangled from an amazing, wild-looking bush, and waiters offered Thai chicken stuffed with crabmeat. In the center stood a splendid old oak, its great arching branches laden with glorious gold leaves, an unruly lineup of crows, a small beehive, the knock knock of a woodpecker, a dozen crickets, and ten thousand errant insects—a force of nature, the rogue heart of the museum.

Like wars and weather, Scotty's face had stoked the nightly news for years. Most Americans knew who he was, and he craved the citizens' starts of recognition when he sailed into a room. He thrived on patting five-year-old heads at rallies, the tumble of applause after his speeches. But they made you need them, he knew that—got you addicted to the ringing phone, the fat mailbags, the goddamn newspaper. The maelstrom of reporters, aides, reps, pols, and voters left you five hours a night or less for sleep and, especially after his wife Eva fell ill, it had become too much like being chewed up all day and then spit out to fend for yourself in the darkness.

"Mr. Speaker, how are you? Welcome," said Dr. Masters.

"Nice to be here," replied Scotty. "Beautiful tree."

"Yes, yes, we give it extra fertilizer."

Mrs. McGwire, of McGwire Pharmaceuticals, major funder of the exhibition and owner of several spectacular folding screens from Japan, joined them.

"Why Scotty, how have you been? Haven't seen you since the drug bill."

"Maggie, what a surprise! Didn't know you were an art collector."

"Gives me an excuse to get over to Japan."

"Speaker Preston! Welcome to the museum!" A trim, pleasant young woman dressed in navy silk joined in. "It's sprinkling, isn't it?"

"Yes. We need it, though, don't we?"

Night Work

"Yes, I suppose we do. I'm Andrea Knowles from the research office."

"Oh yes? And what do you work on?" inquired Scotty.

"I translate inscriptions on the Chinese paintings mostly."

"I'll bet you know a bunch of languages."

"Chinese, Vietnamese, French, English."

"Wow. Let me shake your hand. That's impressive"

"I have a ways to go with Vietnamese. But the poetry is so beautiful, it's an incentive. You must've traveled just about everywhere yourself."

He resisted a reflexive tendency to self-promotion, to embellish the truth. He was among scholars, after all, with their fidelity to the facts.

"Just about everywhere in Pennsylvania!" He wanted to serve on more boards; it lent a pleasant polish to his career. His wife Eva had loved things Japanese, but he was not exactly ready to be a trustee for a museum with a famous Asian collection. He had an aversion to that part of the world because of the bitter Vietnam War years in Congress, not to mention the rupture with his own children, especially his daughter Abby, over his "attitude toward Asians." The subject wearied him from way inside.

"So you help the curators?"

"Yes, and of course I do my own research."

"Of course. You know I've never spent much time in this museum. I guess I'd better come by more often, since I'm official now."

"That'd be great. Here's my card. I'd be glad to take you around or answer questions whenever you'd like."

He liked her, even if she was a bookworm; he actually liked most people, at least at first; that was part of his talent as a politician. People felt that Philly's Congressman Preston was really listening, like a neighbor. Yet his game in committee was hardball. He got things done.

Nevertheless, he realized these were not people he could ever understand. Scholars were not action figures. They were afraid to say anything unless they cited a hundred authorities. And for what? To prove that some pre-Christian horse gear was really made in Mongolia, not Siberia? Speaker Preston had certainly elongated the stats to get crucial bills through committees; he couldn't take the time to check every single thing. Still, the way they studied and knew distant realms, their insistent caution, drew him. Except for Dr. Masters, they seemed free of the deep channel of worry that he inhabited.

The fall air, crisp as a wet forest, embraced and uplifted Scotty. In the courtyard beneath the colossal oak, he felt a surge of wind; the branches, still stately, were swaying, and wide yellow leaves floated to earth. Like an uncertain prowler, there came a drop of rain, another, then ten drops; punches of wind, more drops. Caterers hustled to clear away the perfect food, and people shuffled indoors; wind and rain swung at the mother oak in fits and dribbles, then drove itself home in sheets.

Scotty slipped through the courtyard doors and into the main museum lobby, from which corridors and galleries fanned in all directions. Dr. Masters, rubbing his hands together, pushing his glasses back up, crossing and uncrossing his arms, was occupied chatting to the guests. It was late, and Scotty had chauffeured himself this evening, but the car was a block away. He didn't feel like getting soaked.

Now the leaves were aroused, the storm roaring, as if a reckoning with the gods was imminent. He sipped some mineral water and made his way through the fast-thinning crowd, passing down a wide, arched hallway and into the *Folding Screen* exhibit. Inside was a Tiffany screen formed of stained glass, ripe with violet grapes, blue clematis, golden pears, and next to it, the blurred edges and stark reds and blacks of a Rothko, as sad and sublime as the Tiffany was joyful and abundant. Six panels of green and white camellias attracted him to a Japanese group, which included another six-panel screen, used as a room divider in a wealthy household, painted with people and animals. He had never been to Japan but remembered that Kyoto was spared from bombing in World War II, although evidently not spared incursions by the giant, Shuten Doji, depicted on the screen, who in the tenth century had taken to kidnapping and devouring young noblewomen. Scotty liked the gold borders, red robes, and green pines in the pictures but he wasn't in the mood for dead horses and warriors and bleeding, and he couldn't follow the complicated story. What would Eva have said? He still forgot sometimes that she was gone, and when he remembered, he felt lost and clumsy, as if he'd banged against a bruise and been left limping.

Each screen was creating its own folding room, the sum a crazy house of beauty, sorrow, war, longing. He was thrown off balance. He wanted to keep moving and walked on through, soon becoming aware of Italian marbles and French impressionists. As the swells of talk receded behind him, he encountered a gallery of American paintings—robust, cheerful portraits of humorists: Mark Twain, Will Rogers, Jack Benny; next was a small show of movie posters. He slung his jacket over one arm, loosened his signature red tie, and roamed—settling in, curious, enjoying the place.

In *Tea Room*, bowls, caddies, boxes, and trays for the Japanese tea ceremony were positioned, accompaniments for a social occasion in which every gesture was completely lucid—even the pitch of tea streaming from teapot to cup had been perfected for centuries. Doesn't seem like much of a party, Scotty thought. The curator had written an entire booklet—twenty-four printed pages—about one tea scoop. For the Speaker, accustomed to the feeding frenzies of politics, this was a phenomenon of nature like continental drift, for which there was no counterpart in his experience. He approached the scoop, lying patiently beside a plain black tea bowl, knowing he could never in a thousand years see there what the scholar sees. The teleprompter in his brain flashed questions: Did that curator ever suffer from volcanic scandals? Two hundred reporters a day?

Suddenly, the track lighting that was cocked discreetly toward the side walls clicked off. A few ovals of brightness still hovered in distant corners, so it wasn't disturbingly dark; in fact now he could see the agreeable shine of droplets splashing on the window panes. The rain completely enveloped this gallery and all the other rooms in its steady, safe music, and listening and pausing in the presence of the simple tool and the passionate study it had begotten, the Speaker was calmed. He decided they wouldn't mind all that much if he stayed a little longer. He didn't really feel alone, amidst the remains of so many civilizations. He was tired. So tired his shoulders were tingling and aching, and he wanted to take his shoes off, rotate his ankles, flex his feet to work away the stiffness. Putting the tea booklet into his pocket, he edged into a sculpture gallery, feeling strangely reassured by a stone, lion-faced chimera guarding the doorway. There was a bench in the center of the room—maybe he'd go in and stretch, sit for a minute.

He seemed to be surrounded by statues of divinities from all over Asia, some tall and upright, with arms outstretched, some with hands folded at their waists, eyes lowered; several astride welcoming lotuses. He stopped in front of a golden boy-god from Sri Lanka, legs playfully awry, head tilted quizzically—these were not the kind of gods he was used to, not at all—and the effect was startling and soothing, as if he had wandered into a stand of firm, wise, young and very ancient trees. He wanted to rest. The bench looked good, very good, and he moved toward it.

Four steps in, he bumped hard into something, with his chest, knees, forehead. A free-standing exhibit case. On impact the walnut base shifted across the floor, making a slight brushing noise. The Speaker closed his lips and held his breath; the rain stopped. Everything went very quiet.

There was a thud. Not a crash, but a small hit, like a full cup riding down too hard, irretrievably, to a tabletop.

The Speaker righted himself and from his pants pocket, pulled a slim flashlight, soldered to his keys so the keys and the light couldn't get separated, so he could see his front door lock no matter what time it was, but as he reached for the light, he forgot about the keys that he must also handle, and the keys rattled in their familiar noisy way; it was just that right now he wished to be totally inconspicuous.

He detected a drip of perspiration on his left eyebrow and dabbed it with his sleeve, again causing the keys to shift, the tiny clink of metal on metal enough, he was afraid, to rouse the guard half a building away.

In his beam of light, a small goddess lay toppled absurdly from her dainty pedestal. She was energetically curved and bejeweled, arms raised, hips flaring. Brass prongs, which had adroitly supported her fragile spine and waist from behind, were now twisted and exposed. Her exuberant breasts and serene smile were intact. Her shoulder was badly cracked.

He read the label: her name was something unpronounceable that meant "musk-scented one." From Southeast Asia. "I'm sorry," he whispered. "Look at that broken shoulder. What should I do?" A headline unfurled in his mind: "Former House Speaker found babbling in art museum."

He had a security detail, personal assistants, attorneys, accountants. He dealt with fear by caucusing his staff, taking another opinion poll. He was a shoot-'em-up politician. Presidents worried over his views. He had finessed tax returns, defamed secretaries of state, derailed senators. He had brokered bombing raids and semi-larcenous contracts. He knew how to brush away his tracks. But here, alone in the dark, he was anxious about this little accident.

No alarm had sounded. Was there a way to reach in and put her back? Would they notice if he took his goddess away to be fixed and then returned her? Should he say he saw someone else hit the case?

He wasn't thinking clearly; he was so damn tired. He spotted the bench, still there, still inviting, and ambled over, loosening his tie on the way. He turned off his flashlight and lay down. It was so good to stretch out, so nice to listen to the rain. That was the last thing he remembered.

Serena was licking smears of cherry pie from the tips of her fingers, leaving a baggie of raw carrots untouched, when on the monitor for security camera one she observed a crumpled figure on the floor in Gallery Seven. It was five a.m.

"Sweet lord, Dora got in here. During the reception maybe. Oh lord, a destitute Jesus freak." Hadn't she completed a final patrol around eleven? Her instructions were to radio for assistance in the event of an intruder, but she thought she'd better just hustle Dora out, poor lost lamb.

Serena revved the microwave, boiled water, and plopped a tea bag in, fixed a lid onto the Styrofoam cup, and with the tea in one hand and her industrial-sized flashlight in the other, she left her post for the gallery.

It was still raining, but a drip-drip rather than an uproar, the drips interspersed percussively with the tap of her shoes down the corridor, which she made no effort to conceal. As she set forth, Serena glanced out the window and saw the forlorn "Adore" sandwich boards arranged lean-to fashion on Dora's grate, as though someone was trying to keep dry. Sure enough, Dora wasn't there.

The tea would help revive her, get her out of the building faster. Serena quickened her stride, tacking through the gallery of folding screens, and on through Galleries Three, Four, Five, Six, the tea warming her hand. No, she did not want Dora living in the museum.

Into the gallery of gods strode Serena, clicking her light at the sleeping form on the floor, next to the only bench in the room. There was a monumental snore: the person spending the night in Gallery Seven was not Dora.

She recognized him immediately as Scott Preston, former Speaker of the House, now honorary this and that, she wasn't sure what, but he was unmistakable: white hair, round glasses still resting on his nose, trim—he'd starred in a whole ad campaign on physical fitness—and that red necktie. She'd seen him the evening before at the reception. For a few years, that face had been almost as familiar as the president's, but at this moment he resembled a pile of laundry except for the arm flung across the floor and legs pulled toward his chest. His shoes were placed in a neat pair under the bench.

"So is this allowed? Because he's a V.I.P.? Did someone forget to tell me something?"

Serena was sure of two things: he wasn't dangerous, and he wouldn't want anyone to know. She crept closer, focusing the light so she wouldn't disturb him just yet.

"Why Serena, god bless you!" came a lilting voice from behind.

Serena jumped, the tea dribbling from beneath the lid of the cup. Dora was yawning near a huddle of clothes at the base of Lord Shiva. With a leisurely cat stretch, she drew to her knees, bowed her head.

This was too much, way too much. Two people camping? In here? Inside the museum?

"Dora, get out of here!" Serena was hoarse. "How in the hell did you get in?"

She tiptoed over to Dora who, implausibly, always smelled like rosewater, and pulled her up by the elbow. "Come on, honey—you have got to scoot—right now!"

"All right," she nodded, bowing again to Shiva, dancing inside his ring of flame, as Serena led her away. She gave Dora the hot tea, unlocked the museum door, and settled her outside in the drizzle near the sandwich boards.

"How fresh the pavement is. Washed by the rain."

"Now how did you get in? Tell me, please."

"The lord let me in," answered Dora. "It was raining and I was needed inside. So he let me in."

"God almighty I can't take it any more. *Do not* sneak in again! I'll lose my job and then who's going to give you biscuits? Please, honey, stay out of the building, okay? Please!"

"God bless you, Serena," nodded Dora, curling inside her lean-to, yawning. Serena checked the visitor log. The last two persons to sign in were Ho C. Min and Speaker of the House. Serena maneuvered the second cup of tea with her right hand and the telephone with her left. The tea took fifty seconds to brew; the phone call to the hospital took thirty seconds; and the walk back to the gallery two minutes. The morning sun would bring the next security shift, and it was imperative she deal with the sleeping Speaker immediately.

Scott Preston loved security people. During his tenure in Congress, the good officers at the Capitol had intercepted four incendiary devices. With the help of security, he had confined his daughter to a hotel room during the 1968 Democratic convention when she wanted to run away from the family. When a psychopath barged into a rally pointing a gun at Scott, a guard took the bullet, suffering a terrible leg injury, and in gratitude Eva and Scott had put the officer's son through college. This fall morning, Scotty opened his eyes to swirls of luminous clouds visible through the skylight above and a grove of gods and goddesses on the ground. He was feeling quite rested, if a bit stiff, and to make things even better, a security officer with skin the color of caramel was leaning over him with a cup of hot tea. He actually felt happy.

"Good morning, sir. How do you feel?"

"Pretty well! I must've conked out. Slept great." He had no idea how or when he had relocated from the bench to the floor. And were there roses somewhere?

"Will you drink some tea?"

"Sure, yes, thanks." He propped himself on one elbow, let his legs stay loose. "I dreamed someone was praying for me," he smiled.

"We'd better get you to a hospital," urged Serena.

"You're nice to help me," said Scotty, "but really I'm fine. I think I'll go on home."

She helped him sit up, encouraging him to sip. Then she glanced around the gallery, suddenly registering in her sights, like a ticking bomb, the disrupted exhibit case.

Then: "Officer! Mr. Speaker?" rose the near-shrieking voice of Dr. Masters, appearing like bad news, from absolutely nowhere.

The fallen goddess swung into the crosshairs for Scott Preston, Dr. Masters, and Serena at precisely the same moment. Scott looked at the statue, at his black wingtips, patient under the bench; at the clouds, at the statue; he looked at Dr. Masters, examined his own red tie. Dr. Masters was extremely dismayed, for he had simply intended to accomplish his rounds early. Not only did he have a semi-prone distingué on his hands, now wrung to the bone, but a perhaps fatally broken Cambodian sculpture. He didn't know which to attend to first but he knew better than to dwell on the Speaker's shortcomings as a guest.

No one said anything. Serena felt dizzy. A fresh spattering of rain tilted the silence, and the director circumnavigated the exhibit case.

"Oh no. My god. What happened?" Distraught as he was, he refrained from probing as to why the Speaker was still in the building eight hours after the reception had ended.

"Careless visitors. Or derelicts. One of them might've stumbled in here. Could've happened yesterday. And there was that thunderstorm thrashing the building."

Still crouched near Scott, Serena was thinking Yes, let it be the thunderstorm, and no, you bastard on the floor, you couldn't have done it because people like you are never guilty of anything; you don't bash into furniture like ordinary idiots. *Sir, I have to tell you that Miss Dora, the homeless woman we see sometimes, was in the gallery. I found her here this morning and escorted her out immediately. It is possible that she accidentally hit the statue.*

But those words could cost her. They could make her unemployable as a security guard. Serena knew she should say those words, but she could not make them form on her tongue. Rain blasted the roof again; the oak tree shimmied and threw down a load of leaves and bugs.

"It was me," Scott spoke up. "I hit the case and she fell."

"Nonsense," said Dr. Masters. "You don't remember. You're not well!"

"It's hazy, that's true. But I was wandering around and I bumped into the case. I think so, anyway."

"I think you got lost in the museum and passed out. Anybody could've done it."

"Not with your excellent officers on duty. Nobody else was here. It must've been me. Besides I remember. I'm sorry. I'll pay to fix it."

Serena extended her left hand to Scott to help him stand; they collected his shoes, keys, jacket. "I'll tell the ambulance there's no need. I'm off duty—I'll drive you home," she announced. Dr. Masters' hands relaxed as he began to grasp the advantages of the Speaker's contrition.

"Well, you go rest. I'll talk to the officer later," he said.

Serena took Scott by the elbow and squired him past Lotus-Eyed Krishna Longing for Love; past Vasudhara, Buddhist goddess of wealth with her six arms—one hand holding a water pot; one, a scroll of small lies; one, a sheaf of corn; one, a cluster of jewels; the remaining two hands at rest; and on past the paunchy elephant god Ganesha, remover of obstacles. Aligning their paces, they continued unhurried through corridors and galleries and through the hall that ran alongside the courtyard with its mighty, teeming tree.

Serena slipped into her raincoat, slung her bag over a shoulder, and the two kept going, to the parking lot. On the windshield of Serena's Toyota, tucked under the wiper, was a note smelling faintly of roses: "God bless you, guardian spirit."

The Best Doctor

Galveston 2000

Dr. Parek? Oh, hello Dr. Parek. You know we need to run to the store for milk and after that we need gas, but I wondered if it would be all right for me to call you back around noon because we're a little worried about our mother. This is Beverly, her daughter. Or you could call us. Thanks.

So, message one concerned Mrs. Wilkens, on whom Jay had operated that very morning. He readied his pen for message two.

Hello? Hello? This is Beverly Wilkens again. Wanted to let you know that I can't call you at noon, like I wanted to, because the electrician is coming, but let me leave you my number. Can you call me back this afternoon? You just say when and I'll be right by the phone.

Jay had to search his patient database, because she didn't leave the number on the machine. He punched it in. But his temples were pulsing and without intending to, he hung up after three rings. Her calls were from earlier, when he was in surgery, so he presumed the problem had resolved itself. He cycled through the endless queue of messages.

Hey Edward, can you get the baby to stop crying? I'm going to tell the

243

doctor. We want our mother to reach her one-hundredth birthday. Hello? Dr. Parek? It's three o'clock. I'm going to call the hospital. This is Beverly Wilkens. Mama isn't feeling very good. Dizzy.

He recalled this woman from a pre-op interview. She was chatty and not well informed about her mother's condition. There were five other brothers and sisters—a middle-class black family with good insurance.

Dr. Parek? Hi, it's Connie Ardennes. I'm having a terrible spasm in my back this morning. It's my birthday, too. Can you send me some pills?

This office, Jay thought, needs an aquarium. Little red and yellow fish. Whirls of seaweed. He patted down his thick black hair and straightened his glasses, gulped seltzer water. He liked the flesh and intensity of surgery, the nurses, monitors, and instruments, and took inherent pleasure in meticulous execution of a task. All this led to amazed gratitude, something he took for granted, from patients who would wake up with restored digestion or a clear throat. The operating room was the closest thing to a home he'd encountered in America: a den where you lock arms with good men and women and work along, riveted on each other's every gesture. But the daily riff of sick people was not his best arena; the phone calls, consultations, and small talk with patients wearied him. Often he'd let his machine take a message on purpose so he could avoid yakking with someone.

Connie was a young mother and a chemistry graduate student, and he hated for her to be in pain on her birthday. He rang back, got her answering machine.

Mrs. Ardennes, this is Dr. Parek. I suppose this pain is similar to the spasms you've had before? Along the shoulder blade? I'm going to call in a prescription; it should relax you and reduce the pain. Call me back if you need anything else.

He tried the Wilkens family again; after twelve rings an answering machine clicked on: *We're so sorry to miss your call. Please leave a message and have a wonderful day.*

To which Jay replied: *I understand your mother is not quite well. I hope she's feeling better. Please call me if you have more problems. Good luck.*

He picked up his briefcase and empty lunch box, headed to a dentist's appointment, after which he'd go home, a one-bedroom condo four blocks away, where he'd lived alone since he began his residency. He hadn't had a single live conversation all afternoon and felt a hint of despondency. He flashed to the beauty of the backwaters and his home in Kerala, where paths wound through serene palm groves among friendly houses. He knew every man and woman, boy and girl, in the village; as a child he drank tea in their kitchens, did homework on their porches, fished from their docks.

But as he grew older, he'd been driven mad for a chance to be alone once in a while. Every dinner at home included more neighbors and cousins than he could count; his mother would tend people with extra dal, rice, and chapatis, and there were always mangos and good tea. He couldn't sit down with a book without being interrupted a dozen times by five-year-olds, fifteen-year-olds, seventy-year-olds. And now here he was in Galveston, close to the ocean, relieved in a way of the crowds in India, but in another way, unsettled by a viral silence that beset him after a day of e-mail, voice-mail, and memos. The desire for solitude competed constantly with his loneliness; he was surrounded by perfectly nice people, friendly people. Yet, he was aware that he came across as too clinical, even impatient. Well, he was just all screwed up, rudderless on the hot Gulf Coast of America.

"Wow," Janet exclaimed, her two thumbs positioned on his lower front gum. "Great graft!"

"Mmmmm," responded Jay.

"Sonia! Can you come in here for a second? Look here! See how fine the scar line is. That surface is perfectly flat."

"Where?" She pinched his lower lip with her index finger and thumb, so that now three hands were tugging at Jay's mouth. "Oh, yes. Great!" Sonia spoke in heavily accented English. She looked genuinely pleased as though she'd just solved the crossword and won a mug.

"Dr. Young did it. Four years ago. He'd have lost that tooth otherwise. Any trouble with the flap, Jay?"

To the best of his ability, Jay shook his head no. Sonia let his lip loose and turned to x-rays. Janet rambled on.

"You know, Sonia, Jay here took a trip to New Orleans this spring. Have you ever been?"

"Not yet. It's on my list. I heard about New Orleans back in Macedonia. Famous place."

Jay's mouth remained winched open by Janet's formidable hand, and she continued to stab his soft tissues with sharp instruments. Several minutes went by, punctuated by wincing from Jay, as the two women conversed about Mardi Gras.

Suddenly Janet retracted her hands and swiveled backwards to study a folder. "You have a crown, don't you? Dr. Young's?"

Finally able to speak, Jay answered: "Yes. From two years ago."

Without explanation, Janet left the room for about five minutes. She then resumed probing and scraping at Jay's teeth and gums, amid talk of family car trips and praise for the American highway system.

"What are you doing tomorrow?" she asked warmly. Tomorrow was the Fourth of July, and Jay planned to take a picnic to the beach and enjoy fireworks. In fact, he wanted to get blasted. But with his mouth immobilized, he could not explain this. Sonia beckoned to Diego, a hygienist in training. Now everyone grabbed Jay's lips to again admire the dentist's craftsmanship. Jay had been prostrate in the chair for forty-five minutes, and the hygiene seemed only now to be commencing. He wasn't in a hurry, really, but he felt mildly annoyed. How much did these people accomplish in a day? Was Janet doing a professional job or was she distracted and slow? When she finally finished polishing his enamels, still perky, still ruminating aloud about Independence Day, he paid with a credit card and escaped to his condo.

Gulf of Mexico had in Jay's loneliness sounded almost as seductive as *Malabar Coast,* and though Galveston Island didn't have cashew trees or rice paddies, it possessed a medical school, and its wide beaches, burly heat, abundant oleanders, and rowdy tourists gave Jay a certain rough succor. He sometimes missed dwelling among Hindus, and so, though he wasn't a believer, he made a point on holidays to fashion offerings to a small Ganesha: marigolds, caladiums, pine cones, candles; whatever was handy here in Texas. On American Independence Day, at ease in his breakfast nook, he smiled and prepared a shrine with strawberries, white oleander petals, and blueberries. And jasmine incense.

On the first Fourth of the second millennium of the common era, Jay hit the beach, with his state-of-the-art Gore-Tex backpack, filled with peanut butter, samosas, coriander chutney, bhel puri, and Kingfisher beer. He settled his yellow chair low to the ground and close to the water, so that waves swept under his bottom, bathing his feet and spraying his contented legs. Good-humored masses of people were streaming north, south, east, and west—girls in red, white, and blue bikinis hovered and swished past, like patriotic butterflies. People spread mats over the sand and set up wind breaks and umbrellas amid a convergence of plastic plates, coolers, volleyballs, soaring kites, and icy beer. Squealing children dashed in and out of the surf. Every brand of picnic sprouted forth: fat-free veggie chips and kiwi fruit served on recycled paper; jalapeno poppers, fish sticks, and burritos on Styrofoam. A couple slathered each other's backs with suntan lotion, then, giggling, lay down on their blanket propped up on elbows. They passed an egg roll back and forth; he bit off his end and conveyed it by mouth to his girlfriend; she bit her end, passed it back. They split the last morsel and kissed. Jay caught himself staring, even smiling, rather too obviously; the pang of envy surprised him.

Around eight p.m. there came awesome, drenching rain. Ten-minute downpours followed by slight clearing and wet wind, quickly interrupted by another ten minutes of pounding thunder and more thrilling rain. Within minutes the beach had metamorphosed into a carnival of blue tarps and gay umbrellas—everybody soaked and huddling under makeshift shelters and still in good humor. Jay decided to pick up and struggle through the crowd toward the huge performance stage, which had been erected near a beautiful pier that stretched like a wing out over the sea. Latin superstar Ricky Martin was prancing and singing under a giant canopy, to the utter delight of the crowd. Britney Spears, idol of millions of eleven-year-olds, was holding up her own umbrella—wow! The Texas A & M band elected not to march through the storm, but pounded out Sousa tunes from their metal folding chairs beneath the canopy. The rain was a nuisance, but the adversity energized and entertained an already jovial crowd and spirits stayed high. For a couple of hours roaring showers and crazy wind were interrupted by brief quiet breezes, during which respite gangs of people would scurry from shelter to shelter.

Under an overhang by the stage, Jay found himself beer in hand, mashed up against two old ladies in wheelchairs. Each had short, white, curly hair and big glasses; each wore a T-shirt and khaki slacks, Nike walking shoes, and thick socks. Both were covered head to toe in what appeared to be a year's supply of plastic. Old lady number one sported an umbrella-shaped cap—it perched on top of her head and spread its red, white, and blue crown widely enough to keep rain off her hair. Old lady number two wore a clear plastic shower cap, just the thing for wet weather. Her American flag earrings dangled below the elastic edge of the cap. A poncho tumbled over her shoulders and bunched into her lap; more sheets of plastic were wrapped around and around her legs. She resembled a whole sheep, ready for the freezer, and also prepared if necessary, to rev up her wheelchair and storm into the eye of a hurricane. Dr.

The Best Doctor

Jay, sometimes bored by old people in his practice, was amused.

Suddenly lady number one sneezed passionately and seemed unable to stop. Jay, barely protected from the elements in shorts and sandals, felt mildly alarmed. He adjusted his pack.

"Good madam, are you all right?"

The sneezer paused. "Oh, yes. This happens in weather."

"Well, you certainly look protected against the rain."

The two old ladies laughed. "Peggy, there, my daughter, wrapped us."

"Are you sisters?"

"Friends! I'm Evelyn and she's Betty."

"We worked together for thirty years," explained Evelyn.

"Phone company," added Betty.

"We've been retired for twenty," Evelyn said.

"Came for the fireworks," confirmed Betty.

They dissolved into a long, infectious bout of laughter.

"What?"

"I don't know," Betty answered, dabbing her eyes.

"We get like this some times," Evelyn gasped, trying to find her breath. "Get each other started. On a jag. Can't stop."

By now daughter Peggy and the inquiring doctor were also grinning.

"Where are you from?" said Betty.

"I come from India."

"I look awfully pale next to you. I should get out more."

"In my country we have seasons of rain like this every year."

"Oh those terrible cyclones."

"Occasionally. But the regular monsoon rains can be very heavy."

"Monsoons. Palm trees bent double. Software deliveries delayed. I've heard!" More laughter.

"Good luck with the fireworks."

"Do you think they'll cancel them?" asked Betty.

"Oh no. They can shoot them no matter what the weather."

"Hope so," said Evelyn.

"Hope so," said Betty. "We drove two hundred miles just to see 'em."

In that minute, the sky exploded: yellow pinwheels, green starbursts, and red and white girandoles shot up through the drizzle and bloomed above the cloud bank. The crowd sang out its approval, and Jay and Peggy and the old ladies applauded, their spirits borne aloft by the rough exalted voice of Ray Charles: "Oh beautiful for spacious skies, for amber waves of grain, for purple mountain majesties...from sea to shining sea."

Hello Jay, it's Robert. Evidently Beverly Wilkens couldn't get you on the phone. Jay, there's a problem regarding this family. Please call me right away, okay? If I don't hear from you in a half hour, I'll stop by your office.

Jay checked his watch. It was ten o'clock, and the message was a half-hour old. Sure enough, an impatient knock rattled the door.

"Jay, how are you?"

"I'm well. You?"

"Okay, I guess. Listen, you performed an exploratory day before yesterday on Mrs. Wilkens, the elderly African American woman with stomach cancer?"

"Yes. To check the intestine." Jay felt his diaphragm tighten. He tended his cuffs, arranged his clipboard so it was perpendicular to the edge of the desk.

"Apparently Mrs. Wilkens seemed fine until she got home. Collapsed on the way from the car to the house, and her daughter managed to get her to bed. She was conscious by then and said she was dizzy and wanted to rest. So they let her sleep. Said they left you a message, but didn't hear back. About four o'clock they called 911 because she was incoherent."

"I did call back. I left a message."

Dr. Robert Bentley had been leaning against the door jamb

The Best Doctor

with his arms crossed. Now he took a chair, proceeding in a softer tone. Dr. Bentley had clear blue eyes and white hair, had been chief of gastroenterology for twenty-five years. Dr. Parek had graduated in the top ten percent of his med school class, but had been practicing for only five years. Dr. Bentley had performed two surgeries on the old woman; for the exploratory procedure, which involved a small incision in the stomach wall, the family had requested Dr. Bentley—*We want the best doctor*—but he was unavailable. *I'm sure you're very good but we had gotten used to Dr. Bentley, and I guess if he says you can do the procedure it will be fine but we wanted to meet you first.*

"So the stomach wall was compromised?" Jay took pride in mastery of the latest techniques, but now his breath was short. The details were hailing down on him like pellets of ice.

On the way into the operating room, the nurse and anesthesiologist in their scrubs had fitted the ninety-nine-year-old Patty Wilkens with a plastic cap and I.V. and joked with her. How do you like your chapeau? Mrs. Wilkens was stable, alert, and chuckling. "But of course! I look good in hats. Can I hold somebody's hand, though? I'm so damned old."

"Exactly. The medics brought her into emergency. There was an outcry from the family that they don't know how they got you in the first place and to please call Dr. Bentley. I went in and cauterized the incision. The old woman had to be awake for a good part of it. It was hard going; she's so elderly and already very sick. She was woozy but pulled my head down to her and whispered that it meant something to the family for her to hang on."

"So I didn't close the wound?"

"Right."

"I've never made that mistake before. Are you sure the disorientation was caused by the procedure?"

Mrs. Patty was the first black woman in Galveston to cast a vote.

"Absolutely. Anyway, I did what I could and told the family their mother was in danger, but after rest, she might rebound. Two of the sisters were crying. I think she has a slight chance to pull through but she lost a lot of blood. Of course, she also has incurable stomach cancer that'll get her in a few months. You were off yesterday for the Fourth, and I was glad to watch her. But she's not doing well."

"I'll go see her later this morning. If they knew what her insides look like, they wouldn't be so anxious to keep her going."

"The family is insisting that you stay off the case."

"I see. They refuse to acknowledge that these procedures have risks."

The ancient, amazing Mrs. Wilkens had a website, selling caladiums online.

"They say you didn't explain, and there was no form to sign. But also that you always seemed impatient and distracted, like you were thinking of anything but their mother."

Our mother raised us kids on her own through the Depression and war, and two went to college in the 1950s. Guess which one of us knows Chinese. South Texas black kids.

"Since she had an endoscopy recently, I didn't think it was necessary to go over it all again."

"But you need to remind people. They're not going to remember that stuff four months later. I told them you were conscientious and had quite a few patients, so you might seem hurried. But you know how important it is in this hospital to treat people with respect. Like you have all the time in the world; we give them potted plants to take home. We recommend a fertilizer."

Ms. Beverly Wilkens, her three brothers and two sisters, assorted spouses, and several small children had marched into Jay's office, talking nonstop. Almost completely silver gray, the hair of one sister was fixed in cornrows and little braids and red and yellow bows. Silly, at her age. She was managing twins, about five years old. "Doctor, this is April and this is May. Born at midnight on April 30. They did my hair; I decided to leave the bows in; it tickles the kids."

"My accent bothers people some times."

"This has nothing to do with your accent. It has to do with their mother dying." Dr. Bentley left abruptly, not bothering to pull the door closed behind him. Jay had always admired Dr. Bentley's honesty and was stung now by his attitude. An amorphous loneliness overcame him, like a muddy wave. It was true, he tended to just see a patient's ailment, snipped away from its effect on loved ones.

Our mother Patty Wilkens is ninety-nine years old. She was a miracle, born on Sunday, September 9, 1900, the day after the great hurricane in Galveston.

He walked home, flicked on his air conditioning, made a cup of tea. He had no wife or children; and he had chosen to live a world away from his family. He clung to the admiration of his colleagues; it connected him to them, to something; now he found himself rummaging for a phone number.

It was seven in the morning in Kerala. His father answered.

"Oh hello, Jay! I am just out of bed. How are you? It's not my birthday, is it?"

"No, no, I just wanted to see how you are."

"We're fine. Your mother's gone for a walk; you know she loves early morning. Your sister and the kids are staying here for a month. It's warm, but in paradise the heat doesn't bother you. I know it bothered you, sometimes."

"It's plenty hot here."

"I know, I know. I'm rubbing it in. What are you reading lately?"

"Oh, medical journals. Sometimes a mystery story. What about you?"

"I'm deep into the newspaper. That's about it for me these days."

"What about your fishing? You still like it, don't you?"

"Yes, I do. I go on Tuesdays and Thursdays."

"Tell everybody hello for me, will you?"

"I will do it. Take care of yourself, son."

Next morning, at 7:30 a.m. Jay checked his sort-of shrine. He lit a candle and cranberry incense and dusted off his Shivas, as though his race memory was telling him to summon the help of the gods. The thought of his father, calling him "son," warmed him.

When he reached the hospital, the nurse greeted him. "Why

hello Dr. Parek. How are you today?"

"Tired. How are you?"

"I have to tell you that Mrs. Wilkens died an hour ago. The family's in the room with her."

The unkind thoughts he'd had about the Wilkens family suffused his mind and body, and his skin went hot and soft in shame. One afternoon, after a bunch of them had vacated his office, he'd pictured brown pelicans, beaks in constant motion with ungainly wingspans, bumping into his bottled water, kicking his sticks of incense, threatening his striped yellowtails from Baja, and he didn't even have an aquarium. They had not, of course, touched a thing. Did they remind him of mobs at his mother's house? He thought of his grandmother who died at the age of fifty-five, so young, and her funeral pyre. The fire had frightened him, and the sight of the ashes ascending made him sick. He felt his cheeks again damp, as when he had cried for her, the one person who always whispered to him as if he were the only boy on earth. It didn't matter to her children how lucky Mrs. Wilkens had already been, to live so long, or how merciful a quick death might seem to some doctor.

He peered through the high window in the patient's door. The room was dim, crowded. Tall candles and vases of roses and calla lilies were arranged on the side table. Mrs. Wilkens stretched the length of the bed with her arms folded over her chest. Her head was propped on a pillow, hair nicely combed, the picture of serenity and grace. But the rest of the sad room was grayed out, homeless.

Beverly's head lay in her dead mother's lap. April and May were silent; each held one of Patty's hands. Edward held her feet, rubbing them. A son and daughter, Ben and Serena, were sitting on the side of the bed, sobbing. Ben's twin brother, Reginald, stared out the window. Daughter Charlotte had covered her own face with a handkerchief. Her son's arm encircled her. Patty Wilkens, her stomach riddled with nodules of cancer, had stopped breathing. Her hair was thin; her flesh spotted and pocked and wrinkled. She'd told the nurse that when she looked in the mirror she saw someone else, an alien, not the healthy eighteen-year-old who lived inside.

Jay remembered sideswiping a car in Madras. He scratched the passenger door and had knocked off the side mirror. He'd left a note and phone number: "So sorry. I swerved and nicked your car. Please call me and I will make amends." He wished he could do that now: "So sorry, I cut into your mother and nicked her and she died. I am very very sorry."

He knocked, opened the door slightly, not going into the room.

"I am so sorry for your loss. Mrs. Wilkens was a fine person, a friendly woman, and I know how hard this must be."

The family fell completely quiet, astonished to see him. No one spoke or moved.

"Do you know?" said Beverly, at last. "Really?"

"I may have made a mistake during the procedure. I'm sorry. I'm sorry." His eyes filled.

"Well, can you fix it?" That was little April.

Edward came over to him. "You seem upset and we appreciate your words."

"We're not going to sue you, doctor. She's been spared a lot of suffering. It's just that we all wanted her to reach a hundred. And we didn't want to let her go," said Charlotte.

"If I can do anything to help, please let me. I'm so sorry." Jay backed out of the room, pulled the door. He went to the staff cafeteria for a cup of tea but in a few minutes was hurrying back to that corridor.

The blind on the Wilkens' high window was not quite closed, so that he might look in without the family noticing. He forgot about the nurses and visitors traversing the hall, who would wonder why a doctor was outside a sick chamber, staring in.

Yes, he could see inside, a sliver of the room. Charlotte was lighting candles; hints of flame flickered off the dark blue stone on her ring. Brothers and sisters and grandchildren were holding hands, in twos and threes, and the little girls were whimpering. Patty Wilkens, almost one hundred years old, washed in pure love.

He had no place to go, except an office that had no bright fish. An apartment and its wilted shrines. He could not leave her window yet. He wanted to stay a while longer, he wanted to find tears.

CPSIA information can be obtained at www.ICGtesting.com
Printed in the USA
BVOW040948011212

307026BV00001B/7/P